The Girl Who Killed Her Mom

## ALSO BY McGARVEY BLACK

Trust Only Me
The First Husband
My Sister's Killer
The Woman Upstairs
Twice On Christmas
The Baby I Stole
The Girl Who Killed Her Mom

# THE
# GIRL
# WHO
# KILLED
# HER
# MOM

## McGARVEY BLACK

Joffe Books, London
www.joffebooks.com

First published in Great Britain in 2024

Cover art by Nick Castle

ISBN: 978-1-83526-766-0

# CHAPTER 1

I was barely fifteen when I killed my mother. Even now twenty years later, I only remember bits and pieces from the weeks and months after it happened. Everyone was pointing fingers. The police buzzed around our house day and night, and never left us alone. It was a crazy time.

And the day my mother died is still a convoluted mess inside my head. Thousands of times I've tried putting all the puzzle pieces together, but they never fit, no matter how hard I pounded on them. One of my therapists said it was because my mother's death was too painful, and it was my way of protecting myself. Of course, my therapist didn't know the real truth. I know it and I don't agree. I block stuff out because of guilt, to keep the images of that day from rising to the surface. Maybe I should be grateful for my scattered memories. Remembering every moment would be so much worse. Then, I'd have to face who I really am.

* * *

*Twenty years ago*

My lids are so heavy that I can't open my eyes. Exhausted, I leave them as they are, shut tight. I'm lying on something

1

soft, with no energy to move a single part of my body. I'm hungover and everything hurts. If I move at all, I'm going to puke, so I just lie still.

*How many pills did I take?*

After all the constant partying the last six months, my brain is like a bowl of oatmeal now, sluggish and thick. There's a throbbing pain between my eyes that won't freaking stop. I must have taken a lot . . . more than my usual.

Opening one eye, I stare straight up at a white ceiling. A vaguely familiar-looking round light fixture is directly above me. There's a crack in the ceiling next to it. I turn my head slightly to the right, causing a sharp pain to shoot from one ear to the other. Squinting, I glance around the room, trying not to move because I know any movement will hurt. A wooden dresser with brass handles is against the wall. That looks familiar, too. I must not be fully awake, because it takes me another second to understand where I am. I'm in my mother's bedroom.

Pushing my body up slightly with my left hand, I catch a glimpse of myself in her mirror. I look like shit. My long brown hair is matted and stringy. My reflection makes me cringe. The whites of my brown eyes are red and my skin is blotchy and gray. I look like I'm forty, and tell myself that I need to cut back on the partying. I lay my head down again to rest.

*Why am I in my mother's room?*

Golden amber light streams through the windows, telling me it's the middle of the afternoon. I rub my eyes with my hand before pushing myself up into a sitting position. The minute I do, the room starts spinning. I take a deep breath to steady myself. It will stop in few minutes, it always does.

Out of the corner of my eye, I spot something large across the room on the floor. I blink my filmy eyes a few times to clear them and slowly things come into focus. That's when I see her. The thing on the floor . . . my mother.

Confused, I wonder why my mother's home in the middle of the day. *Why isn't she at work?*

"Mom?" I shout.

She doesn't move.

"Mom!"

My stomach does a few flips while I try to control the increasing nausea in my gut. The room continues moving, as I squint and look at her again. "Mom?"

*Why is Mom on the floor?*

That's when I notice a splatter of red spots on the white wall behind her. They remind me of the Jackson Pollock paintings we studied in art class . . . when I didn't skip class. I stare at the red dots on the wall trying to work out what they are and why they're there. Then I remember, my mother's on the floor.

*Why isn't she at work?*

I shake my head to snap out of my stupor. I can tell I'm still drunk and high as I turn slightly to examine her. As soon as my eyes focus, my breath catches in my throat. Blood is trickling from three separate spots on my mother's chest, forming a red puddle around her.

I scream as I watch the dark liquid ooze from her body and seep into the beige carpet. My mom's beautiful light blue eyes are wide open, fixed and still.

"Mom?" I say again, in a loud whisper, as if I didn't want to disturb her. She doesn't answer. I lean forward to get a better look. Her chest isn't moving. Slowly swinging my legs off of the bed, I try to stand. As I put weight on my feet, something falls from my hand onto the floor. It's a gun.

Foggy and seriously nauseous, it takes me a few moments to process what's really happening. I'm in my mother's room. Is she okay? Stepping away from the gun, I slowly move towards my mom, dreading what I already know in my soul. My mom is stone cold dead.

I back away, falling onto her bed and begin to convulse. Curling into a fetal ball, I sob and hug her pillow to my chest, hoping to pick up her familiar scent one last time.

The past few months we'd been fighting a lot. She said she was going to call the police. She threatened to kick me out.

At least, I think that's what happened. Most of the past year is a blur. I had taken so many different kinds of drugs, I don't remember much of anything.

I think Travis got a couple of bottles of vodka and some of that sweet wine I like. I remember washing down a handful of yellow and white pills with the wine. After that, the rest is kind of blank.

Frozen, I stare at my beautiful mother, tears dripping down my face. I said terrible things to her. I didn't mean them. I so desperately wanted to be grown-up. I didn't want her telling me what to do.

"*I hate you!*" I had screamed. "I wish I could live anywhere else but here. Why don't you just die?"

Her face looked so sad when I said that, but I was so wound up and angry. I didn't care if I hurt her feelings. I wanted to cause her pain. She was trying to ruin my relationship with the man I loved. But I didn't really want her to die. I never wanted her to stop being my mom. Everything she did was for me. How did everything go so wrong?

I hug her pillow closer to me, aware that the raging anger I'd been carrying around for the past year is suddenly gone. I don't hate her anymore. I never did. I love her. She's my mom.

Right now, I'm filled with overwhelming grief and regret, a much worse feeling than anger. It feels like there's a heavy wet blanket on top of me pushing me under the ground. I can't breathe, so I close my eyes to shut everything out. I don't want to look at her anymore, not like that. It hurts too much.

My mind goes to one of the last conversations she and I had. Truthfully, it was more of a fight. I lashed out at her because she was trying to ruin everything between Travis and me. But even during that terrible argument, I didn't hate her, even though I said I did.

What I want is to tell her how much I love her, but I can't.

She always laughed and joked around with everyone, even strangers. She was like that with me, too, until I pushed her away. Why did I do that? A part of me knows she was desperate to get through to me, to 'save' me, she said on more than one occasion. I didn't want to hear that bullshit. I wanted to live life my way, on my own terms. I look down at the gun on the floor and notice the tiny green shamrock on the grip. I know that gun. It had been my father's, a souvenir from his time in the Vietnam war in the early 70s. My dad's mother was Irish, and he had that shamrock put on his gun for luck. He gave it to my mother years ago, when they still liked each other, long before they got divorced. She kept that gun in a safe in her room, although I'm not sure she even knew how to use it. She didn't know I knew the combination to the safe, but I did. Kids always know more than their parents think they do.

I try to piece a timeline together of what happened, but my brain fog is too thick. I was furious with her for trying to destroy my happiness. She had no right to come between Travis and me. The more she came down on me and criticized my lifestyle, the harder I pushed her away. She didn't get it.

Now, my eyes fix on her body, still slumped on the floor. I want to remember happy times, but the only images that flash across my mind are of me screaming at her and slamming doors.

I hear her voice asking, "Where did my beautiful little girl go?" Tears sprung from her eyes when I raised my fists at her. I had no answer to her question. I didn't know what had happened to me, either. I just knew I wanted to be with Travis. It was that simple.

Still on her bed, I stare down at my mom's body. Her shoulder-length brown hair is loose and free. She usually kept her hair swept up in a ponytail. "It's easier that way," she'd say, when I suggested she wear it differently to look cooler. Now, it's wet and matted with blood, and her beautiful face is frozen into a mask of disappointed surprise. I start to cry again, and am filled with so much remorse. I never intended to go through with it.

My mom didn't deserve this, especially not from me, her 'little angel'. That's what she used to call me. I may be little, but I'm the furthest thing from an angel. Still, none of this would have happened if she hadn't interfered in my relationship. I had to stop her from going to the police. She would have ruined his life. I couldn't let her send Travis to jail.

# CHAPTER 2

Sobbing uncontrollably, I reach for the phone stuffed in the back pocket of my jeans to call my boyfriend. Travis will know what to do. He always does. Whenever things get crazy, he's the one who keeps a cool head. That's why all the kids look up to him. They call him 'the mayor'.

His phone rings four times, and I start to lose my mind when he doesn't answer. Where is he? Why isn't he picking up? Panicking, I leave an incoherent voicemail punctuated with crying and heaving breaths. I end the message begging him to call me immediately. Before I hang up, I mutter something about killing myself if he doesn't call me back in five minutes.

Seconds later, his number flashes on my phone.

"It's me. What's wrong?" says Travis, his voice blasting out from the speaker. "I couldn't understand what you were saying on your message. Why are you crying?"

Between sobs, I try to explain. "Travis, I think . . ."

"What?"

I take deep breath and let it out. "I-I-I think she's dead."

"Who? What are you talking about?"

"Her . . . her . . . blood's all over the room. It's on the walls and the rug. It's everywhere."

7

"Whose blood?"

"*My mom's!*" I scream as I burst into tears again.

"Ok. Try to calm down," says Travis, his voice steady. "You need to stop crying, okay? Tell me exactly what's happened."

"I don't know. I didn't mean to do it," I say through my tears. "She could be a bitch sometimes, but I still loved her."

"What are you talking about?" he says again.

"I know she was trying to break us up, but I didn't mean for this to happen. We talked about it, but I really didn't want her to die. We were just saying stupid stuff. What am I going to do?"

Nearly five years older than me, Travis remains calm and speaks in soft consoling tones. Somehow, the methodical rhythm of his voice takes my temperature down a little. As I listen to his measured words, I actually start to believe he *can* fix this.

"Are you sure she's dead?" he says, after I tell him about all the blood on the rug and walls.

I stare at my mother.

"Focus," he says raising his voice. "Is she dead?"

"Yes."

"You're sure? Did you check her pulse?"

"I don't know how to." I burst into tears again and begin to hiccup. "I'm afraid. You need to come over here, please. You've got to come."

For a second, he doesn't answer me.

"Travis?" I whisper into the phone. There's a faint sigh on the other end.

"Listen to me," he finally says. "Do exactly what I tell you. First, don't move at all. Stay where you are. Don't call anyone or touch anything. I'm in my car only a few blocks from your house. I'll be there in less than five minutes."

He hangs up and I remain curled up on the edge of my mother's bed. My mind drifts back to that terrible day my mother found my journal. Why did she have to go into my room and read it? None of this would have happened if she had stayed out of my business. That journal was private.

Mostly I wrote about Travis, and how I was madly in love with him. There were pages about the two of us being soulmates and how amazing he made me feel when we made love. In one of my last entries, I talked about his upcoming twentieth birthday and the party I wanted to have under the bridge. That's how she found out Travis wasn't seventeen, like I'd told her. She went ballistic.

Later that day, when Travis and I stopped by the house a little drunk and slightly high, my mother was on a rampage and confronted us. She had torn my room apart and started screaming the minute we walked through the door. She said she was going to report Travis to the cops for statutory rape and have him put away for good. She kept saying that he was an adult and I was just a child. I screamed at her and told her I hated her. Then Travis and I left and after a few stops went to the underpass by the highway to meet up with our friends. We got totally wasted.

That afternoon, Travis wasn't his usual cool calm self. He was pacing and ranting, saying he couldn't go to jail and my 'bitch mother' was trying to ruin his life.

I tried to calm him down and told him to relax, that in a few weeks my mom would get over it.

He made a face like he didn't believe me and went off to score some Molly and tequila from one of his friends. Later, after the pills and booze kicked in, we chilled and smoked some weed and started goofing around about getting rid of my mother.

"Maybe we should just kill her," I said, laughing and pretending to slit my own throat with my finger. "That would solve all our problems. Or we could run her over with your car, Trav. How about that? We could nail her when she's coming out of church on a Sunday in front of the whole congregation."

Travis laughed. "Or, how about we turn up the gas on her stove," he said, "and close all the windows in your house. *Adios, mama-cita.*"

"Good one," I said, as I leaned over and kissed him. "There's always poison. She eats graham crackers with peanut butter every single night before bed. We could put poison in her peanut butter."

High as kites, we spent the next thirty minutes devising crazier ways of bumping off my mother. We didn't mean any of it. We were just fooling around. So, how did this all happen?

Suddenly, I'm jolted back into reality when I hear Travis's voice coming up the stairs. "Where are you?"

"Up here," I yell.

When he enters my mother's bedroom and sees her blood-soaked body on the floor, his dark-brown, almost black, eyes widen and nearly pop out of his head.

"Oh, my God. What did you do?" he says, shaking his head.

I open my mouth to speak, but nothing comes out. Instead, tears pour from my eyes, and I slump back onto the pillows. Travis comes over to the bed, lifts me up and holds me in his arms. Sobbing, I cling to him, wishing the whole thing would go away.

He rocks me and whispers in my ear.

"It's gonna be all right," he says. "I'm here now. I'll fix this. I promise."

# CHAPTER 3

Travis is true to his word, and somehow fixes everything. I'll never know how he did it. Then there was the gun. I didn't want to touch that thing ever again. Travis took it, put it in his car and said he'd get rid of it. After we set up the scene in my house to make it look like an angry mob tore the place apart, we call the police. He and I give sworn statements. We tell the cops that we'd come home together that afternoon and found the house ransacked and my mother's body upstairs.

For weeks, the police investigate my mother's death. Ultimately, they determine it was a house robbery gone horribly wrong. Apparently, there had been a couple of other home invasions in Connecticut, so they ran with that theory.

The cops never consider me, not for a second. I guess it's because I'm so young and small. The few adults left in my life try to protect and console me. Everyone whispers how they want to give me the softest landing possible, as I've already been through enough trauma. That part's true. I have been through a terrible time, just not in the way they thought.

The courts assign a victim's rights advocate for me. Her name is Linda. She tells me I can talk to her about anything. I desperately want to talk to someone, because I've got so much bottled up inside, but I don't dare.

"Whatever you and I discuss is completely confidential," Linda says, patting my hand during our second required meeting. "You do understand what 'confidential' means, don't you?"

"It means that no one else will ever know what I tell you," I say. "It's a secret."

Linda smiles. "That's right. Everything you say is between you and me, for our ears only."

I know what *confidential* means, but I don't entirely trust Linda. She's nice and probably means well, but I'm not about to tell her that I killed my mother. I may be a kid, but I'm not completely stupid. I'm pretty sure if I say anything to Linda that implicates me, it will go directly back to the police. I choose to keep my mouth shut.

Once I decide never to reveal what happened, I only tell Linda what a great mom I had and how much I miss her . . . which is true. Mainly, I cry all the time, partly because I miss my mother and also because I'm so filled with guilt. There's a ball of misery growing inside of me right now and it's tearing me up. The only one I can talk to is Travis. He listens to me some of the time, but I can tell, he doesn't want to talk about it. When the police begin asking more difficult questions, Travis starts pulling away from me.

For a while, the cops take a hard look at my father. According to the ballistics tests, the gun used to kill my mother was the same caliber as a gun registered to my dad. The police ask him to produce this gun, and he can't do it. For a while, the missing gun moves my father up the list into the number-one-suspect position. I know he didn't do it, because I know what really happened. I was there. It was his gun, but he didn't pull the trigger.

My dad told the cops that he had given that weapon to my mother for self-protection before they got divorced. The police make some inquiries with some of my mother's friends, and they corroborate his story. Dad also has an alibi for the day my mother died. Eventually, the cops rule him out. I would have come forward and told the truth if they had ever actually arrested him, but they never did.

I was so messed up on pills and booze the day it happened that I could barely walk. The fact that I was somehow able to open the safe and get that gun is astonishing. Much of my memory is still blurry. Maybe it's a form of self-protection. If I can't remember most of what happened, it seems less painful. But is it really?

A few weeks go by, and things between Travis and me get weird. Every time I look at him, all I can think of is the terrible thing I did. Guilt spills out of every pore in my body. I guess it's the same for him, because our relationship deteriorates. Ironically, my mother was the one who had been hell-bent on splitting us up. Now, her death is what's tearing us apart.

The day my mother died, I stopped all drugs and alcohol. I'm not sure how I put one foot in front of the other without the help of chemistry, but somehow I have. After a year of constant pills and booze, I'm dealing with life sober, and it's not easy.

Two months after that awful day, Travis calls and asks me to meet him at the gazebo in the center of town. He says he wants to talk. I'm staying with my dad now. My father's been watching me like a hawk. He's terrified that I'm about to crumble and have some kind of mental breakdown. After a few white lies, I manage to get out of the house and walk the three miles into town. When I get to the village green, Travis is waiting alone for me inside the large, white, wooden gazebo.

He doesn't see me at first and I take a moment to just look at him. He's so handsome in a rugged, dangerous sort of way. His nose is slightly crooked, but the first time I saw him, I was hooked. His long dark hair, usually worn loose and hanging down past his shoulders, is pulled back into a ponytail.

He spots me and waves me over.

"You made it," he says, his dimples engaging as I climb up the steps into the gazebo. I sit next to him and try to give him a kiss. He pulls away, as if he doesn't want me to touch him. I'm not going to lie; it stings.

"What's wrong?" I say, reaching for him again only to be swatted away a second time. "Babe? What's going on?"

He gets up and walks to the other side of the wooden platform, his hands in his pockets. Once he gets to the railing, he turns and faces me.

"Let me speak before you say anything, okay?" he says. He looks around, presumably to make sure no one else is within earshot.

I nod, worried now.

"I can't do this anymore," he says shaking his head. "Everything in Warwick is too intense right now. I'm suffocating. I can't go anywhere without people staring at me. I've got to get out of here."

"To go where?"

"I don't know, maybe California. The cops said they're done talking to me. I need a fresh start somewhere else. There's too much shit going down, and besides, there's nothing here for me anyway. I'm leaving in a few days."

I feel myself tremble as I walk over to him.

"I feel the same way," I say. "I can't take it here, either. My father's driving me crazy with all his questions. He's constantly 'checking in' with me. The police and reporters will never leave me alone. Let me go with you, and we can start over somewhere else together."

Travis' bottom lip curls down as he pulls a cigarette out of a pack and lights it.

"I'm going alone," he says.

"But you can't leave me here," I say, my eyes getting teary. "Without you, I have no one. All my old friends stopped talking to me when I started hanging out with you. Let me come with you."

Travis takes a drag from his cigarette and blows out a huge billow of smoke.

"No," he says. "I'm going alone."

"Please, I can get some money and we can—"

"You can't come with me," he says firmly. "You just turned fifteen. You're still a minor. I'll be twenty in another week. If you leave with me, I could be arrested for kidnapping.

I'm in enough trouble as it is. I'm not going to jail for that. I've got my whole life ahead of me."

The finite tone in his voice sends me reeling. Deep down, I know there's no amount of pleading that will convince him, but I try anyway.

"You can't just leave me here!" Tears start to flow as I reach out my arms. "What am I supposed to do? Everything that happened was for you. You can't just walk away from me."

Travis comes over to me, his face red and scowling.

"Don't put this on me," he says coldly. "I never told you to shoot your mother. You did that all on your own. I was just the person who cleaned up your mess."

I let out a sob. "I was so screwed up that day. Whatever I did . . . it was to protect you. You said it yourself. She was going to call the cops on you."

When I reach for him again, he pushes me away, which makes me cry harder and want him more.

"When my mom said she was going to report you for statutory rape, you were scared you'd go to jail. You kept saying we had to stop her. We talked about ways to keep her from going to the cops. Remember?"

"That was just stupid bullshit," says Travis, moving away from me again and turning his back. "I didn't mean it. I certainly never intended to actually do it. You're the one who took things too far."

I reach my hands up to my pounding head as I cross the gazebo and stand directly behind him.

"I didn't mean for it to happen. I took so many fucking pills that week. I only did it to save you because I love you . . . and you love me. You said we were soulmates. You can't just leave me here in Warwick by myself. I'll die."

Travis turns around, his face is knotted up. He's furious. My heart drops into my stomach. He's pulling away from me. I'm so terrified of losing him that I start to shake uncontrollably.

"I gotta go." He moves towards the gazebo steps. I plead with him to reconsider, to take me with him, but he only shakes his head as he walks away.

Over the next few days, our conversations grow shorter and more contentious. Eventually, we speak to each other like two robots, all emotion gone. I'm exhausted on so many levels. I'm barely fifteen, my mother's dead and my father's a waste of space, especially after he has a few drinks. On top of all that, I have this terrible secret eating me up a little more each day. And now, the man I love is leaving me.

My life totally sucks.

Two weeks later, when my father is out, Travis comes to say goodbye.

We're barely speaking to each other at this point. Still, every time I think of him leaving, I feel like I'm going to die.

"You'll be okay," he says giving my upper arm a squeeze. "You're tough, stronger than you think. And you're smart. You'll get through this, if you keep your mouth shut."

I make a half-hearted attempt at changing his mind, but it falls on deaf ears. He's leaving. He's explained it to me a hundred times.

"Warwick is over for me," he says. "I'm going someplace where I can become a huge success. One day, I'll drink champagne and eat king crab legs every night of the week. When you can do that, you've made it."

"We could do that together."

He shakes his head. "You don't get it. When I helped you cover up your mom's murder, I became an accomplice. I can't stay here anymore."

Deep down, I know he's right.

Travis was only nineteen when it happened, but legally he was an adult. If the cops ever figure out that he helped me, he'd be in a lot of trouble. He'd go to jail.

Sobbing, I reach for his arm as he gets into his car. My grip is tighter than I'd planned. I catch a look of annoyance on his face as he peels my hands away and frees himself. My nose is running like a faucet. I wipe my face with the backs of my hands and black mascara is smeared all over them. I must look awful.

As he closes his car door, there's pity in his eyes. It startles me.

"Please don't leave me," I shout as he puts the car into drive.

"You'll be fine," he says, as his car starts to move, "but only if you keep your mouth shut. You got that?"

Those were the last words my soulmate said before he hit the accelerator and vanished.

# CHAPTER 4

Several days later, though I'm still devastated, a strange sense of relief washes over me. It takes me a while to understand why. I was so numb when Travis left me behind. Even though his presence in Warwick was a constant reminder of the unforgivable thing I did, now I feel so alone. Turning inward, I barely speak to anyone. No one here knows the truth. There's a strange comfort in that.

As the days go by, the guilt over my mother's death increases. It's like I'm carrying a basket of sin around on my back. I isolate, eventually refusing to leave my shade-darkened bedroom. My father tries to talk to me through the locked bedroom door, but I rarely respond. I have nothing to say. What's the point? My mom's dead and that can't be undone.

After Travis leaves, well-meaning people crawl out of the woodwork trying to be my friend. A young female school counselor loosely connected with the police stops by my dad's house. She's smiley and brimming with enthusiastic optimism.

I don't like her.

Without asking me, my father lets her into the house so she and I can talk. It doesn't go well. I shut down after a couple of minutes. She leaves, but not before giving me her card, which I immediately toss in the waste basket. What's the point of therapy when I already know I'm the worst human being in the world? You can't ever fix something like that.

My mother's younger sister, Aunt Eileen, lives in New Jersey and calls me every day. I usually take her calls but only give one- or two-word answers. Anything more than that is beyond my abilities. I can't share my secret with anyone, and it's slowly killing me. I did one of the worst things anyone could ever do so Travis and I could be together. What kind of person does that make me? Then, after all that, he left me anyway.

I hate myself for a lot of things. I regret taking all those drugs, the terrible fights I had with my mom, but mostly for ending her life. I really miss her. I wish she was still here.

"You can't stay inside this house forever," says my father, sitting in his beat-up recliner in the living room, smelling of whisky. "It's an awful thing that happened to your mother. We can't change that. What are the odds that those criminals picked that house? I'm just so grateful you weren't there when it happened. I could have lost you, too. But you weren't in the house and you've got to keep living. That's what your mother would want."

I know he's right. Mom wouldn't want me to be in so much pain. She loved me with all her heart. That's why I ask myself a thousand times a day, how did everything go so wrong?

Without asking, my father makes an appointment for me to see a therapist named Dr. Langford, who specializes in teen trauma. The first time I go, my father walks me inside. He and Dr. Langford go into her office to speak privately. I sit in the waiting room mindlessly thumbing through old tattered magazines, wondering if the therapist can smell the bourbon on my father's breath.

When her office door opens, my father shakes her hand and walks out, saying he'll wait for me in the car. Dr. Langford is a pretty woman in her forties with long blond hair and dark-framed glasses. She smiles at me and signals that I should follow her into her office.

With no way out, I walk through the doorway and sit down on a small beige sofa. She takes a seat on a nearby chair and smiles at me again. It's not a smile that comes from amusement or joy. It's a pity smile, and I hate it. No one likes to be pitied, especially after you do something indefensible.

"So, how are you doing?" the doctor says, with yet another encouraging smile.

"How would you be doing if your mother was just murdered?" I say, deliberate contempt in my voice.

Bonus points for her, because her expression doesn't change. That half-smile remains on her face despite my obvious hostility.

"You must be in a lot of pain," she says. "From what your father tells me, you've been through a lot. He said you've been keeping to yourself since your mother died. Would you like to talk about what happened?"

"No," I say instantly, which isn't true. I'm dying to talk to someone. Keeping everything inside is awful. But I won't tell Dr. Langford that. If she finds out the truth, she'll be obligated to go to the police. There's no confidentiality when it comes to murder. I'd most likely go to jail — or, at the very least kiddie jail, which is supposed to be awful, too. As much as I want to get everything off of my chest, I can't risk it.

After forty-five minutes of an unproductive one-sided conversation, the therapist announces that our session is over. She texts my father, who's waiting in the car. Moments later, he knocks on her office door.

He looks awkward and sad when he comes in to get me.

"How'd it go, kiddo?" he says, with manufactured optimism.

"It was a start," says the therapist diplomatically. "These things take time. We'll get there."

I don't say a word as I follow my father outside to the car. I already know I won't be going back to see Dr. Langford again. What's the point if I can't tell her what really happened? Isn't getting to the truth the cornerstone of therapy?

When we get home, my dad mentions the idea of me going back to school. It takes me by surprise. I'm not ready. I don't think I'll ever be ready to see all the sad looks from the teachers and the other kids.

Aunt Eileen made arrangements with the school district for tutors to come to my father's house, so I'd be able to finish out the school year without falling behind. Like I care about school now. I just want to get out of this town. I'm like a prisoner now, unable to see my old friends and unable to party. Though truthfully, I don't feel much like partying anymore, not after what happened.

My aunt promised that I could stay with her in New Jersey over the summer. It's only early May, and school isn't out for another five weeks, so I've got to suck it up until then. Outside of my father and my aunt, I speak to no one. Travis hasn't contacted me, which surprises me a little. He and I had been so close for over a year. I've tried to call and text him, but I think he changed his number. I never get through. I really miss him.

After my tutor leaves early one afternoon, I'm feeling very restless. My father comes to my room and wants to talk to me about my feelings. I roll my eyes. I can't go there with him. I mutter something about needing a walk and grab my baseball hat and sunglasses and go outside. I don't have a destination. I just want to get away from the house. Wandering aimlessly for over an hour in a daze, I find myself walking past Blessed Sacrament Church. I made my first holy communion and confirmation at Blessed Sacrament. My mother used to take me to that church every Sunday. She also took me there for confession.

As I stare up at the big stone building with stained-glass windows, it hits me. I could confess my sins at church. I could go to confession. God would forgive me, and no one would ever tell the police. I learned about it in religious studies class. Every priest takes an oath to God and promises that everything he hears in the confessional booth is confidential. It's called the Seal of Confession. It's a pledge stronger than iron. No matter what I tell the priest, he will never, ever tell anyone.

Feeling lost and miserable, I put one foot in front of the other and walk up the church steps. At the top, I pull on the oversized, heavy wooden door. It creaks as it opens, and my heart beats so hard that I can feel the thumping in my toes. Beads of sweat form on my upper lip as I walk down the far-right aisle of the dimly lit church towards the altar.

Halfway to the front, several parishioners are lined up waiting for their turn to absolve themselves of their sins. Once inside the confessional, they'll presumably bare their souls to the dark talking shadow on the other side of the sliding screen window.

I look at my fellow waiting sinners, certain that I'm the worst of the lot. They all look pretty ordinary to me. There's an old woman with white hair in a blue coat using a walker. What kind of terrible sins could she have committed? No one here has a sin as bad mine. None of these people look like murderers.

Do I?

# CHAPTER 5

I wait my turn to cleanse my soul, thinking how I'd love some weed right now. When the door on the right side of the confessional booth opens, a woman who works as a cashier in our local supermarket steps out. She looks at me, but doesn't seem to recognize my face. That's a miracle, because my mother's murder was front page news for weeks, and my picture was in the Warwick paper a dozen times.

After the cashier leaves, the light above the confessional door turns green, indicating the booth is now available. It's my turn. My heart's pounding increases as I walk twenty feet, open the wooden door and go inside. The tiny dark cubicle is sparse, with a small seat and a kneeler placed up against the center wall. A black-screened window sits above the kneeler. It's my choice whether to sit or kneel. Given the severity of my sins, I decide the kneeler is appropriate and take my place there.

Waiting on my knees, I listen to the low rumbling of the priest on the other side of the wall. He's talking with what sounds like a male sinner in the adjacent cubicle. The man has a loud voice, and I catch a few words here and there. It sounds like his wife has a boyfriend and he's been fighting with her. In the sin department, he's got nothing on me.

I'm sweating now as I wait for Father to open the small window between us. I've been in this booth many times before. I started going when I was eight, right after I made my communion. I didn't have anything to confess then. If you go to confession, it's required that you have sins to report to the faceless man behind the screen. So I made stuff up. My mom used to take me to confession periodically over the years, until I finally refused to go.

I remember confessing to sneaking an extra cookie or not doing my chores on time. Father Cleary would tell me to say a few Hail Marys and to 'try to be a better girl this week'. Then the little window would close and he'd turn his attention to the sinner on the other side. And just like that, my eight-year-old filthy little soul went from black to white.

Today, only weeks after my mother died, Father isn't going to hear a confession about laundry not folded or a cookie I took. Today, Father Cleary is going to get an earful.

My knees are sore from kneeling when the priest slides open the window. Both of us are partially hidden by the darkened screen.

When the window opens, it's my cue to speak first.

"Bless me, Father, for I have sinned," I say softly. "It's been three years since my last confession."

"Welcome back. Three years; why so long?" he says, in a soft, friendly voice.

The cracks in the fake leather on the kneeler dig into my skin. I shift my weight around until I find a more comfortable position before I answer. I hadn't anticipated him asking me why it had been so long. Right now, that seems to be the least of my worries.

Why *had* it been so long? Was it because I'd become a spoiled brat and rebelled against everything my parents asked me to do? Or maybe when I turned thirteen and started hanging out with a wild crowd and experimenting with drugs, boys and alcohol, I just didn't have time. Or was it because for the past two years, I didn't care about anyone but myself?

I search the depths of my soul for the appropriate answer. When nothing comes, I'm about to make up a lie when I remember why I came in here and change course. I can't hold it in any longer. No more lies. I'm here to tell the truth.

"That's a good question, Father," I say slowly. "I don't know exactly why I haven't been here for a while. Things have been difficult at home, I guess."

"I see," he says kindly. "Would you like to tell me about it?"

For the first time, I'm not afraid of him or the confessional. It used to terrify me. Confession had always been this weird, faceless, uncomfortable process. But this time, it feels different, and I wonder if it could be my salvation. Suddenly, I'm bursting to get everything out and can't wait to talk.

"Yes, Father, I want to tell you what's been upsetting me," I say softly, wondering if he recognizes me. "But before I start, can I ask you a question?"

"Of course."

"Is it true that no matter what I tell you, even if it's something terrible, you can never tell anyone else?"

"That's correct. We take an oath to God," he says. "Anything you tell me is between us and the Lord."

"Even if it's something really bad, Father? Something horrible, like a crime?"

"Even then."

With his assurances, and with me on the brink of combusting, I take a deep breath and begin. Like a balloon slowly deflating, I tell him about everything — the drugs, the fights with my parents, my relationship with Travis and how my mother threatened us.

"My goodness," says the priest, calmly.

"Also, Father, Travis and I were . . . you know . . . romantic."

"Can you explain what you mean by that?" he says softly.

"We were, like . . . doing it," I say, barely getting the words out and feeling myself blush.

"I see. And did your parents know?"

"My mother found out when she read my journal. She shouldn't have read it. It was private."

"She was probably worried about you."

"If she had just left it alone, none of this would have happened."

"Can you be more specific? What exactly is troubling you?"

At this point, my tongue is sticking to the roof of my mouth and I'm having trouble speaking.

"My mom knew Travis was a *little* older than me. She thought he was still in high school. But he wasn't."

"Why did she think that?"

"I told her he was seventeen, but that was a lie. Travis graduated from high school a few years ago. I'm fifteen, and Travis is almost twenty. My mom would have freaked out if I told her his real age."

"That's a big age difference," says the priest, stating a fact, but without any judgment.

"When my mother learned how old he was and that we were, you know, together, she went crazy. This one day, my boyfriend and I stopped at my house after school. As soon as we walked in, we heard my mother upstairs screaming and slamming things. She had torn my room apart and found weed, pills and a bottle of vodka. It was all in a pile on my bedroom floor."

The priest leans closer to the screened opening. "I'm sure you can understand your mother being upset, can't you?"

"Yes. But things got out of control. She was holding up my journal in the air, and kept saying that I was just a child and that she knew how old *he* was. She kept pointing at my boyfriend and told him never to go near me again. She was really angry. She told him that I was a minor and that she was going to call the police and report Travis for statutory rape."

I explain to Father how after the fight with my mother, Travis and I ran out of the house. I tell him what then happened. "On our way to meet our friends, we stopped at the public library and looked up all the laws on statutory rape.

When he read that the cops could put him away for twenty years, he went insane. We left the library, met up with our friends and downed a bunch of pills with some beer. Travis said what happened at my mother's house was 'messed up'. He kept saying that he couldn't go to jail and that we had to stop her from calling the cops."

"And then what happened?" says the priest.

"The next day, Travis told me he thought he should leave town before my mom went to the police. I lost my mind. Travis was my person. We were soulmates. I couldn't stand the thought of him leaving me. I hated my mother for trying to destroy the one good thing in my life."

There's a rumbling on the other side of the confessional. The person waiting in the adjacent booth is growing impatient. I look at my watch. I've been talking to Father Cleary for nearly thirty minutes. Clearly, confessing the mother of all sins takes time.

I peer through the tiny holes of the wooden door separating me from the interior of the church. A line of waiting sinners has formed and people are getting antsy. I've stalled long enough. It's time to tell Father what I came here to confess.

I turn my head again towards the small screened window. Water springs from my eyes and trickles down my face. I lean in close to the screen and whisper.

"Father, are you sure God will forgive any sin?"

"If you are truly repentant, he will."

I swallow. "I shot her, Father. I killed my mother. I was the one who killed Midge Lester."

Fifteen minutes later, I emerge from the confessional, head down and face streaked with tears. Walking past the line of waiting parishioners, I pass the man at the head of the line. He's middle-aged, with a big stomach and has a weary look on his face. He appears to have the weight of the world on his shoulders. It occurs to me that he was standing only feet from the tiny dark closet where I had just confessed to killing my mother.

*Did he hear what I said?*

I brush past him and for a split second our eyes meet. It's fleeting, but I'm sure I detect a look of fear, confusion and . . . maybe *pity* in his eyes. Wondering if I'm being paranoid, I race out of the church, gasping for air. Did that man hear what I told the priest?

# CHAPTER 6

The police investigation into my mother's death continues for a long time. Warwick is a small town; the cops have little to no experience with murder. Most of the crimes our police deal with are small — shoplifting, parking violations, noisy parties . . . stuff like that. The last murder in Warwick happened several decades ago. Before I was born.

My mother's murder is front page news for weeks, and the investigation is discussed regularly in the local papers. The cops leave no stone unturned. They even interrogate gang members and drug users in the county looking for a lead. In the end, the police come up with nothing.

Throughout the investigation, I'm feeling so alone. My best friend since first grade, Kathy Peluso, no longer calls me. We had been so tight growing up. But when I started hanging out with Travis and his friends, she pulled away from me. We had been inseparable until Travis. She didn't like him or any of the other kids he hung around with. She told me I should stay away from him. Deep down, I probably knew she was right. But that wasn't going to happen because Travis and I were in love. We were soulmates. Kathy was a straight arrow: no drugs, booze or anything like that. She didn't understand true love like I did.

When she stopped talking to me, I really missed her. I don't blame her at all. We were on different paths. She chose the high road and I slid slowly onto the low. Travis's pull over-rode any sadness or regret I may have felt about losing Kathy.

I started sneaking out of my mother's house several nights a week to meet up with Travis and his friends. We'd congregate anywhere that provided a cloak of privacy — empty parks, under bridges, vacant ball fields at night. I'd consume any drug or alcohol put in my hand. I started skipping school and my grades went from straight As to failing in most of my classes. The funny thing is, I didn't care.

Travis was my one and only priority. At first when he started paying attention to me, I was a little afraid, but also flattered that *he* was interested in me. After a few weeks of his attention, all I could think of was him and how much I loved him. I was sure Travis Ritter was my destiny and that one day we'd get married.

School and family, once at the center of my life, became an afterthought. Nothing mattered to me except Travis . . . and partying. My mom wasn't stupid. After a while, she noticed the change in me. Before Travis, I shared every detail of my life with her. After he and I got together, all communication with my mom pretty much stopped. I lied about everything and shut her out completely so I could be with him.

At one point, she asked me if I was drinking or taking drugs. I gave her an accusatory stare and lied again.

"How can you ask me that?" I demanded, fury in my voice. My fabricated indignation must have worked, because she backed off. After that, I lied about everything and never gave it a second thought. But eventually, what I was doing to myself was hard to disguise.

Like anyone using a substance, my behavior and appearance changed. It was impossible to ignore or excuse. My mother confronted me again and again. We fought all the time, and eventually she grounded me. She attributed all of my problems to Travis and said I was not to see him again.

I hated her for trying to stop me from being with the man I loved. She had no right to tell me what to do.

At that point, my mother still didn't know that Travis *wasn't* seventeen. Looking back, I know she was only trying to protect me. But at the time, I didn't see it that way. Travis was everything; I would have done anything he asked me to do. Anything.

Now, I have to live with that terrible decision.

I really miss my mom.

# CHAPTER 7

*Nineteen years later*

*Abbie Sterling*

I don't deserve my wonderful husband, Jason. He loves me dearly, and I'm happier than I've ever dreamed I'd be or deserved to be. We have a beautiful home and family, and my life is filled with positive happy things like raising my two girls and volunteering. Over the years, I've found that helping other people makes me feel good. It's how I get through the day or the week.

"So, what do you think of the place, babe?" Jason said, as he and I walked out onto a long, gray, wooden dock. The magnificent twelve-thousand-square-foot home in Eastport, Connecticut was right on the Long Island Sound, and just went on the market.

"It's your decision," Jason said, smiling at me. "Is this the one? Your call. It's only a little over an hour train ride into Manhattan, and they have great schools here. It could work."

"I don't know," I said tentatively, marveling at the splendor of the property. In my wildest dreams, I never expected to live in a place like this.

"It's totally your decision," he said, walking along the water's edge and skimming a stone. I watched it bounce six times. "I want you to be happy. If you don't like this one, we can look at something else."

I let out a contented sigh.

"Are you kidding? This place is amazing," I said, looking out at the water. "The kitchen's fantastic and has amazing light. Did you see the appliances? There's a walk-in refrigerator, just like they have in restaurants."

"What's not to like?" interrupted our real estate agent. She was a sixty-something woman wearing a blue pantsuit two sizes too small. It was apparent she was counting her potential commission, and it was making her salivate.

"I'm tellin' you, you should grab it," she continued. "This place is a little gem. If you like it, Jason, you should put in an offer. There are several other parties interested in this house. It's gonna go fast, trust me."

"What do you think, girls?" shouted my husband. Our daughters were playing on the swing set on the lawn.

"Can we get a dog?" shouted Luna, only six and already a shrewd negotiator like her father.

"We'll see about a dog. What about you, Gracie? You want to live here?" My husband ran his fingers through his thick, shiny, black hair. "We could get you a slide to put next to those swings. Maybe I'll even build you a treehouse. Would you like that?"

Grace, who had just turned four and would do anything for her father, came running over. "I like the house if you like it, Daddy. Can we get a trampoline, too?"

I shook my head and gave my husband The Look, which meant: 'absolutely not; our children will die on a trampoline or at the very least end up in wheelchairs'.

He understood and laughed. A lot of men look forward to sons, but not Jason. I never met a man who loved being the father of daughters as much as he did. He was born to raise girls. And his daughters would do anything to make their father happy.

I met my husband right after he sold his first technology company. I had put myself through college waiting tables and driving a private school van filled with rich kids. I got a degree in accounting, and my first job out of school was doing bookkeeping for the small start-up company that Jason had recently founded.

There were only nine employees when I started. I was number ten and had a crush on him from the first time I met him. I used to get tongue-tied whenever I passed him in the hall. He took me out to dinner six months after I joined the company.

From the start, Jason was charming, kind and easy to be with. At the same time, he exuded steely confidence after founding, building and selling a multimillion-dollar company before turning thirty. When I met him, he was on course to do the same with his next company. I guess you could say he had the Midas touch. There was no stopping him. On top of all that, he was really kind, too.

Meanwhile, I was living paycheck to paycheck. I walked everywhere in Manhattan, to save the subway or bus fare. Unless it was torrential rain or a snowy blizzard, I got around New York on foot.

"You're spoiling me," I said to Jason, on one of our first dates. It was in a restaurant I could never have afforded to go to.

"Good. That means I'm doing all the right things," he had said, his dark-brown eyes twinkling as he took my hand. "If anyone deserves to be spoiled, it's you, and I intend to do it."

I remember thinking at the time, *He would never say that if he really knew me and what I'd done. He wouldn't want to sit at a table or even in the same room with someone like me.* I didn't deserve to be spoiled. I *deserved* to be in a federal prison, for killing the one person who loved me more than anyone else in the world.

Five months after our first date, Jason Charles Sterling, once listed on the *Forbes 30 Under 30*, asked me to marry him.

When he got down on one knee in Central Park and surprised me with a five-carat diamond and platinum engagement ring, I was truly blown away. My first thought: *I need to tell him the truth*. It would be unfair to enter into a marriage harboring my deep and disturbing secret. I told myself that if I really loved him, I wouldn't withhold the truth. He had a right to know who he was marrying.

Staring down at the glistening gemstone in the little black box, my guilt stopped me from saying yes to his proposal. He waited for my answer, angst on his face. When I offered no response, his brows knitted together.

"If you don't like it," he said, concern mixed with tenderness in his voice, "we can find something else. You can pick out whatever you want. I just want you to be happy."

A lump formed in my throat because I had no right to someone like him. None.

"We can go to the jeweler tomorrow," he said, still full of hope that I'd say yes.

I remember thinking that the engagement ring he selected was the most gorgeous one I'd ever seen. I never dreamed of a ring like that or of finding someone as amazing as Jason to love me. People like me don't get to be happy. Yet there he was, right in front of me, asking me to be his wife.

I stared at the ring, wrestling with whether or not to tell the truth or continue with my lies. If I said nothing, I could put the beautiful ring on my finger and go on to live a wonderful life with an incredible man.

Or I could do the right thing and be honest with him. Taking that path would mean I'd probably lose him, someone I truly loved and respected, and who made me laugh. I wrestled with myself. It would be impossible for him to rationalize marrying a murderer, a woman who killed her own mother to save her teenage boyfriend. But if I really cared about him as much as I thought, how could I *not* tell him the truth?

Even if Jason somehow accepted that I was remorseful and a different person now, it would open up a whole new can of worms. By telling him, I'd be making him complicit in my crime. Then, he'd have to keep my secret, too. My heavy burden would become his, circling like a black raven over our marriage and future family. I loved him far too much to ask him to do that.

After an agonizing mental debate, I made a decision and stretched out my left hand. He smiled and slipped the diamond ring onto my ring finger. I knew then I was making a deal with the devil by staying silent, but I didn't care. I desperately wanted to be happy.

"I love you so much," I said, tears gathering in my eyes as I looked at my future husband. "The ring is perfect. I don't want another one, and I can't wait to start our lives together. It will be a fresh start for both of us."

Jason cocked his head. "Fresh start?" he said. "What have you ever done that you'd need a fresh start? You're the kindest person I've ever known. You never say anything bad about anyone. You're practically a saint."

I smiled and let out a little self-deprecating laugh to diffuse my inner loathing.

If he only knew the truth.

# CHAPTER 8

We got married the next summer on the beach in Montauk, New York. It was a fairytale wedding, and Jason was my handsome prince. My father, who had thankfully stopped drinking by that point, was there to give me away. Dear Aunt Eileen, with her flaming red hair, was dressed in royal blue, and was my maid of honor. Through the years, my aunt had tried to fill in for my mother the best she could. She and my mom looked so much alike, except for the red hair. Sometimes, I even pretended she *was* my mother.

After Jason and I got married, I continued to work for his company. But six months after our honeymoon on the Amalfi Coast, I found out I was pregnant. We both decided I'd resign when I went on maternity leave. Not long after Luna was born, Jason sold that company and made another small fortune.

Now, nearly a decade later, he's founded and built an angel investment group. When he's shorthanded, I still do some bookkeeping for him, to keep my skills up. I also volunteer to help local women who are starting businesses. We don't need the money, so helping these women get a leg up is a labor of love for me.

These days, my life is delicately balanced. I maintain our home and family as a way to stay sane and keep the ancient demons out of my mind. Having order and beauty around me and doing things for others helps block the terrifying images of my mother from creeping into my consciousness. It doesn't always work though, especially not at night.

When it's dark, the worms start crawling around in my brain. Then the nightmares begin, and my screaming follows. Jason holds me when that happens. Every time it does, he asks me what's wrong, what's troubling me so much? Obviously, I can't tell him. I'll never tell. If I did, my family and my life as I know it would disappear. That's why my secret has to remain one until I go to my grave or I'm arrested . . . whichever comes first.

There are some parallels between my life today and my childhood. My mother was only a few years older than I am right now when she died. We lived in Warwick, Connecticut, which is only twenty minutes northwest from where I live now. But that's where the similarities end.

Warwick was a working-class town then and still is today. It's a place where people work two jobs and have drawers full of unpaid bills. Our family was no different. Eastport, on the other hand, where I live now, is inhabited by more of a working leisure class. On any given weekend, you'll find Jason and me along with dozens of other parents cheering at one sports field or another while our children play soccer or lacrosse.

To someone looking in from the outside, it appears I lead a very privileged life. That's because I do. But my life is also a well-crafted illusion. If you look close enough, I'm wearing a cheap mask with frayed edges. I work hard to keep that mask on.

Once a year, I drive over to Warwick to see my dad. I hate going there because it stirs up awful memories. Even after all these years, there's still a little gossip around town about my mother's murder. A lot of people still think my father did it. Obviously, I know that's not true. He was nowhere near the house the day she died. Chances are he was drunk somewhere, his usual condition at the time.

Despite my father having nothing to do with my mother's death, the stink of public opinion was all over him. Given that, it's ironic that I came out of the whole mess smelling like a rose.

"Are you kidding?" people in town would whisper. "Tom Lester's as guilty as sin. His ex-wife is dead, so now all his alimony payments go bye-bye. You do the math. If it walks like a duck . . ."

The summer after my mother's funeral, Aunt Eileen drove up to my dad's place. She told him in no uncertain terms that I was going to live with her in New Jersey. She said it 'wasn't up for debate'. My father was so drunk he just sat there nodding but said nothing. After getting little to no reaction from him, Eileen packed up all my things and whisked me back to her home in northern New Jersey. Single, warm and loving, she made me feel safe again.

After the murder in Warwick, the cops collected DNA from our house. None of it provided a match to anyone in the system. They found my prints and Travis's along with a few friends and neighbors but that was to be expected, they said. Our house safe had been left wide open, and things were missing including Mom's jewelry, silverware, cash and her handgun.

The working police theory at the time was that a group of crazed drug addicts looking for something to steal and sell broke into what they thought was an empty house. Since my mom had come home early from work that day, her case was categorized as a 'wrong place/wrong time' crime. In layman's terms: it was rotten luck.

Long before Jason and I got engaged, I told him about losing my mother — how I had come home and found her bleeding on the floor of her bedroom. It was a beautiful New York summer day. He and I were sitting on a bench looking out at the East River at Carl Schurz Park. Barely able to get the words out, I got very weepy as I slowly shared the official story of my mother's death and the home invasion. Jason put his arm around my shoulders, drew me in and held me for a long time.

"I'm always here for you," he had said. "Nothing's going to harm you, not while I'm around. Remember that."

For the first time since my mother died, I finally felt safe. After that day in the park, he never brings it up unless I want to talk about it, which I never do.

Today, my mother's murder investigation is as cold as a snowball. The files are probably stashed away in some old metal storage unit gathering cobwebs. From what I understand, that's not unusual after so much time has passed. I've learned that murders in this country go unsolved by the thousands. I'm counting on those statistics working in my favor.

I still hear from the Warwick Police Department when something new pops up. Every time they reach out, my heart skips a beat. I think to myself, *This is it. It's over. I'm going to prison.*

Thankfully, none of the new police leads have ever amounted to anything. So, I go on living my life. I raise money for new soccer field equipment, volunteer at senior living centers, sell Girl Scout cookies and sometimes teach adult education classes in bookkeeping.

I don't keep in touch with anyone from Warwick. After I left there with my aunt, I was a physical and emotional train wreck. All the drugs and uncontrolled teenage anger had taken its toll on me. In the years that followed, my monumental guilt nearly killed me. I was very depressed. Travis had been the only thing that mattered to my misguided fifteen-year-old self. After he blew out of town and left me, I never heard from him again. I didn't think so at the time, but it was a good thing. I had to move on with my life.

Once I was in New Jersey with my aunt and away from all the bad influences, I started to mend. At first, I thought I would miss the wild crowd and all the partying we did. But after what happened, I never wanted to party again. Eventually, I became a model high school student and even achieved high honors.

My new friends were decidedly different from the ones I hung around with when I was in Connecticut. My Jersey crowd was nerdy, and a much better fit with my true personality. I was no longer that badass I pretended to be in Warwick. Drugs and alcohol were in the past, and I discovered volunteering. Doing things for others made me feel less bad about myself.

The boys I hung out with at my new high school were on the track team or in the theater club. Turns out when I wasn't intoxicated, I could run pretty fast and had a knack for acting. I lived with my aunt until I finished high school and then headed off to college in Virginia.

Over the years, I saw my father a few times. My aunt insisted he meet me in New Jersey when he wanted to see me so that I didn't have return to Warwick. Eventually, my dad started to clean up his act. He quit drinking and pulled himself together. We're not close, but I'm glad he's in a better place. Now, we have a cordial relationship, and he's really good with the kids. We never talk about my mother. It's too hard. They were divorced, but I'm pretty sure he was still in love with her.

Flash forward now to our life in Eastport. Jason and the kids keep me pretty busy. On any given day, I'm carting my girls from one activity to the next: dance rehearsal, soccer, art class, piano lessons, lacrosse. I even make their Halloween costumes from scratch. I want them to have everything I didn't.

I also try to remember to do a little self-care from time to time. I go hiking and, when I can, take an exercise class at the local gym. I have a vegetable garden in the backyard, bake my own bread from time to time and try to adhere to a healthy Mediterranean diet for my family. I'm trying to do everything to be a good mother, wife, friend and neighbor.

And, I was totally nailing it . . . until today.

# CHAPTER 9

Sitting in my car in Bianca's driveway, in front of her large white clapboard house, I honk the horn twice. There's a flutter in one of the upstairs bedroom windows followed by her face mouthing "sorry" while she holds up one finger. That's Bianca-speak for 'give me five more minutes'.

My best friend is always running late, so I settle in. Rolling down my car window, I notice that everything is green and dewy, and I take in a deep breath of the beautiful spring morning air. Fiddling with the radio to find music to fit my mood, I pick a classic country station, and sit back to wait for Madame to arrive.

Moments later, Bianca signals again. This time, she's standing in her front doorway holding up two fingers. That's code for 'it will be another five minutes before I actually get into your car'. I roll my eyes and smile. Everyone knows Bianca's always late, but nobody minds. She's so darn nice and supportive that people give her that extra wiggle room. We all build a few minutes into our schedules to accommodate her.

Bianca and I are the co-chairs of the outreach committee for the Eastport Community Council (ECC). Our group does all kinds of public service activities for different programs throughout the county. We do everything from raising money to help poor families at Christmas to driving cancer patients to doctor appointments.

Bianca was the first real friend I made here in Eastport. Over time, she's become more like a sister to me, one that I never had but always longed for. After what happened with my mother, I've always been guarded with friendships and relationships. I don't make friends easily. I guess you could say I have some trust issues.

But Bianca is a positive force, just like my Aunt Eileen. Bianca's contributions volunteering have made huge differences in our community and the surrounding towns. I loved her the minute we met. She's so darn happy; I just like being around her.

A door slams, and I look up as Bianca runs down her front steps, her arms full. She's carrying a large open cardboard box filled with several dozen bottles of tiny floral arrangements. Yesterday our outreach committee got together and assembled all of them. There are two big jugs of water in the back of my car that we'll use to fill up the little vases when we get into the rooms at St. Vincent's Senior Living Center.

"Put the box in the back with my stuff," I shout, as I pop open the lift gate of my SUV.

"Sorry, I'm late," Bianca says, as she climbs into the passenger seat and lets out a big dramatic sigh. "I was running around like a madwoman this morning—"

I smile because Bianca starts every conversation with 'sorry, I'm late'.

"—Dave forgot to feed the dog before he left for work," she says. "When I went to get the dog's food, the container was empty. I had to go down to the basement to find a new bag and—"

"Don't worry about it," I say, putting the car in drive. "We'll get to the senior living center in plenty of time. The photography books the library donated are on the back seat. We'll pass those out as well."

One of the ECC's primary initiatives this year, aside from our recycling initiative, is to expand our senior outreach. We host frequent holiday events at senior centers, and also do regular visits to nursing homes and assisted living facilities around the county. So many older people never get visitors. Our goal is to fill that void and bring in a little sunshine. I really like working with older people.

"I've never been to St. Vincent's before," says Bianca, checking her messages on her phone.

"Me neither. I spoke to the director last week. She's thrilled about the program we're doing. She gave me the rundown on the whole place."

"Anything juicy?"

I smile. Bianca's always on the lookout for drama.

"Don't get your hopes up. Nothing too exciting," I say. "St. Vincent's is primarily funded by the Catholic Church, and they've got a little over a hundred residents. Most of them are laypeople, but there are a handful of former clergy . . . nuns, priests, brothers. The director told me their oldest resident is about to turn a hundred and four."

As we drive through the scenic wooded backcountry roads lined with stone walls, Bianca rattles off a laundry list of items our steering committee needs to address.

We pass the sign for St. Vincent's.

"Here we are," I say, interrupting her as I turn into the facility's parking lot. I look for a spot near the front entrance because we have a lot to carry in. Luckily, just as we pull in, a blue Toyota backs out of a space right next to the main entrance.

We get out of the car, stretch our legs and look around the campus. The St. Vincent's Senior Living Center is a large, colonial, red-brick building flanked by pastoral gardens. Nestled on a large piece of property surrounded by acres of woods, it's so quiet that all you can hear are the birds chirping in the trees.

"Not a bad place," says Bianca, taking it all in. "I could live here."

"You're only thirty-five," I say, with a smirk. "You've got time before you need to pack your bags."

Gathering up the boxes of flowers, vases and books, we string half a dozen full tote bags over our arms and head into the building. An older woman with white hair and glasses is seated at the reception desk. She smiles as we approach.

Minutes later, the director of patient services comes out to greet us. She gives us a map of the place and tells us we have free rein throughout the building.

"Stay as long as you like," she says. "Feel free to visit with anyone you want to. Our patients love it when people come here. We're so grateful to your organization for doing this. It makes a real difference."

After giving us the lay of the land, she explains how some in their population would not benefit from our visit due to their compromised condition. To maximize our time, she gives us a list of room numbers for those residents she thinks will enjoy interacting with members of our committee.

We look at the map. St. Vincent's has one main building with four wings jutting off from the center. Each wing is named after trees — Birch, Maple, Pine and Oak. The administration offices, medical and dining areas are housed in the Oak Wing; the residents live on the other three.

Bianca hands me the list of approved rooms. There are a couple dozen in the Birch Wing, the same in Maple and just a few in Pine. Since we're supposed to come here weekly, Bianca makes a suggestion.

"I think we should split up? That way each of us can spend more time with individual patients and get to know them better. Otherwise, we're going to be racing through to get to all of them."

I nod.

"You take the Birch Wing," she says, "and if you don't mind, I'll take Maple, because my uncle's sister-in-law is a resident here and she's in Maple. When I told my uncle I was doing this project, he was so happy. I promised him I'd spend time with her every week when we come. Is that okay? We'll meet back here in an hour and do the Pine Wing together at the end."

I pick up my box and bags and head down the hallway towards Birch. The wing has three stories and twelve rooms on each floor. I look down at my list for the room numbers. As I start to move, I notice that each resident has their own room, with a name plate on the outside of the doorway so I'll know who I'm talking to.

In the first room, I meet Alberto Sala, a World War II veteran. He's nearly a hundred years old and has significant physical limitations. He needs help getting in and out of his wheelchair, but after we chat for a few minutes, it's clear that he's mentally on the ball. We have a nice conversation, and he thanks me for the flowers and picture book.

"You'll come to see me again?" he says, with an encouraging smile.

I smile back. "Of course, Mr. Sala. I look forward to it. I'll be coming every week."

"If you're gonna be here all the time, you better call me Albie. That's what my friends call me."

Feeling pretty jazzed after a successful first visit, I check my list of rooms and head to the next one, B107. The plaque outside of the room says *Joan Wilson*. A nurse passing by stops me in the hallway and asks me if I'm lost. I explain why I'm there and she lets me know that Joan Wilson is a retired nun.

"You should address her as Sister Joan," she whispers. "It will help get the ball rolling. She's an interesting woman."

Having gone to Catholic schools, I stand up very straight before I enter Sister Joan's room. My recollection is that nuns were always sticklers about posture. Why, I don't know, but it was definitely a thing.

I enter her room and introduce myself. Sister Joan seems unaware that I'm there. Her eyes are open, but she doesn't acknowledge my presence, even after I say my name twice and explain the program.

46

At this point, I relax my back and neck, figuring if she doesn't know I'm there, she won't be evaluating my posture. Standing at the foot of the old nun's bed, I try to make conversation again. This time I speak a little louder and slower.

"Good morning, Sister Joan. My name is Abbie. I've brought you some fresh flowers. This room could use some brightening up, don't you think, Sister?"

The nun finally turns her head and looks directly at me.

"Got any gin in those bags?" she says, suddenly alive and sporting a wicked smile.

I stammer. I wasn't expecting that response.

"I've got to go to prayers soon," she says. "Can you turn on *Wheel of Fortune* for me?"

"I think that show is only on at night," I say.

"Are those flowers for me?" she asks, her face softening as she smiles again. I explain a third time who I am and that I'll be coming once a week.

"I never get visitors anymore," says the old woman, shaking her head. "What's your name?"

"Abbie."

"I used to live in an abbey," she says, starting to laugh. "Those days are gone. Now, they've stuck me in here."

We continue our disjointed conversation while I try to follow her unique logic. After about ten minutes of confusing chatter, I look at my watch and tell her I've got to get going.

"I enjoyed your visit," she says. "You will come again, won't you?"

"I will," I say with a smile, before I head out into the hallway. My conversation with Sister Joan hadn't made much sense. But she seemed happier when I left. That's why I was there, so I guess it was mission accomplished.

# CHAPTER 10

Struggling down the hallway with my heavy load of floral arrangement stuff, I spot an empty metal cart shoved into a corner. No one appears to be using it, so I 'borrow' it. I actually groan as I place the heavy box of posies and multiple shopping bags onto the cart.

Moving on, I meet six more residents, giving each flowers and books along with friendly conversation. Like the first two people, their physical and mental conditions vary. One woman was asleep the whole time I was there. I waited a few minutes, but then left the flowers and vase on a tray next to her bed. I also left a handwritten note, introducing myself and saying I'd be back next week.

I check the time. I'm supposed to meet Bianca at reception in fifteen minutes. Looking over the diagram of the Birch Wing and the list of room numbers, I need to go up a flight to finish. I take the elevator to the third floor for my last two rooms. I finish one and then wheel the cart to the doorway of Room B304, the last on my list. The name plate on the outside of the room is missing. I'll have to wing it on introductions.

"Good morning," I say, with a big smile on my face as I march into the sunny room. A very old man with wisps of white hair and wire-framed glasses perched on his nose is sleeping in a wheelchair by the window. Seated in a chair next to him is a woman I guess to be in her sixties. She's wearing blue scrubs and has a large metal cross hanging around her neck. I presume she's a nurse.

"Are you lost?" she says. "Who are you looking for?"

I look down at my paper. "They didn't give me a name, only a room number — B304. I'm with the Eastport Community Council," I say. "We're doing weekly visits to nursing homes. I've brought some flowers to spruce up the room for Mr . . ."

"It's Father," she says, as she gets up, taking me by the elbow and leading me to the other side of the room. "He's napping right now. Poor man doesn't sleep well these days. I'm afraid he needs his rest more than flowers. I'll give them to him later when he wakes up."

She takes my vase and goes into the adjoining bathroom to fill it with water. I glance over at the sleeping man slumped in the chair. I hear the water turn on in the bathroom sink giving me a few seconds to look around.

It's tidier and sparser than the other rooms I've been in. In fact, there's no decoration of any kind — no cards or festive balloons like some of the others had. The only thing in here that wasn't supplied by the hospital is a silver picture frame on the window ledge, containing a black-and-white photo. I walk over to get a better look.

I pick up the small frame. It's a group shot of seven young smiling priests wearing black robes. There appears to be some kind of ceremony going on. I wonder if this was the sleeping man's clerical ordination. A priest on the far left of the picture is very handsome. He also looks vaguely familiar, but I don't know why.

Before anything concrete forms in my memory, the nurse returns. Her name pin says Sister Peggy Hannon, R.N. Now I understand. She's not only a nurse, she's also a nun . . . a formidable combination.

"There," she whispers, carrying the little vase and flowers over to the table next to the sleeping priest. "When Father wakes up, he'll be able to see the flowers quite well from here."

"There was no name outside the door for this resident," I say, looking down at all my papers again. "That's why I didn't know who he—"

"His old nameplate was badly discolored. Father deserves a nice nameplate for his room, don't you agree? I've requested a new one from maintenance, but they haven't replaced it yet. Everything takes so much time these days."

"Seems that way," I say, not knowing what else to say. "Can you give me his name for my records?"

"Father Cleary," she says, waving her hand at the sleeping man. "Father Michael Cleary. He's a wonderful man."

When I hear that name, a bolt of lightning hits me between the eyes. My past comes flooding back like a tidal wave sucking me under. I'm ten years old again and in Warwick. I'm sitting in a pew next to my mother at Blessed Sacrament Church on a Sunday morning. We used to go every week to listen to the priest's sermons and receive holy communion. Images flash through my mind and I can see the face of the pastor of our church, Father Michael Cleary, saying mass. He officiated at my first holy communion, my confirmation and later . . . at my mother's funeral. He was someone I saw around and about my entire childhood.

It's been nearly twenty years since my mother died. My memories before, during and right after it happened have always been hazy at best. I've tried to put the puzzle together a million times, but it never works. I tell myself it's because of all the drugs and booze. Or maybe I just don't want to remember because it's too awful. Sometimes I think my partial amnesia is a form of self-protection. If I can't remember it, I don't have to relive what happened. Honestly, not remembering the details is a blessing.

From time to time, fleeting visuals of that day randomly flash before my eyes without warning. Anything can trigger it. When that happens, it cuts me to the core. I could be in the supermarket ordering halibut or putting the finishing touches on a new craft project and — *bam!* — my mother's body is on the floor right in front of me. After, I'm a mess for days.

I've read a ridiculous amount of self-help books, and concluded that I didn't like myself very much when I was a teenager. I think I 'projected' all my teenage angst onto her, which was unfair. When I look back, it seems like I hated everything and everyone, except for Travis and his friends. I thought partying with them under the highway overpass was my salvation. It wasn't.

For nearly two decades, I've been carrying around the guilt and the fear of the truth coming out. Guilt is like poison. It bores a hole into your soul and festers. I may not be in a physical jail, but I'm still in a prison of my own making. In some ways, it's worse.

Today, I live in a constant state of regret, forever sorry for everything that happened. My mom wasn't at my graduation from high school or college. She didn't attend my wedding or see her granddaughters born. She'll never be able to know them, or they her. She would have loved them so much and my girls would have adored her. Grace is so much like her.

Every day of my life since then, I grieve the loss of my mother and hate myself a little bit more. Carrying around that secret, unable to tell anyone, is almost worse than going to jail. Travis was the only person who knew what happened that day. He helped me out and never told. Years ago in Manhattan, I ran into an old classmate from Warwick. She had just been to her tenth high school reunion. We got to talking about some of the kids we both knew. She told me about a few people who had died. That's when I found out about Travis. He was one of them. She said he died in a car accident about seven years after he left Warwick.

I remember feeling a mixture of sadness and relief. I had a momentary flash of remorse, but it was quickly replaced with gratitude. I hated myself for feeling that way, but with Travis gone, my secret was safe . . . I was safe.

After learning about Travis's car accident, I felt able to move on. I married the love of my life, and we had our family. I put my past behind me. Twenty years ago, alone and afraid in that darkened confessional booth, I asked for God's forgiveness for the terrible thing I'd done. Father Cleary heard my confession and absolved me of my sins. He was old then . . . I always figured he was long dead by now.

My heart pounds as I stare at Nurse Peggy. With each breath, I can literally feel it slamming up against my ribcage. While a million horrifying thoughts race through my mind, four questions reverberate.

Does Father Cleary remember what I told him?

Did he keep his vow of silence like he was sworn to?

Am I safe? Is my family safe?

# CHAPTER 11

After hearing the priest's name, I try to steady myself and focus my attention on Nurse Peggy. To counteract my increased anxiety, I plaster a smile on my face in an attempt to hide my paranoia. I move closer to the sleeping priest to get a better look. Nurse Peggy's eyes stay on me.

*Does she know something?*

The nurse/nun remains seated next to the old man as I fuss with the tiny flower arrangement. While I'm messing around with the vase, she picks up a black hairbrush from a tray and gently combs the priest's remaining strands of thin white hair. Glancing at the flowers, she gives me a half-smile. I can't figure her out, but she definitely gives me the creeps.

I try to present myself as cool and calm. But on the inside, my nervous system is buzzing like a beehive. After all these years, I've come face to face with the only person left who knows what I did. Panic sets in, and I start making inane small talk. I tend to do that when I'm nervous.

"They've got a beautiful campus here, gorgeous grounds," I say. "Do you work here or are you a volunteer like me?"

"I work here part-time, *and* I volunteer." She gets up and places the brush in a drawer next to Father Cleary's bed. "I'm off duty right now. There are several nuns and priests who are residents here at St. Vincent's that I spend time with. I take care of Father Cleary every day. It's the right thing to do for a man who gave his whole life to God and his parishioners. He was selfless. Nowadays, we get old, and everyone forgets about us. I'm not going to let that happen to Father."

I press my lips together and nod.

"That's what always happens," says Nurse Peggy, in an accusatory tone. "I don't think that's right, do you?"

I shake my head vigorously. "No. It's not right at all."

As the words leave my mouth, Father Cleary sits up straight in his chair and lifts his head towards the ceiling.

"*Cum sancto spiritu in gloria Dei Patris,*" he says, with a strong bellowing voice that echoes off the bare walls. "*In gloria Dei Patris . . . Amen.*"

Alarmed, I look at the nurse. She's nodding and smiling at the old man.

"Amen," she says. "Yes, Father, indeed. Amen."

He looks at her. "Jesus said we must turn the other cheek," he says. "People don't do that anymore, do they, Sister? I sometimes fear our savior's message has been lost to Sodom and Gomorrah."

"We can always pray, Father," Nurse Peggy says, patting him gently on the shoulder. "Look at the lovely flowers this young woman has brought for you."

I'm surprised she thinks they're lovely, since her reaction to me thus far has been decidedly on the chilly side. I start yammering to the old priest about the Eastport Community Council and how I'll be visiting every week.

Suddenly, Father Cleary starts preaching in Latin again.

"*Et revel abitur gloria Domini,*" he says before leaning forward and pointing his finger at me. "A man with a mustache was here this morning and stole all my clothes. He wore a green shirt and pants and had a knife. It was big and sharp."

"Oh, my goodness," I say, not wanting to use my usual 'Oh, my God' in front of a priest and nun.

"He took my clothes right out of the closet," says Father Cleary, in a loud whisper as he looks around for imaginary danger. "He stole my favorite camel hair sweater, the one that Sister Peggy gave to me last Christmas. He told me to keep my mouth shut or he'd slit my throat wide open."

My eyes must look as big as dinner plates, because Peggy starts clucking, shaking her head and patting the priest on his arm.

"Now, you know that's not true, Father. You're scaring this poor woman. The man you're referring to is George. He's on staff here. You like George. He brings you your meals every day and tells you funny stories."

"I don't like him," says the priest, his face now in a snarl. "I don't like him even a little bit."

Nurse Peggy pats his hand again. "Father, that's just not so. You do like him. George always stops by to see you and tells you jokes that make you laugh. I'll bet this morning what you saw was George putting your clean laundry into the closet."

The nurse walks across the room and opens his closet door. Inside she retrieves a camel-colored cardigan on a hanger and takes it out. "See, here's your sweater, Father. No one took it. It's right here."

"He had a big knife," says the priest dubiously, shaking his head. "It was like a machete. I saw it."

"Hmm," the nurse says, as she closes the closet door, "I'll bet he used that knife to cut up your fruit this morning. He told me he brought your breakfast today."

The priest looks confused but nods. After a moment, he notices that I'm in the room.

"Who are you?" he says, peering at me.

"This is Ms. Sterling," says the nurse, reading the name sticker on my shirt. "She's a volunteer, and apparently, will be visiting every week. She brought you these pretty flowers. Aren't they nice?"

The priest follows her gaze until his eyes land on the small vase with flowers sitting on the table near his bed. He blinks twice. Then, slowly, his face relaxes.

"They're very pretty. Thank you," he says, in a totally normal tone. "Nice to have something fresh and new in the room for a change. This place can get very depressing now and then. Nothing happens here . . . except for old people dying."

I'm marveling at the sudden change in the man's lucidity. He went from totally out of it and speaking in another language, to normal, in five seconds flat. I'm trying to work out the whole situation when a young man with a mustache, wearing green scrubs, enters the room. His name tag says *George Butler*. I presume he's the same machete-wielding George the priest just told us about.

"Sorry to break up the party, but it's time for physical therapy, Father C," says George, with a grin. "Your PT told me she's going to work you hard today. We've got to get those legs of yours moving. No pain, no gain."

"She's a task master, that one is," says Father Cleary genially, as George unlocks the brakes of his wheelchair and pushes him towards the door.

"Nice meeting you, Ms. Sterling," says the old priest, over his shoulder. "Come see me again, won't you? I enjoyed our visit and look forward to continued conversations."

## CHAPTER 12

Once the priest leaves for physical therapy, I'm left alone with Nurse Peggy.

She smiles at me, but only with her mouth. Her eyes stare right through me.

"Does he often speak in Latin?" I say.

"Father has his moments," she says, letting out a sigh. "He occasionally reverts to Latin because it feels familiar to him. Sometimes he concocts bizarre and often frightening stories about all sorts of people. It can be about anything or anyone — the man who waters the plants or the person who delivers mail. Sometimes Father swears he sees strangers' faces out the window. We're on the third floor, so obviously, that's impossible."

I look out the window. She's right: seeing a face there would not be doable from up here.

"Right before he left the room, he was totally normal," I say. "He was calm and in control. Is that change typical?"

The nurse nods. "That's the peculiar thing about dementia," she says. "Every day it's different. Sometimes Father is his normal self for most of the day. But his cognition comes and goes. I've heard him tell the most outrageous stories."

"You mean like George stealing his clothes?"

She smiles. "Father's got quite an imagination, I'll give him that. He gets things confused inside his head. I've become pretty good at deciphering his facts from fiction."

"How can you tell? A few things he said could have happened."

"If it sounds preposterous, it usually is. His short-term memory isn't very good. But I find his long-term memory is excellent. He can still recite the entire mass in English *and* Latin. It's impressive."

The nurse walks over to the window and looks out.

"He remembers almost everything that happened twenty, forty or even fifty years ago," she says. "He can tell you details about people he counseled in 1986, or families he helped back in the 1960s."

"That's amazing," I say.

She turns and faces me. "At the same time, he often can't remember who he met yesterday, this morning or even fifteen minutes ago. Sometimes he has very frightening delusions and nightmares."

As I listen to the nurse speak, one overarching question burns in my brain. Does Father Cleary still remember what I told him in that confessional twenty years ago? And, if he does, has he told anyone else?

"When Father has these more outlandish delusions," I say, trying to appear only mildly interested, "is there ever any truth to them?"

Nurse Peggy purses her lips before she speaks and then stares into my eyes.

"Father Cleary and I are close . . . very close. He tells me everything. There are some things I probably shouldn't know."

I swallow as my pulse quickens. At this point, I clock my anxiety level at sky high, and worry if I'm going to make it out of the building without falling apart.

"Unfortunately," the nurse continues, "Father doesn't have a filter anymore. He mentions things to me, personal things that people have told him over the years. These days, he's sort of like a river overflowing its banks. Once the water starts flooding the streets, it's hard to stop it."

She walks over to his bed, fluffs the pillow, and then lovingly smooths it.

"You seem very interested in Father Cleary," the nurse says as she straightens the blanket at the foot of his bed. "Why is that, Ms. Sterling?"

I clear my throat to buy myself a few seconds so I can come up with a plausible response. When I was kid, everyone called me Abbie, never my full name, Abigail. I decide to use Abigail at St. Vincent's. I don't want to trigger any ugly or incriminating memories for Father Cleary, if I don't have to.

"Please, call me Abigail," I say, with a smile. "I'm interested in all the residents here. If I'm going to come every week and be an effective outreach person, it's helpful to have a clear understanding of each person's medical condition. It will improve the patient experience."

I thought that sounded pretty good. But I can't tell if old Peg buys what I just said. Thankfully, she gives me no indication she thinks my little speech is bullshit, even though it totally was.

"You have to understand," the nurse says, as she straightens the hanging clothes in the closet. "There are bits of truth to all of Father's stories. Sometimes he mixes up the players or combines two people into one. But most of the time, I've found he's remarkably accurate when you investigate it."

Her words unnerve me. Does she know something about me? Did he tell her about my confession?

Walking over to me, she leans in as if we were co-conspirators in some secret endeavor.

"Father Cleary once told me a staff member here was being rough with him," she says, in a loud whisper. "At first, I didn't believe him. All the staff here seemed so nice. But Father kept complaining. At one point, he showed me a bruise on his upper arm. I couldn't imagine how he would bruise himself like that, so I took action. When you know something, you've got to do something about it."

I gulp. "What did you do?"

"I may be old, but don't let that fool you. I'm very tech savvy. I put a hidden camera in Father's room — you know, one of those nanny cams."

"That was so clever of you," I say, thinking Sister/Nurse missed her calling. She should have worked for the FBI.

The nurse nods. "Cameras don't lie. Sure enough, everything Father had told me was true. One of the aides showed gross negligence and was abusive when he interacted with Father Cleary. I saw him shove Father several times and act very rough with him. I called the police right away and showed them the video. That same employee is sitting in jail right now, paying his dues for what he did."

"Sounds like you saved the day."

"Don't underestimate Father Cleary. He knows what's going on. He sometimes gets confused, but he knows."

"Maybe people shouldn't underestimate you," I say, feeling slightly sick.

"Someone has to look after him and the others. Father has no family that I'm aware of. It's my honor to take care of him. You could say it's my calling."

I nod at her again, like a bobblehead doll, because I don't know how else to respond. Clearly, she's a little obsessed with the cognitively-impaired priest, which makes me nervous.

"You'll be back next week, then?" she says.

"That's my plan. Our group goes to several other facilities, but I'll most likely be working here at St. Vincent's."

"I could tell Father liked you. He seemed at ease, almost like he knew you. He's not like that with everyone, especially not new people."

Part of me wants to say that I'm flattered because I've never met him before. But something tells me not to lie. It would be easy enough for the tech savvy nun to find out that I grew up in Warwick and went to the same church where Father Cleary was the pastor. Nurse Peggy strikes me as the kind of person who would do a deep dive on anyone coming near *her* priest.

With a million negative thoughts running through my mind, I feel my throat closing up as I say goodbye, grab my things and leave. Out in the hall, as I lean on my cart for balance, my legs start to buckle underneath me. Thankfully, there's a chair in the corridor and I sit down to catch my breath. I lean forward, and gradually my heart rate begins to slow.

"Are you okay?" says a familiar voice.

I look up. Bianca is standing over me. Her beautiful smiling face is a welcome relief.

"I'm fine now," I say. "I don't know what happened. I got a little lightheaded all of a sudden. I probably should have eaten breakfast."

She makes a tsk-ing sound. "I don't know why you skip the most important meal of the day. You need to eat something in the mornings," she scolds, as she whips a bag of almonds from her purse, rips it open and hands it to me. "Eat. The flowers can wait."

For the next twenty minutes, Bianca and I deliver the remaining flowers, vases and books throughout the third wing. As we go room to room, she chatters about clothing drives and charity dinners. I'm only half listening, because I'm completely focused on the fact that Father Cleary is alive, a patient here and a potential time bomb. I need to find out what he remembers and who he may have told.

On our drive back to Eastport, Bianca, who sits on a dozen different committees, makes a string of phone calls. This gives me some quiet time to think about the whole situation and to plan my next move. My first question is, will seeing me trigger Father's memories and ultimately cause him to share my secret? Going there every week might be a bad idea.

I pull up in front of Bianca's house.

"Thanks for driving," she says, as she opens her car door. "Today was fun and eye-opening. Some of the residents are really sweet but others don't even know we're there."

"Yeah," I say, "it was great. But I've been thinking about the time required for this project, and I may have overextended myself."

Bianca closes the car door. "You can't bail on me now. We're a team. It's only once a week."

"I know, but I have so many other obligations. And—"

"But we were always going to do this together," says Bianca, going into full pitch mode. "Besides, the school year is almost over. You know what it's like trying to find volunteers during summer. It's impossible. I won't be able to get anyone to replace you at this point, with summer right around the corner."

"I know, but maybe we can—"

"I'll make you a deal," says Bianca. "Just do St. Vincent's with me until school starts in the fall. Then our committees will be in session again, and if you still can't do it, I'll find a replacement for you."

My persuasive friend finally gets out of the car, only after I agree to continue with the program through September. I really have no choice. I signed up for this, and she's right, there isn't anyone to take my place over the summer. Waving to her as I pull away from the curb, another terrifying thought crosses my mind. Lucid Father Cleary was a kind man of principle and integrity, someone who took his vows very seriously. The man I knew back in Warwick would never violate the sanctity of the confessional or his oath to God. But cognitively-impaired Father Cleary is an unpredictable wild card. If he hasn't told anyone yet, he could let the cat out of the bag at any time.

It occurs to me that it might be risky showing my face to the old priest.

*Would seeing me cause him to remember? I'll have to take that chance. I have to know for sure if he can connect the dots.*

As I pull into my driveway, I know what I need to do. I'll give Father Cleary a little test to see if he has any recall of my face.

# CHAPTER 13

By the time I get home from the senior living center, it's around 1:30 p.m. When I walk into my kitchen, my entire body is still one giant rush of adrenaline. I'm so jittery and anxious that I feel like I'm going to jump out of my own skin.

Desperate times call for desperate measures, so I pour myself a small glass of red wine. That should calm me down before my girls get off the school bus. *Note to self: don't make a habit of mid-afternoon cocktails.*

The house is deadly silent, so I flip on the TV to a news station to create some noise. Sitting on the couch, I wrap my arms around my shoulders, give myself a hug and play back the events of the day, trying to make some sense of them. After all these years, I've come face to face with Father Cleary again. The one thing I know is, one wrong comment from him could blow up my life.

I take another sip of wine, feeling the warmth move through my body while trying to convince myself that the priest hasn't told anyone about me yet. If he has, I'll soon be sitting in a jail cell. Still, I have to be a realist. With Father Cleary's intermittent dementia, he could out me at any time without even realizing it. All he has to do is suggest what happened to my mother, and it would be all over for me. Everything would explode — my family, my husband, my entire world. What would something like this do to my kids if it got out?

When I left Warwick and moved in with my aunt, I put everything behind me and tried never to think about what happened. Years later, in a college psych class, I learned that's called 'compartmentalizing'. Over the years, I've become very good at that. I'm so good at it that sometimes I don't think about my mother for months. I like to pretend she's away on a fantastic trip somewhere exotic.

At one point in my late teens, I almost convinced myself that it didn't happen, and that I didn't do it. I imagined that there really had been a home invasion. That was the official story, and that's the narrative I've clung to all these years.

But now there's a new danger — a ninety-seven-year-old land mine with dementia. Father Cleary being not in control of his thoughts puts me at significant risk, and I don't know what to do.

I finish my glass of Cabernet feeling slightly more relaxed, but still on edge. The school bus will be here in twenty minutes, and then I won't have a moment to think. The kids will barrel through the door, grab a snack and then, minutes later, we'll be on the go for several hours of lacrosse and Girl Scouts.

When we get home, they'll start their homework while I get dinner ready. Jason's away on a business trip until tomorrow night. It will only be the three of us for dinner tonight. Given the shock I had today, I'm not in the mood to cook. We'll stop at the market and pick up sushi and dumplings for the girls and a Cobb salad for me. Thinking about the errands I have to run is a welcome distraction. With all the racing around I'll be doing for the rest of the day, I won't have time to think about my precarious situation until after the girls go to bed.

The high-pitched screech of brakes on the old school bus pierces the air as it stops at the foot of our driveway, letting me know my kids are home. As I walk to the front door to unlock it and turn off the alarm, an old saying pops into my head — *keep your friends close; keep your enemies closer.*

I open the front door and watch my girls climbing off the bus. They wave to their friends as the large yellow vehicle heaves twice and moves on down the road. From the street, Grace and Luna see me standing in the front door. Their faces break into smiles and they run towards me. That single moment fills me with so much joy. My entire face smiles, and I wave as they get closer. No matter what, I can't let my past ruin their future or their father's.

As they run up the driveway towards me, a plan forms in my mind. I *will* keep my enemy close. I'll become the most devoted volunteer that St. Vincent's has ever had. I have to find out exactly what Father Cleary remembers and if he's ever told anyone about me. I've got to protect my family.

It's nearly 6:30 p.m. when the girls and I finally pull into our driveway after a busy afternoon.

"Daddy's home," both kids say in unison when the garage door opens and we all see that Jason's navy-blue SUV is parked inside. My husband had taken a trip to Seattle for a series of tech meetings and wasn't due back until tomorrow. It's a nice surprise for me, too.

Before I turn off the engine, Luna and Grace are out of the car and running up the basement stairs to the first level of the house. I look in the back seat, they've left all their practice gear in the car.

Huffing and puffing up the steps lugging their bags, I walk into the family room and drop everything on the floor. Luna and Grace are sitting with Jason on the couch peppering him with questions about his travels. He looks up at me, smiles and gives me a wink. He's loving every minute of their undivided attention.

"Did you go to the top of the Space Needle, Daddy?" says Luna.

"Not this time, sweetie. I was pretty busy with all my meetings," he says.

"Did you take a ferry ride in the harbor, like we did when we were there last summer?" says Grace, snuggling in closer to her father.

My husband shakes his head and laughs. "Girls, I think you're forgetting. I wasn't on a vacation. I was working. There wasn't any time for rides and trips to the Space Needle."

"Poor Daddy," says Grace, my little one. "Work doesn't sound like fun at all."

"That's why they call it work. But it can be fun, if you do it right," says my husband, looking at me standing in a pile of sports equipment. "Girls, go help your mom with all your gear."

Because Daddy asked, they immediately get up and collect their equipment. When Jason asks them to do something, they can't do it fast enough. With me, not so much. I usually have to ask a few times. They both pick up all their things and run up the stairs giggling.

"Your dirty clothes go in the laundry basket . . . not on the floor," I shout up the stairs before sitting down on the couch next to my husband.

He puts his arms around me and gives me a kiss. "Hey you," he says. "Long couple of days. It's good to be home."

"I thought you weren't going to be here until tomorrow night," I say, leaning into his shoulder.

"I wasn't, but my last meeting was canceled. I could have stayed, but there's a guy I want to meet with in New York tomorrow. I've heard he's got this interesting system that converts methane gas from cows into renewable energy. A few of my partners have been looking into his company, and their early assessment is very positive."

"Methane gas?" I say. "From cows?"

"Sounds crazy, but if what he claims he can do is true, it could be huge. I'm still mad at myself for not jumping on the cannabis movement earlier."

"You'd invest in cows?" I say, mildly curious about this unusual idea.

"If it works. Renewable energy is a different beast, and we have to solve it. If this person's legit, we may jump into the water."

"It sounds kind of exciting," I say drifting off, my inner thoughts swinging back to Father Cleary.

Jason gives me a look.

"Everything okay, babe?" he says, scrutinizing my face. "You don't seem like yourself."

*Damn. He reads me like a book.*

As the girls bang their way down the stairs, I use the distraction to avoid giving my husband a truthful answer.

"Me? I'm great," I say, getting up and walking towards the kitchen. "I picked up some sushi and dumplings for the kids. There's enough for you. Let's eat."

# CHAPTER 14

Over the next month, Bianca and I go to St. Vincent's every week, rain or shine. I've learned that I love interacting with seniors and am more committed than ever to working with them. At the same time, I have a dual purpose — keeping tabs on the confused and chatty priest. But first, I had to find out if he remembered me at all. If he did, I couldn't go back.

On my second visit to the center, when Nurse Peggy stepped out of Father's room to help another patient, I sat down next to the priest. Once Peg was out of earshot, I took out a bunch of photos, including an old photo of me from when I was fourteen. It was a wholesome picture taken on Mother's Day, the year before my mom died. I placed my picture in with the other photos of my family and friends.

"Would you like to see some pictures of my daughters, Father?" I said.

"Ok," he replied, staring out the window.

I shuffled through a dozen shots of my kids and friends with my fourteen-year-old picture mixed in.

"This is Luna, and this is Grace," I said, showing him the first few images.

"They look like good girls," he said.

68

I showed him another picture of my girls with some of their friends, and then the one of me at fourteen.

"That's my neighbor's daughter." I pointed to my image and studied his face looking for a glimmer of recall.

"She looks nice," he said, with no more emotion than he had when he looked at my daughters.

With that unscientific test completed, I figured I was semi-safe continuing to volunteer at St. Vincent's. If my teenage face didn't trigger his memory, my thirty-five-year-old face shouldn't either. That means, I can still stay close to him and see what he does remember.

For today's project, we're putting together small living plants in ceramic planters. Bianca and I have brought seedlings for each patient, so they can take care of them and watch them flower and grow.

As we walk into the building, Bianca suggests that we do all the rooms together for a change. That won't work. I need alone time with the priest.

"I don't know," I say. "Some of the residents might find different volunteers confusing."

After a minute of gentle yet firm debate on my part, Bianca gives in. She'll continue to work the Maple Wing and I'll stay on Birch.

Walking through the building to see my peeps, I keep my eyes peeled for Nurse Peggy. Even when I don't see her in the hallway, I get the nagging feeling she's lurking somewhere nearby. I've made a few innocuous inquiries with one of the aides about Peggy. I learned that she started working part-time at St. Vincent's about two years ago. According to the aide, the Catholic diocese assigned her to tend to all the retired clergy members in this facility. Once I understood that, Nurse Peggy's protective behavior made a little more sense. That's why she hangs around Father Cleary so much. Maybe she's not as strange as I thought. Technically, it's her job to look out for him . . . but still, she's odd.

This morning, when I enter Father Cleary's room, I'm relieved. Florence Nightingale is absent. Something about that woman puts me on edge. Maybe it's because she's so close to the one person who knows my entire secret. Regardless of Peg's motivations, I need to keep an eye on her, too.

As I put my things down on an empty chair, I notice the old priest is awake. Today will be my first opportunity to do a little fishing away from Nurse Peggy's prying ears and eyes. Father Cleary is fully dressed and sitting in his wheelchair facing the window, his back is to me.

"Good morning, Father," I say with manufactured enthusiasm, as I walk towards him. "We've got another beautiful day. The birds are singing, and all seems right with the world."

I wait for his response to determine if I'll be talking to lucid Father Cleary today, or cognitively-impaired Father Cleary. Several seconds pass with no response. I'm just about say something else to get the conversation rolling when he finally speaks.

"It *is* a beautiful day. Turn me around so I can see you," he says gently. I walk up behind him, grab the handles of his wheelchair and swivel it so it faces the interior of the room. Then, I stand in front of him so I'm in his sightline.

"I know who you are," he says pointing a finger at me, "and I know why you're here."

I freeze.

"You're the woman who brings flowers every week," he says. smiling.

I let out a breath and force a smile.

"That's right, Father. I'm with the group from Eastport."

"You're Mrs. Sterling," he says. "What's your first name?"

I hesitate for a moment, not wanting to trigger old memories by saying my name. Hearing it might help him make a connection.

"It's Abigail."

"You don't hear that name much anymore. Did you bring more flowers today?"

I smile. "Not flowers, Father, but I did bring some small succulent cactus plants. They'll live for a long time."

"I don't know how much longer I'll be here," he says. "But Peggy will take care of it when I go."

"I'm sure you'll be around for a long while," I say half-heartedly.

He looks away and seems to drift off into another place.

"Father?" I say.

"*Vivamus moriendum est*," he shouts, as he looks out the window.

I grab my phone and type a version of those words into Google translate. In layman's terms, what he said was 'life is short'. I smile nervously not knowing how to respond, either in Latin nor to his somewhat accurate comment about his imminent death. That's when it occurs to me. If the priest expired, it would solve all my problems.

"Are you not feeling well?" I ask, not sure if I'm hoping he'll say yes.

He smiles and turns to me. "I don't have much longer here. I'm ready whenever the good Lord calls me home."

I refrain from doing a happy dance after hearing about the priest's self-prognosis, but truthfully, I am relieved.

"Father, where were you stationed when you were an active priest?" I'm not sure if 'stationed' is the correct terminology, but my meaning seems to get across.

"I was a chaplain in Korea with the U.S. army. When I got home, they sent me to a brand-new church in Florida. It was too hot there for me, so they moved me to a parish about forty minutes from here, in Warwick. Stayed there for nearly fifty years."

I sit down on his bed so we can look at each other face to face.

"It must have been gratifying to be in one place for so long. I imagine you got to know all your parishioners quite well."

He nods and then smiles ruefully, but doesn't answer my question.

I try again. "I'll bet you helped people get through some dark times," I say, hoping to start him talking.

He nods. "Sometimes things were tough. But it wasn't all sad. There was a lot of joy, too — weddings, baptisms, communions. And don't forget the holidays. You should have heard the choir at Midnight Mass."

"I love Christmas, too."

"I have a secret," he says, tipping his head towards me and lowering his voice. "Terrible stage fright. Every time I said mass, I shook like a leaf."

For a second, the old priest's confession stuns me. I remember all those Sundays sitting in Blessed Sacrament with my mother watching him preach before the altar. I never would have guessed he was nervous. He always seemed in control, so confident, a true man of God.

"I'm sure no one ever noticed," I say.

"It's time for me to go," he says, starting to shout. I watch his face scrunch up as he becomes visibly agitated. "I want to go now. Take me, Lord. I'm ready. Take me."

For a second, I want to say something to give him hope. I want to tell him that there are lots of things he can do and so much to look forward to. But I stop myself because I know it's bullshit. The man is nearly a hundred. He can't walk or see very well, and slips in and out of dementia without a moment's warning.

Before I can respond with my hollow encouragement, there's a noise behind me.

"Good morning, Father," says a sharp voice. Nurse Peggy looms in the doorway, hands on her hips. "Oh. You're here again."

"Every Wednesday," I say, as I stand up and face her. "And sometimes, other days if our schedules don't work for Wednesdays. It depends."

"There seem to be an awful lot of flowers and odds and ends around the room since you started coming," she says, clicking her tongue in obvious disapproval. She makes a point of looking over my shoulder at the collection of vases and bric-a-brac I've brought that now line the window ledge.

I hold the smile on my face, so I don't give away what I'm really thinking. Before I can respond to her comment, Father Cleary begins to shout.

"*Extra Ecclesiam nulla salus. Dominus vobiscum,*" he says, in a quasi-Gregorian chant, the kind usually reserved for a mass or a horror film. He waves his right hand in the air, giving the sign of the cross as he continues his Latin rant.

"What's happening?" I ask Nurse Peggy. "What's he saying?"

"He's ministering," she says calmly. "It's what he knows how to do best. He's been preaching to his flock for over seventy years."

"Bless me, Father, for I have sinned," the old priest shouts, as he points and looks directly at me. "Bless me, Father, for I have sinned. *Extra Ecclesiam nulla salus. Dominus vobiscum.*"

"What does all that mean?" I say, looking at the nurse.

"It means outside the Church there is no salvation," she says.

"Why is he looking at me?" I say taking a step backwards.

"Maybe he thinks you have sins to get off of your chest."

Nurse P and I are now locked in a death stare. I look into her eyes trying to detect a deeper meaning to her words.

"They stole my shoes," says the priest, becoming more distressed and looking to us for some kind of resolution. "It was that woman who brings my food. She took my shoes. She drinks my milk and only gives me the empty containers. I see what she does. She thinks I'm asleep but I'm not. She pours the milk into a plastic bottle and takes it home to make rice pudding. She spits on my food, too. I've seen her do it."

"Now Father," says Nurse Peggy, going over and placing her hand on his shoulder, "you know that's not true. No one here spits on your food."

"She does. She brings big dogs with sharp teeth here. She spits on my food when she thinks I'm not looking, but I know."

The nurse tries to calm the old man, but he becomes increasingly defiant and redder in the face.

"She hits me and steals my ice cream. I need to get out of here," he shouts as he tries to push himself out of his wheel-chair and stand up. "I'm leaving. I'm going home now."

Nurse Peggy firmly pushes him down and looks up at me.

"Well, don't just stand there," she says. "Help me keep him in the chair."

"But if he wants to get up . . ." I say.

"Father Cleary can't walk. If he somehow gets himself up, he'll fall and crack his head open."

At this point, God forgive me, I'm thinking that wouldn't be such a bad idea. Regardless, I go over to help her and place my hands on the priest's shoulders. To aid in calming him down, I sing a folksong I sang when I was a kid.

Within a few minutes, the old man relaxes and retreats quietly back into Latin.

"*Signum Fidel, Signum Fidel*," he says over and over.

I look at Nurse Peggy. "What does that mean?"

"Sign of faith," she says, as she wheels him over to the window.

"Do you think anything he says is true?" I say. "You know, about people stealing or spitting on his food."

Nurse Peggy rolls her eyes dramatically, clearly conveying she thinks I'm an imbecile . . . which is uncalled for, in my opinion.

"Father often makes up stories about people he sees around St. Vincent's," she says.

"How do you know what's true and what's not?"

"I know. Yesterday, the woman who regularly brings his meals brought her toy poodle in with her. Most of the patients love it when she brings in her dog."

The nurse pauses a moment and straightens the cross around her neck.

"Occasionally," she says, in almost a whisper, "I've seen her take uneaten wrapped packages of cookies and crackers and slip them into her purse."

"Then, Father Cleary isn't completely wrong."

"No, he's not totally wrong. He has trouble deciphering real from not real. But he doesn't miss much. If you show or tell him something once, he never forgets it. Ever."

# CHAPTER 15

That night, after hearing Father Cleary's Latin diatribe, I'm wide awake in bed. Jason quietly snores next to me. Disconnected memories from when my mother died run through my mind on an endless reel. I can't turn them off, no matter how hard I try. Tossing and turning, I ask myself a million 'what if' questions. Eventually . . . gratefully, I drift off to sleep.

Later, I'm suddenly awakened by screams, followed by a voice calling out to me.

"Abbie, can you hear me? Abbie, wake up. You're all right," the voice says.

*But I'm not all right. I'm never all right.*

Someone's shaking me hard. I'm afraid and try to push them away.

"Abbie, please wake up," the voice says again.

I feel myself shaking uncontrollably. My eyes are closed but my mouth is open. I'm gasping for air. I can't get oxygen into my lungs and I feel like I'm drowning.

*Am I having a seizure?*

Someone shakes me again. My eyelids spring open. Jason's face is directly over mine. He looks concerned. No, it's not concern, it's terror written on his face.

"Abbie, it's okay, sweetheart," he says stroking my hair. "I've got you. Breathe. Breathe for me."

"Is Mommy okay?" says a tiny voice from out in the hallway.

I turn my head. Grace and Luna are standing in the doorway in their pajamas, clinging to each other. Grace is crying.

"She's all right, girls. Go back to bed," says my husband. "It's just another one of Mommy's bad dreams. She'll be fine. Go to your rooms and I'll be there in a few minutes to tuck you in."

"I hope you feel better, Mommy," says little Grace, walking towards me and handing me her favorite lavender-stuffed lamb. "Alvin will stay with you so you're not scared."

Luna takes her sister's hand. I watch my two sleepy daughters turn and leave the room. Jason continues holding me, and over the next few minutes, I start to calm down.

"Was I screaming again?" I whisper, while trying to regulate my breathing.

My husband nods.

I let out a breath. "I'm sorry. I didn't mean to wake everyone up again."

"I know you can't help it," he says gently. "But this has been going on for too long. Tonight was one of your worst. You scared the shit out of me and you really upset the kids."

Every time this happens, Jason asks me what my dreams are about. He wants to know what terrifies me so much. I always tell him I can't remember, which of course is a lie. The truth is, I know every detail of the dreams, because they're almost always exactly the same.

It starts in my old house. I'm fifteen again and alone in my mother's bedroom sitting at her vanity table. Her perfume and makeup is strewn across the top of the table. Looking in the mirror, I try on some of her jewelry and brush my hair with her brush. I feel very grown-up sitting there in her special spot. All of a sudden, I see my mother's reflection in the mirror. She's standing across the room by the bed folding clothes from the laundry basket. I look down at the vanity. There's a

76

red lipstick sitting there, and I ask her if I can put some on. She tells me 'no', that I'm 'too young for cosmetics', and not to ask her again.

Then my dream gets dark. I don't know where it comes from, but suddenly there's something heavy in my hand. I look down and see I'm holding a gun. I turn and face my mother. She has a confused look on her face when she sees what's in my hand. Her mouth opens but she says nothing. For a moment we just look at each other without speaking. Then, the gun fires all by itself. It shoots off three times and my mom falls back and onto the floor. When I see the blood spurt from her chest, I start to scream. I keep on screaming until I eventually wake up.

"I'm so sorry I scared you and the girls again," I say to my husband, as he sits me up and takes me in his arms. "I have no control over them."

"I know that. But, we've got to face the facts. It's been happening more often and it's getting more intense. You need to see someone about this, Abs. Your nightmares used to be short and only happened once or twice a year."

"I know, but—"

"Let me finish. For the past month, it's been happening almost every night. Each time, it takes me that much longer to wake you up. I almost didn't go to my meeting in Denver last week because I was afraid to leave you alone overnight."

I look up into my husband's beautiful brown eyes and feel a tear trickle down my cheek.

"And tonight," he says, "I was shaking you so hard, I thought I was going to hurt you. You wouldn't wake up. You scared the hell out of me, not to mention terrifying the kids. We can't keep doing this."

Another tear runs down my face.

*If I tell him the truth, he'll hate me. I'll lose him and my girls. I'll be all alone . . . again.*

My husband's right. The nightmares *are* getting worse, and they *have* increased in frequency. Seeing Father Cleary at

St. Vincent's has turned everything upside down. I've spent years trying to make amends by building a good life with my family. Now, it's all crashing down around me.

Priests aren't supposed to tell what they hear in confession, but what about a priest with cognitive impairment? Father Cleary says all kinds of bizarre things. What if he tells someone about me? Nurse Peggy has made it clear that she's his confidant. For some reason, she doesn't like me. Did he already tell her about my confession? Does she know?

Jason gets out of bed to check on the girls. When he returns, he brings me a cup of chamomile tea.

"Drink a little of this," he says glancing at the clock, which is flashing three thirty. "Maybe we can still get a couple of hours of sleep. I've got a big day."

I take a sip and let the warm, soothing tea run down my slightly sore throat. Screaming will do that.

"Are you sure you don't want to talk about your dreams?" he says, as he lies down next me. "People say I'm a good listener."

I shake my head. "I told you, I can't remember them. I only know that they scare the hell out of me."

Of course, getting the whole thing off my chest might improve my nightmare problem, but it would create a bigger one. Jason's my best friend and I really want to tell him, but I can't.

"I want you to go see a therapist," he says as he leans over, kisses me on the cheek and turns out the light. "Maybe a professional will be able to help you get to the bottom of this. All I know is, we've got to try something."

I agree to go to counseling, but in my heart, I know I won't tell the therapist anything that could actually help me get better. That would mean revealing the truth, and I can't go there.

I have to always remember . . . there's no statute of limitations on murder.

# CHAPTER 16

Jason makes an appointment for both of us to go see Dr. David Goldberg. He's a licensed therapist specializing in sleep disorders and comes highly recommended.

A few evenings later, we get the babysitter situated in the family room, put a Disney movie on for the girls and set off to have my head examined.

On the drive over, I contemplate what I'm about to get myself into. There's no question I need help. But I'm a little freaked out about talking to someone. What if I slip? All these years I've kept my own counsel and it's worked for me . . . except when I'm dreaming. Talking to a therapist now could unleash things that I don't want to see the light of day. I promise myself to be on my guard at all times. No matter how genuine and caring this man seems, I must never reveal the truth.

Always the optimist, my husband chatters cheerfully the entire twenty-minute trip trying to put a positive spin on our upcoming shrink session. We pull into a parking lot in front of an antique wooden building with yellow clapboard sides and white trim, typical in this part of Connecticut. He turns off the engine and we both sit in the car for a moment without speaking.

"Don't be nervous, babe," he says as he shuts off the engine. "Goldberg came highly recommended from numerous sources."

I turn my head and look at him with an accusatory stare. "How many people did you tell about me? Does everyone in Eastport think I'm a raving lunatic?"

Jason shifts slowly in his seat, faces me and gently takes my hand.

"Abbie, I know you're feeling hyper-sensitive right now. I promise, nobody knows anything about you or our family. I would never put you in a bad light with anyone. I told a few people who I like and respect that *I'm* having some sleep issues, that's all. I asked them if they could recommend a therapist for *me*. Not you. Okay?"

I let out a sigh and squeeze his hand before we get out of the car. My snippy overreaction to his comment is a result of my emotions being on overdrive. I don't really care if other people know I'm seeing a therapist. There's no shame in it. I sure as hell went to plenty of shrinks after my mother died; it won't be a new experience. We get out of the car and Jason takes my hand. As we walk towards the front door, I realize he's right, but for different reasons. I have bigger problems than people knowing I'm in therapy . . . much bigger.

Ever since I saw the priest at St. Vincent's, my life hasn't been the same. I'm convinced that seeing him again after all these years is what triggered my recent string of nightmares. For all I know, he could be in his room right now blabbering in Latin to Nurse Peggy about me being a homicidal maniac. His thoughts may often be jumbled and nonsensical, but those crazy ideas could potentially destroy the life I've built. Sure, he's out of it half the time, but occasionally he makes perfect sense. And, when he does, that nurse nun is always there . . . listening to everything he says. What would she do if he tells her the truth about me? My guess is she'd head straight for the nearest police station and sing like an operatic canary. Without realizing it, even a confused Father Cleary could take me down.

Jason and I walk through the parking lot towards the small two-story building. There's a shingle hanging out front with Goldberg's name on it. Jason holds the front door open for me as we walk into a tiny vestibule lined with brass mailboxes. The door to the right is the one we're looking for.

We enter the small waiting room containing a beige sofa and a black lacquered coffee table piled high with magazines. There's a closed door over to the left. The doctor must have some kind of silent alarm because he comes out to greet us before we have a chance to sit down.

"Good evening," he says, as he gestures for us to follow him into his office. The man is about fifty, wearing jeans and a sports jacket. His brown hair is receding and his lower face is covered by a trim brown beard flecked with gray. I notice his eyes bulge slightly, making me wonder if he has a thyroid condition. We walk past him into his office and sit on a brown leather couch. Smiling, Goldberg sits across from us in a matching leather chair.

"So, tell me how I can help you," he says, holding a notebook and a pen in his hands.

My husband starts first by filling Dr. Goldberg in on my night terrors and their increasing frequency.

"And about how long have these nightmares been going on?" he asks.

Jason looks at me. "Since I've known you, right? But in the beginning, it only happened once or twice a year."

I nod.

"But for the past few months, it's been several nights a week," he says. "When I first met Abbie, they were short and mild. She sort of moaned a little and was easy to wake up. Recently, they've become much louder and last longer. Also, now my wife is far more terrified than she used to be."

"Would you agree with that, Abbie?" says the therapist.

I nod again.

"Sometimes, she wakes up the whole house," Jason adds, explaining how my 'episodes' are affecting the entire family.

"I'll be perfectly honest," says Jason. "It's scaring the hell out of our kids."

Goldberg looks at me. "Do you agree with Jason, Abbie?"

I begin to feel like a bobblehead doll, when I nod a third time. The last thing I want to do is terrify my girls. I see how my nightmares upset them. But I also don't want to go to jail and leave them. I remind myself to be very careful of what I say to this seemingly helpful man.

For the next fifteen minutes, Jason and I fill in the therapist on what's been going on. When we finish, Goldberg suggests we use the remaining thirty-five minutes so he and I can talk alone.

After Jason leaves, Dr. Goldberg and I look at each other. I say nothing, trying to wait him out. I know the old rule about the first person who talks loses. But after sixty long seconds, I break first.

"What do we talk about now?" I say, with an awkward smile.

"This is your time, Abbie. What would you like to talk about?"

*We're playing that game. Questions answered with more questions. Newsflash, Dr. Goldberg, you've met your match.*

After my mother died, my Aunt Eileen had me in trauma therapy for a solid five years. She even insisted I keep seeing someone while I was in college. You might say I'm a therapy pro. I know exactly how much info to give up in order to keep a therapist happy. I also know all the right words to say so he'll think I'm making progress.

I clear my throat.

"As my husband told you," I say, "I'm only here because my nightmares are disrupting our family. If it was just me, I could deal with it by myself. But since it's affecting everyone in the house, I need a way to get it under control. I'm hoping you can help me do that."

"I'll certainly try."

He asks me about the content of my dreams. I have to pay close attention, reviewing and evaluating each word before it comes out of my mouth. One slip could be devastating.

Priests may not tell tales from the confessional, but therapists . . . they're obligated by law to report a murder.

I cross and re-cross my legs, giving me some extra time to come up with a story that reflects the testimony I actually gave the police when I was a kid.

"My dreams are always pretty much the same. I'm in my old house in Warwick, where I grew up," I say. "I'm looking for my mother. I call out her name as I go from room to room. After looking from one end of the first floor to the other, I can't find her. Eventually, I climb the stairs and go up to her bedroom. It's empty."

Goldberg leans forward and looks at me in earnest.

*Nice touch. He really looks like he cares.*

"When you get to this point in your dream," he says, "how are you feeling?"

"I'm curious and a little apprehensive, but not scared. I have this sense that something's going to happen."

"Something bad?"

"No," I say. "Not bad, just that a surprise is coming. I'm not afraid."

He writes something down in his notebook and tells me to continue.

"I go over to my mother's dressing table and touch all the little items on the top — a Hummel statue of a milkmaid holding a basket, a robin-egg blue ceramic dish filled with her hair ties and clips, and her bottle of Chanel No. 5 perfume. That was my mother's signature scent. She had those items on her dressing table for as long as I can remember. I wasn't supposed to touch them."

"What happens next?"

"There's a noise and I turn my head towards the bedroom door. I don't know where she came from, but now my mother's in the room. She's smiling at me and I ask her if I can try on a necklace from her jewelry box, or some makeup from her drawer or a piece of her clothing. Each time I have the dream, I ask her for something different. Is that normal for small details to change in a recurring dream?"

Dr. Goldberg looks at me and smiles. "There's no normal when it comes to dreams. Since they're fueled by our imagination, anything can happen. Keep going; what comes next?"

I take a breath, deciding what I will and will not reveal.

"My mother's smile suddenly vanishes. She's become furious, and her face is red like a ripe fall apple. She yells at me for touching her things. I start to cry and close my eyes, so I don't have to look at her angry face. The room goes quiet. When I open my eyes, my mother's body is on the floor covered in blood, and I start screaming."

I feel myself getting weepy as I look up at Dr. Goldberg. He can tell I'm fighting back the tears because he hands me a tissue box and suggests we take a break.

"When your husband called me," he says, "he briefed me a little on your mother's death. He told me how you were the one who found her body. You're obviously reliving that trauma when you sleep. What comes out in our dreams is often fueled by what's bottled up inside of us."

I nod, a bobblehead again.

"What's puzzling me," says the therapist rubbing his beard with two fingers, "is why this has suddenly become worse after all these years? Is there something else going on? Can you think of anything that could be the catalyst?"

I press my lips together and look down at the floor.

*I know exactly why my dreams are getting worse, but I'm not telling him.*

He continues. "I've found the best way to get control of disturbing memories is to let some sunshine in and air them out. Through therapy, I can help you do that."

We talk for a while longer, and he gives me some relaxation exercises to do before bed. I agree to return the following week to continue our conversation.

Walking to the car with my husband, I take stock of my overall emotions. I don't feel any better after the therapy session, but I also don't feel worse. And, I got through the whole thing without revealing anything incriminating.

The big question is, how long I can keep up the charade? I saw all of Dr. Goldberg's degrees hanging on the wall in his office — Princeton, Harvard and Yale, a trifecta of amazing schools. He's clearly no dummy. How long will it take before he figures out I'm serving him up a load of class A bullshit?

# CHAPTER 17

Several weeks later, Jason's off on a two-night business trip to Chicago. He was hesitant about leaving me. I assured him the therapy was helping, even though I'd only been to a few sessions, and that he should go.

The frequency of my night terrors has definitely decreased a little since I started seeing Dr. Goldberg. Maybe talking about it does help, even if I haven't revealed anything remotely significant.

This morning, I drop the girls at school and then drive over to pick up Bianca for our visit to St. Vincent's. Today, the back of my car is filled with colored glass ornaments in the shapes of birds and flowers. They were donated by a local gift shop in Eastport. We plan to hang the translucent birds and flowers on or near the windows in each resident's room. When the sun shines through, the stained-glass shapes should brighten up the rooms and make the entire space feel more festive. That plain vanilla facility could use a little color.

I enjoy going out to St. Vincent's and spending time with the older people. Some of them have had the most amazing lives. But many are alone and rarely have visitors, which is so sad. It makes me feel good to share a conversation with them and see them smile. That alone is worth the trip.

Of course my visits to the senior center serve a dual purpose. While I'm there, I can also keep tabs on Father Cleary. Occasionally, when I've been in his room, I've heard him muttering long drawn-out stories to Nurse Peggy. Sometimes they make sense; often they don't. Regardless, she sits there smiling at him and takes in every word. I'm surprised she doesn't take notes.

Maybe I'm being a little paranoid, but the last time I was there, I could swear she looked at me funny. It was just for a second, but I detected a weird vibe coming from her. A few times when I've entered Father's room, he's been alone and we were able to have a semi-normal conversation. But within ten minutes, that nurse always appears. It's like she has a tracking device on me. Or maybe, she's just always there, never leaving the room . . . just waiting.

For whatever reason, I get the feeling she doesn't want anyone else to be alone with the priest besides her. At one point, it occurred to me that she might have a crush on him. But he's in his mid-nineties and while she's no chorus girl, she's *only* in her mid-sixties. Regardless, this is the hand I've been dealt and I've got to play it. I don't have a choice.

When I was kid, I was known as Abbie Lester. By using Abigail Sterling now, it shouldn't ring any memory bells for Father Cleary. I never know what to expect with him. Sometimes, he's cheerful and friendly and talks about normal things like the weather. He's usually very polite and introduces himself as if it's our first time meeting. I know it's the dementia, so I play along. I don't want to confuse him. Or do I?

Our visits usually go the same way. We start with a few minutes of mindless chit-chat. Then, Father often zones out and rambles about things that happened long ago. Frequently, he becomes unintelligible, using sentences without a beginning or an end. It's pretty clear his short-term memory is shot. But here's the thing . . . he does remember things that happened fifty years ago in vivid detail, just like Nurse Peggy said.

That's not good for me.

The last time I was with him, he talked about his childhood and his early days in the priesthood. He reminisced a little about long-gone parishioners who had invited him to their homes for the holidays. His eyes lit up when he told me about his big trip to Rome to visit the Vatican and his meeting with the Pope in the 1980s. And then, like it always did, the dementia overtook him and he zoned out, sometimes speaking in Latin.

I tried to nod at the appropriate moments, but my mind stayed focused on each word, waiting to hear anything remotely to do with confession.

Then it finally happened.

"I probably heard a hundred thousand sins over the years in those confessional chambers," the priest said, clasping his hands together. "Listening to all that sadness and regret takes a toll on a man. It's not easy keeping all those secrets, but I do it because I swore an oath."

My head jerked up and I stared at him, terrified at what was coming next.

"I can imagine," I said, using a coaxing tone. "It must have been extremely difficult hearing all that and keeping it to yourself."

He smiled slightly. "The truth is, most of what I heard was nothing too serious. Although a few confessions were pretty surprising, and one or two were . . . heartbreaking. Those are the ones that still eat away at me."

I nearly passed out. *Is he talking about me?* Immobile in my chair, I held my breath, waiting for him to point at me and shout 'murderer!'. But he didn't, and within a few seconds he was back in a cognitive haze, rambling in Latin.

Now, all I know is, I've got to find out everything he remembers about my confession without letting him know who I am.

Huffing and puffing, Bianca and I lug the bags of supplies into the building. We wave to the receptionist before parting ways to go to our respective wings. She goes to Maple; I go to Birch. Later we'll reunite in the Pine Wing.

In recent weeks, I've changed my hallway routine to give me more face time with Father Cleary. Now, I try to make my last stop with the old priest whenever possible so I can take extra time. Despite the potential danger he presents, as far as I can tell, he was and is a good and kind man. My mother always liked him and thought he was a man of honor. I don't think he'd ever violate the Seal of Confession knowingly. But his brain doesn't work right anymore, so there's that.

When I walk into his room today, he's alone sitting in his wheelchair in his usual spot looking out the window.

"Good morning, Father," I say brightly to the back of his head, covered in fine, snowy white hair.

"That you, Peggy?" he says, without turning around.

I shudder at being confused with Nurse P and walk across the room into his sightline.

"It's me, Father, Abigail . . . Sterling. I've come to hang some decorations on your windows. I think we can make this place a little cheerier, don't you?"

He looks up at me and squints, the sun in his eyes. "You're not Peggy. Who are you?"

He's confused again, so I touch his arm gently.

"I'm Abigail, Father. I come here once or twice a week to visit with you and some of the other residents."

I reach over and pick up the plant I'd brought him several weeks earlier.

"Remember this? I gave it to you a few weeks ago. It's looking very healthy, by the way. You're taking excellent care of it."

The old man nods, still squinting.

"I know who you are," he says, pointing right at me.

Before I can respond, there's a shuffling sound behind me. I turn my head to see what it is. What a surprise. Nurse

Peggy is standing in the doorway with her usual sourpuss look on her face.

"I know you," says the priest again still pointing his finger at me. He lifts his arm and it begins to shake. "You were there."

The nerves in my entire body are buzzing, and my already dry mouth involuntarily falls open. I take a few steps backwards and try to speak.

Before I can respond, Nurse Peggy brushes past me to get to the agitated cleric. As I back away, he continues to point at me and mutter, "I know you," over and over.

"Try and stay calm, Father," Nurse Peggy says, crouching in front of him at eye level. "Of course you know Mrs. Sterling. She's been coming here for a while now. You like her, remember? She brings you all those little plants that I then have to water."

*Bitch.*

The priest waves for her to come closer. She leans in and he begins to whisper in her ear. I can't hear what he's saying, but she keeps one eye on me the whole time. I watch her expression change from concern for the priest's health to surprise and then . . . alarm.

*What is he telling her?*

When Father finally stops talking, Nurse Peggy stands up and straightens her top, but her eyes remain fixed on me. She gives me a weird smile.

"For some reason," she says, "Father is getting you mixed up with one of his parishioners from a million years ago. He's quite upset right now and needs to rest. I think it's best if you leave."

"What did he just say?" I ask, every nerve in my body tingling and telling me to run.

"Nothing important," she says, as she fusses with the old man. "Father often rambles and gets confused about many things. He sometimes gets people mixed up."

"I understand," I say, starting to lose my patience and sanity, "but what *exactly* did he tell you just now that had to do with me?"

90

Nurse Peggy lumbers over to me and stands so close that I get a whiff of the coffee on her stale breath. It smells awful and I involuntarily wrinkle my nose — which of course, she notices. It doesn't endear me to her.

"Aren't you the curious cat," she says, with no expression on her face or in her voice. "It's nothing for you to worry about. Just the dementia talking."

"But you were alarmed. What did he say?" I ask again.

The nurse/nun looks around and leans in towards me.

"He said," she whispers, "that something bad happened to you a long, long time ago."

## CHAPTER 18

With my face only inches from Nurse Peggy's, my stomach lurches. I want to scream, run out of the room and never come back here. But I don't. I maintain my gaze and smile slightly, as if she's just told me we're supposed to get rain this weekend.

"He said something *bad* happened to *me* a long time ago?" I say, looking down and casually rummaging through my purse as if what was inside was more important than the priest's accusation. "What a funny thing to say."

"Yes, it is. But that's exactly what he said."

"I have no idea what he could be referring to."

She gives me an overly long look before she speaks.

"I wouldn't worry about it," she says, finally leaving my personal space. "He says things like that all the time. Sometimes they're true, but mostly they're not. Still I wonder . . . his memories from his early days and the years he spent at Blessed Sacrament in Warwick are usually fairly accurate."

Now, I'm totally freaking out while trying to maintain a calm, detached composure. There's no doubt that the nosey nurse is acting even more peculiar than she normally does, if that's possible.

I shake my head and mutter. "I can't imagine what that could be. I'm not that interesting."

She smiles, but it doesn't seem genuine.

"I'm sure it was nothing," she says. "I wouldn't worry about it."

I leave the room as quickly as possible and race to the other wing to find Bianca. I need to get out of this place or I'm sure I'll burst into flames.

"But we've only been here for thirty minutes. I still have more rooms to do," she says, holding a handful of glass birds. "You finished with all your people already?"

I obviously can't tell her that a priest with dementia has memories of me connected to a terrible thing that happened twenty years ago. That would open a can of worms. Bianca would never let that go. Instead, I say I'm coming down with a migraine. People never argue when someone says they're getting a migraine. It's the medical version of a Willy Wonka golden ticket.

"You do look kind of pale," she says, as she packs up her things.

As we race out of the building, Bianca calls out to the receptionist letting her know we'll be back in a couple of days to finish our project. Once in the car, I begin to calm down. Thankfully, Bianca happily chatters solo during our drive, only requiring me to periodically say "yes", "no" or "wow, that's crazy". While she rambles on, I analyze my situation.

My overarching questions are, does Father Cleary really remember what I told him? And, how likely is it that he'll say something? My conclusion: he could and he might.

"Do you want to go back there this Friday?" says Bianca, as I pull into her driveway.

"Where?" I say, suddenly pulled out of my guilt-ridden trance.

"To St. Vincent's, to finish the window decorations. Were you listening to me at all?"

*Time to pull out the migraine card again.*

"Sorry. My head is still throbbing. Let me see how I feel tomorrow."

After I drop her off, I stop in town to pick up something for dinner before I head home. Jason won't be home from the airport until late tonight. It will only be me and the girls for dinner again.

When I get to my house, I still have a few hours to myself before the kids come home from school. The minute they walk in the door, we'll be on the go. I do a lot of driving on weekdays, but I don't mind. My mom wasn't around to do these kinds of things for me. I'm so grateful I can do it for my girls.

I fix myself a cup of chamomile tea and open up my computer. I need to find out more about Sister Peggy Hannon, R.N. Who the hell is she, and what is her deep connection to Father Cleary? I'm convinced there's more there than the passing interest of a nurse in a patient.

I begin with some random Google searches. It takes me a while, but eventually I find a few sources of information. Pretty soon, I've put together a loose timeline of Sister P's life.

Margaret Mary Hannon is sixty-five years old, and grew up in Manchester, New Hampshire, aka the 'Live Free or Die' state . . . figures. She went to nursing school in Massachusetts. After graduating, she joined an order and went to work at a Catholic hospital in Wisconsin. Then she went overseas to work in a clinic in Africa. Back in the States, she goes to a Catholic hospital in Maryland and remains there until four years ago. So far, I see no previous connection to Father Cleary to explain her overbearing and possessive demeanor.

Unable to find anything more, I do a search for Father Michael Cleary.

His name is fairly common, but I eventually zero in on the right profile. Sorting through a bunch of random websites, I construct a loose timeline for him as well. Since he's in his nineties now, when I lived in Warwick, he was only in his mid-seventies. Not so old then.

I continue Googling. Father C was born in New York City and went to Regis High School in Manhattan. I found a photo of him at Regis from some old newsletter. He's pictured with a group, all members of the high school's religious studies club.

Just as I noticed from the photo in Father Cleary's room, when Father was young, he was very handsome. Is it possible he and Nurse Peggy had an affair at some point? That could explain her abnormal possessiveness.

I look at the clock on the kitchen wall. Luna and Grace should be getting off the school bus in ten minutes. That still gives me time to do one more dive into the data before my afternoon is no longer mine. My research has brought me way down a rabbit hole, but I'll keep going until the girls plow through the front door.

Typing in a few additional keywords, I get a hit. It's a link to a brief biography of Father Cleary from some Catholic charity dinner program. According to the article, after Father Cleary got his teaching degree at Iona College, he entered the priesthood. He became a chaplain in the U.S. Army and later was assigned to a Catholic Church in Florida. It looks like he stayed there for ten years. Eventually, he lands at Blessed Sacrament in Warwick, where our paths crossed. He finished out his career there.

I'm trying to make some sense out of all the disparate bits of info I've uncovered, when my kids come stampeding through the front door.

"Can we have a snack before we go to practice?" they shout in unison. I smile and shut down my computer, because the rest of my day will be devoted to them. My pursuit of information about Father Cleary, Nurse Peggy and their possible connection will have to wait until tomorrow.

# CHAPTER 19

Jason arrived home tonight around 10.30. I was still agitated after my encounter with Nurse Peggy this morning, but I don't think he noticed. We went to bed and three hours later, I have another whopper of a nightmare. It's a little after 3:00 a.m. when I wake up the whole house. Once I calm down a little, Jason puts the kids back to bed and then holds me for over an hour.

Initially, I had been skittish about speaking to a therapist, but now I crave it. Every time I encounter Father Cleary, it has a demonstrable effect on me. Whenever I leave St. Vincent's, that compartment in my head that holds the memories of my mother is left wide open. I've been keeping everything bottled up inside for so long that it's slowly suffocating me.

I don't have a therapy appointment scheduled for another few days, but in the morning, I call Dr. Goldberg. Luckily, he's got a cancellation in the afternoon and I grab it. Later, seated in his office, we exchange greetings, and he quickly gets down to business.

"You asked for an additional session this week. I presume you've had another nightmare?" he says gently.

I nod.

"You walked me through your dreams in more detail during our last session," he says. "It seems clear that what's causing you pain and stress now is somehow connected to your mother's death. I know it's painful to talk about, but I think the key to the whole thing lies there. Why don't we explore more about what happened when you were a teenager? Maybe you can tell me a little about the year leading up to your mother's death."

*I knew this was coming. I have to give him some kind of answer, but this is where it gets tricky. Talking about a dream is one thing. No one's going to put you in jail over a dream. But talking about reality could land me in a federal prison.*

"Go as fast or slow as you want," says Dr. Goldberg encouragingly. "Why don't you tell me about your relationship with your mother? Let's start there."

*There's no way I can tell him the whole truth. But if I'm not honest with him, I'll never get better. I can't keep living this way or putting my family through this insanity night after night.*

I take a deep breath and begin . . . carefully.

"Everyone loved my mom," I say. "She was really fun, always laughing and acting silly. When I was little, she used to turn on the radio in the kitchen real loud. We'd both dance around while she cooked dinner."

"So they're happy memories."

"Some. She and my father got divorced when I was eight. After that, things were different and money was tight. She tried to do special things with me that didn't cost a lot."

"Would you say you had a good relationship with her?"

"When I was young," I say. "By the time I got into my teens, I was . . . a little rebellious. I was alone a lot. My dad had already checked out, and Mom was always working or out with a new boyfriend."

"Did that bother you?"

"In the beginning. But when I was thirteen, I got interested in boys myself."

"Pretty normal."

"For a while, but then I started hanging around with a wild crowd. At least that's what my mother called them."

"Then your mother *was* paying attention."

"Sometimes. They weren't bad kids, but looking back now, they pushed the envelope quite a bit. Some of them got into a lot of trouble."

"What kind of trouble are we talking about?" says Goldberg.

"You know . . . kid stuff. Drinking, skipping school, smoking . . . drugs . . . shoplifting."

"Now that you're a mother, would you say that would be concerning behavior if it were one of your kids?"

"My kids? You better believe it. But at the time, I didn't see it that way. I was a little miserable and thought I knew everything."

"And how did that work out for you?"

"My mother's dead, so not so well, I guess. My friends were just kids trying to have fun. They accepted me for who I was."

"Did you get involved in those 'extracurricular' activities as well?"

"You mean the drugs?" I say, then nod.

"I'm guessing your mother didn't go for that."

"At first, she didn't realize what was going on. But when she found out, we had terrible fights."

"How did you get involved with those kids?"

I blow out a long slow breath. "Probably the way a lot of people do. I fell in love with a boy. He was older than me and handsome. I was young and impressionable. Looking back now, I would have done anything for him, and I did."

Goldberg shifts in his chair. "Teenage infatuation is very powerful. Tell me about him."

"His name was Travis. He didn't live in Warwick; he was from the next town over. I met him in the park with a bunch of other kids. He was like the mayor there. Everyone was in awe of Travis. Most of the kids who hung out with us were between fourteen and seventeen, but Travis was almost nineteen, practically an adult. Everyone thought he was so cool."

Goldberg makes a note on his paper before looking back at me.

"And Travis, he had already finished high school?"

I nod. "Yeah. One day when I was hanging out after school with my friends, he showed up. He came over to us and told me he thought I was cute. I was just fourteen then, and didn't feel very pretty. Attention from him was like catnip. I couldn't stop thinking about him. A lot of the other girls liked him because he had these intense black eyes which made him seem mysterious. When he chose me, the only way I can describe it was that it was . . . intoxicating."

"That's understandable. You were young and impressionable. That happens to a lot of kids."

I take a sip from my water bottle to buy me time to choose my words carefully.

"Travis could have been on the cover of *GQ*, and he looked young for his age. He passed for sixteen, and did."

"So most people assumed he was in high school?" says Goldberg, as he jots down another note. Part of me is dying to see what's in his notebook, but I don't dare ask.

"When I introduced Travis to my mom, I told her that he was sixteen and a half, a junior in high school. I lied to her. She would have flipped if she knew he was nineteen, since I was so much younger. She thought I was too young for a boyfriend anyway."

"How did you feel about lying to her?"

I look up at the ceiling, wondering if he's judging me.

"I didn't like lying about it, but my mom would have freaked out if I told her his real age."

"You didn't feel like you could be honest with your mother?"

I look out the window. "Not if I wanted to keep seeing Travis. I was so enmeshed with him that I couldn't see straight. I would have done anything to be with him. When I think about it, I did everything a parent *doesn't* want their fourteen-year-old kid to do."

"Why do you think you made those choices?"

I dig deep and think.

*Don't spill the tea.*

"I-I-I guess it was because he made me feel like a woman. I desperately wanted to grow up and get out of Warwick. He and I were in this crazy whirlwind filled with partying and excitement. Half the time, I didn't know where I was. Most of the time we were together is still a big blur."

# CHAPTER 20

I stare off into space while Dr. Goldberg waits patiently for me to continue. While I carefully search for the right words, his phone mercifully rings, breaking the silence and giving me time to think.

"I'm sorry," he says, looking down at his phone. "I have to take this call. I'll only be a minute."

I take another sip of my water as he leaves the room. While he's gone, I assess my overall performance. Reasonably good, I think. A primary objective for this session was to explain the story of my mother's death without incriminating myself. I think I succeeded, because Goldberg seems like he's buying what I'm selling.

Minutes later, my therapist is seated in front of me, ready to roll.

"Let's get back to you and your mother," he says, "and the day she read your journal."

I swallow, to make it appear that I'm digging deep into my soul.

"When it came to drugs and alcohol, my mother didn't mess around. She had zero tolerance for that kind of stuff. Midge Lester could be fierce when she wanted to be."

"But you kept seeing Travis anyway?" says Goldberg.

"I couldn't stop," I say. "It was like he had a spell over me. The day my mother read my journal and found out his real age she threatened to call the cops on him. We bolted out of my house and met some kids under the bridge by the park to get high. Travis was acting kind of crazy that day. He kept saying that my mother was a 'world-class bitch'. He was convinced she was going to pull us apart and that he'd end up in jail."

"How did you respond to this?" says my therapist.

"I was furious with my mother, angrier than Travis was. I felt betrayed. She'd violated my privacy."

Goldberg shifts in his chair before he speaks. "It's understandable that you felt that way, but can you see it from her perspective? You were so young."

"Now, I can. But then, not so much," I say. "And Travis was spinning out. 'Your mother's a crazy bitch,' he said to me. 'She's gonna put me in jail and send you off to some rehab.'"

I look up at the ceiling to buy some more time. Goldberg's eyes remain fixed on me.

*If he's waiting for me to have some kind of epiphany moment, it's not going to happen.*

"I didn't know what to do," I say. "I didn't want Travis to go to jail. I loved him."

"Let's move on to the day your mother died," Goldberg says softly.

I shift in my chair. *Here we go.*

"Ok," I say. "Two days later, on a Friday, I got home from school and the back door of our house was slightly open. Right away, that struck me as odd."

*Stick with the same story you told the police. No more, no less. Do not embellish or editorialize.*

"Take your time," Goldberg says. "There's no rush."

I reach for a tissue on the table and blow my nose to buy myself a few extra seconds. Then, I tell my therapist the exact same timeline and load of bullshit I gave the police twenty years ago.

"After I saw the door was ajar, I wondered if my mother had come home early from work. She normally got home around six, and it was only four. I stepped into the little mudroom right inside the back door and called out to her, several times. There was no answer, so I shrugged it off."

"And then what happened?"

"As soon as I walked into the kitchen, I knew something was wrong. All the drawers and cabinets were open and things were pulled out and strewn around the room. I yelled for my mother again, but there was still no answer. I was afraid someone might be in the house and waited a moment before going into the living room."

Real tears well up in my eyes and I flutter both hands in front of my face to fight them back. This time, Goldberg hands me the entire box of tissues. I take one and blot my eyes before continuing.

"I'm sorry," I say, sniffling. "This is harder than I thought it would be."

"Take your time, Abbie. We can take a break whenever you want."

I put the tissue box down and sit back. "The living room was ransacked just like the kitchen, but I kept going through the house."

"Were you afraid of who might be there?"

"I should have been, but for some reason the house felt empty to me. Somehow, I knew no one was there. Slowly, I climbed up the stairs, still calling out for my mother."

My tears are coming fast now, and Goldberg asks if I'd like to take a break. The truth is, I would love to, but I also want to get this over with. I keep going.

"I get to the top of the stairs, pass my bedroom door and look in. My room had been pulled apart, like the rest of the house. I shout out again. 'Mom, are you here? Mom?' There's no answer, so I continue down the hall towards my mother's bedroom."

My nose is running now, and I nervously bite my bottom lip. Even though what I'm relaying is mainly fabricated, parts of it are true. It's the telling of those bits that's getting to me.

"When I get to my mother's bedroom doorway and look in, the room is a wreck. Everything is pulled out of the closets and drawers and tossed all over the floor. I didn't see her until after I stepped into the room. She was on the other side, on the floor next to the dresser. She wasn't moving, and there was so much blood. From where I stood, I knew she was dead. That's when I screamed."

At this point, I'm sobbing so hard that Goldberg reaches over and pulls several more tissues out of the box in my hand and gives them to me.

"I think we should stop for today," he says, sitting back in his chair.

I let out a grateful sigh. Telling that last lie had been harder than I thought it would be. Twenty years have passed since my mom died, but today, it feels like yesterday.

I gather my things and agree to come back in a few days to continue the conversation. He walks me to the door and gently pats me on the back.

"Therapy can sometimes be painful, but that's how you get to the hard stuff. It's the only way you'll get past those nightmares."

I give him a half-smile as I open the door.

"Abbie, one last thing," he says. "Did the police ever catch the person who did it?"

I shake my head and let out a deliberate sarcastic laugh. "The cops said it was a 'home invasion' because of two other similar incidents in Connecticut the year before. I don't know if they were connected, but no one was ever arrested for my mother's death."

"And Travis? Do you know where he ended up?"

I look away and let out another laugh. "We were over the minute my mother died. It got really weird in Warwick during the weeks after her death. Travis turned twenty and wanted to get out of town and move on with his life. I tried to get him to take me with him. He wanted no part of it. He said something about how I was only fifteen and he would be arrested for kidnapping."

"He wasn't wrong," says Goldberg.

"He left town. After that, I don't know where he went. He blocked my calls. I was devastated and never heard from him again. He didn't want to be mixed up in some murder investigation."

"Do you think talking with him now might help you find some closure?"

"That wouldn't be possible."

"Why?"

I step outside the front door of the building, exhausted and so ready to end the conversation.

"Because he's dead," I say.

After I drop that last little nugget and watch my therapist's eyebrows go up, I turn and walk to my car. After my mom was killed, Travis was my Achilles heel. He knew the whole truth about what really happened. He knew what I'd done. As long as he was still walking around, I was at risk.

When I found out he died, I was finally free to live my life.

# CHAPTER 21

A few days later, I drive back to St. Vincent's alone. Bianca has an early-morning dentist appointment and will meet me out there.

Despite everything that's been going on, volunteering at the senior residence has helped take my mind off the nightmares. When our committee first discussed getting involved in a countywide nursing home program, I jumped at it. My mother's gone and I don't often see my father. Spending time with the older people at St. Vincent's helps fill that hole inside of me . . . a little.

Today, I've brought boxes of cookies baked by members of our group, along with some books donated by our local library. After distributing those goodies today, my primary mission is to get some alone time with Father Cleary and pick his confused brain. I have to take control of this narrative, instead of waiting for an anvil to drop onto my head.

Right after my initial encounter with the priest, I spent days analyzing his words and body language. I was pretty sure the old man didn't recognize me. When you think about it, why should he? I have a different name now and am twenty years older. Abigail Sterling the adult looks nothing like little

Abbie Lester, the skinny, mixed-up, Goth teen covered in piercings, who he vaguely knew back in Warwick.

Twenty years ago, other than the time I spent with him in the confessional, I was just another bored kid reluctantly sitting in a pew on Sunday mornings. He didn't really know me . . . until the funeral.

I pull my car into a space in the St. Vincent's visitor's lot and pop open the lift gate. I grab a large cardboard box filled with donated photo books and all the cookies. We selected this project because some of the residents have difficulty with language and cognition. Looking at pictures seems to both entertain and soothe them. I hoist the heavy box up into my arms, lock the car and stumble towards the building.

When the automatic front doors magically open, the receptionist waves to me and points at something on the far side of the lobby. A woman's legs are sticking out from behind a large white pillar.

"Bianca?" I say, walking in her direction, the box in my arms getting heavier.

She leans forward and looks up at me with her big, trade-mark hundred-tooth smile.

"Oh, my God," she says, as she runs over and scoops up a large stack of books out of my box, thereby lightening my load. "You're carrying way too much. Give me some of those."

We wander down several hallways until we find two abandoned wagons and load them up with our supplies. After agreeing to meet up in an hour and a half, I start my rounds through the Birch Wing.

My first stop today — Ms. Elizabeth Gill's room. At a hundred and one, she's still in pretty good shape. She gets her hair done once a week, is always in full makeup and dripping with costume jewelry. I chuckle whenever I see her, because she's always dressed for a night out on the town, even at nine in the morning.

When I arrive at her room, I dig through my collection of books. There's one photography book with photos of the world's most beautiful cities. I pluck it out of the pile and sit beside her.

Together, we flip through the pages talking about this city or that. After a while, she begins to fade. She may be dressed for a night out, but she's typically got a twenty-minute window before she runs out of gas. When I see her eyes close, I quietly get up to leave.

"You'll come see me again next week?" she says, opening her eyes.

"They couldn't keep me away," I say, pushing my cart towards the door and out into the hallway.

I finish with all of my patients, saving Father Cleary for last. When I arrive at his room, B304, the door is wide open. From my position out in the hallway, I can see Nurse Peggy sitting in a chair next to his bed. She's reading to him. I'm beginning to wonder if she sleeps there.

Clearing my throat, I push the cart into the room.

"Good morning. How is everyone today?" I say.

It could be my imagination, but I could swear Nurse Peggy makes a face when she hears my voice. It was fleeting, but I saw it and stop dead in my tracks.

*She knows something.*

"Good morning, Ms. Sterling," the nurse says, closing her book and placing it on her lap. Her eyes stay glued to mine. "I'm afraid Father's a little tired today."

"I won't stay long then," I say. "I've brought some home-made cookies and . . ."

"Father Cleary is a diabetic." She spits this out like venom. Getting up, she stands between me and the priest as if I were about to force-feed him maple syrup. "A cookie could kill him, you know."

Before I can answer and defend myself, a woman's voice rings out behind me.

"I'm sure Abbie had no intention of giving any patient cookies before getting approval from their doctor."

I spin around. Bianca's in the doorway. "Half my residents were asleep. I finished up early on the Maple Wing and decided to see what you were up to."

I give her a grateful smile and push the cart over beside Father Cleary's bed. When I sit down next to him, Nurse Peggy abruptly leaves the room.

"Good morning, Father. I've brought a couple of photography books that I thought we could look at today," I say, as I hold up two books for him to choose from. "One contains photos of the world's greatest bridges and the other is a compilation of black-and-white pictures of the cathedrals of Europe. Would you like to look at the book of cathedrals?"

The old man nods. I pull my chair closer and open the large coffee table book. Bianca sits down next to me. Slowly, I flip through the pages reading the descriptions of each scene.

When we get to the end, my eyes go to the silver framed photo of the group of priests sitting on the window ledge. "I noticed you have a black-and-white picture over there, Father. Who are all those people?"

"I don't know," says the priest, appearing confused.

"That's enough for today," says Nurse Peggy, as she plows back into the room and stands next to the bed like a castle guard.

"He does seem more tired than usual." I get up and push my cart to the doorway.

"We never escape our sins," shouts the priest, suddenly animated and agitated. "The Lord sees all and the day of reckoning will soon come."

Not knowing how to respond, Bianca and I walk briskly towards the lobby.

"What the hell was that all about?" she says, in a loud whisper. "And what's the deal with that nurse? I got really weird vibes from her."

I shake my head. "Who knows? She's been like that from day one."

"And what's wrong with the priest? Is he always so out of it?"

"Not always. Sometimes, he's pretty normal. Other times he rants in Latin or makes no sense. Today he was okay, until the end when he started to go off the rails."

Bianca laughs. "At least it was in English. Latin always sounds so creepy, like one of those exorcist movies."

I giggle as we push the carts into a storage room and head out to the parking lot, planning our next visit. When I get into my car, I notice a piece of orange paper stuck under the windshield wiper. It looks like one of those flyers from a restaurant or car wash. I grab the paper and toss it onto the passenger seat next to me. As I'm backing out, I glance down at the paper. It's not a flyer. It's a note written with a black sharpie.

*Secrets have a way of finding daylight.*

# CHAPTER 22

After reading that note, my stomach's in my throat. I'm so distracted, that I nearly sideswipe a car as I pull out of the parking lot onto the main road. Halfway home, I have to stop on the side of the road because I'm in the throes of a full-blown panic attack. Frantic, and trying to catch my breath, I call my husband. Hearing his voice always calms me down.

"Hey, babe," he says, when he answers the phone. "Did you go to the nursing home today?"

"Yeah," I say, barely audible.

"Everything okay?"

My voice catches. I can't get my words out. Even if I could, I can't tell him what's really freaking me out.

"Abs?" he says. "What's going on?"

"I was driving home and felt lightheaded and pulled over. I just needed to hear your voice, that's all."

Jason begins to speak. He's calm and reassuring, a skill that has served him well in business. Within five minutes, I'm breathing normally again. My high adrenaline levels subside and my heart rate starts to slow.

"I feel better," I say, in a loud whisper.

"You sure you're okay?" he says. "Why don't you leave the car where you are and call an Uber? I can pick up the car tonight when I get home."

I lie and tell him I'm fine, that I'll see him later. Not convinced, he promises he'll try to get home early.

It's nearly 2:00 p.m. when I pull into our driveway. A FedEx package the size of a loaf of bread addressed to me is sitting outside our front door. There's no return address on the outside. I try to recall what I've ordered recently, but nothing comes to mind. I carry it into the kitchen and place it on the counter next to the sink.

The box is wrapped with a ridiculous amount of strong, clear tape. I try scissors first. When that doesn't work, I reach for a sharp steak knife to cut my way through. I finally open it, and inside is a silver-and-blue wrapped gift box with lots of curly blue ribbons. I dig around in the shipping box looking for a receipt or card, but find nothing.

Inside the gift box is a large, brightly painted wooden doll. Right away, I know exactly what it is — a Matryoshka doll aka a Russian nesting doll. My dentist is Russian and has a display of these colorful figures lined up behind glass in her waiting room. A smaller doll 'nests' inside a larger one. I've always admired them whenever I go in for my cleaning.

I open up the first doll and am intrigued and delighted at the same time. *Maybe they're from Jason?* Slowly, I open each one. As expected, every time I take a doll apart, a smaller one sits inside. I know this is what's supposed to happen, but it makes me happy nonetheless. I guess that's the point. As I continue, the dolls get tinier and tinier. I wonder how small they will ultimately become before I reach the end.

When I finally get to the last doll and open it, I find a tiny spooled roll of paper inside with writing on it. It looks delicate. I unfurl the paper very carefully and unfold it. It's a copy of an old newspaper article. When I read the headline, I feel sick. It's a nineteen-year-old article from the *Warwick Press*.

I can't breathe when I see the headline.

*Who killed Midge Lester?*
*Three weeks have passed and the police investigation*
*still delivers no answers . . .*

The smallest Russian doll drops from my hands and clatters onto the wooden floor. It rolls across the room and stops when it hits the leg of a chair. Still holding the piece of newspaper in my hand, I run after the doll. Sweat forms on my forehead as I climb down under the table to retrieve it.

Standing back at the counter, I gather up all the dolls and place them one inside the other until I'm left with only the big one. I place it back in the gift box and stash the whole lot in my pantry closet underneath a bunch of old grocery bags. Jason and the girls will never poke around in there.

The girls will be home soon. I take another look at the outside of the FedEx box to see if there are any other clues as to who or where it came from. The only thing I detect is that it appears to have been shipped from New York City. Since eight million people reside in New York City, that doesn't narrow it down very much.

Tomorrow after the kids leave for school, I'll call FedEx to see if someone can help me identify the sender. I have so many questions and so many fears. My entire body is pins and needles.

*Who sent that package, and what do they want?*

While waiting for Grace and Luna to burst through the door, I'm lost in thought.

*Is the person who sent the dolls the same person who left the note on my windshield? The only way someone could know about that old newspaper article is if they were in Warwick nineteen years ago. Father Cleary obviously couldn't send this. Is there someone else out there that I've forgotten about?*

There's a commotion at the front door as the girls come stampeding into the house, both talking at the same time.

"Slow down," I say, as they each try to tell me a story at the same time. "Luna, you go first."

"Our class is going on a field trip to the Sawtucket Nature Preserve," says my nine-year-old. "Since you do all the Earth Day events, my teacher thought you might want to be a class mom for the trip. Can you come, Mom? Please."

"Sounds right up my alley. Get me the date. Okay, Gracie, your turn."

"My art teacher picked my picture to be in a show at the library," says my seven-year-old, beaming.

"That's wonderful. Wait until we tell Daddy," I say, as I prepare a snack of apple and cheese for them before our afternoon activities commence.

"I brought in the mail for you," says Luna, placing a pile of mainly junk mail on the kitchen counter. "This was in the mailbox, too."

"What?" I say, my back to her.

"A funny doll," she says.

I spin around. My older daughter is holding up a single nesting doll in her hand.

*Where did that come from?*

"Was it wrapped in anything?" I say, taking the doll from her.

"I don't know," says my daughter, no longer interested and walking away.

"Luna, I'm serious," I say, calling after her. "Was the doll wrapped in a package or was it in the mailbox just like this?"

"Like that," she says, as she and her sister leave the room to get changed for soccer practice.

Alone in the kitchen, I close my eyes and grip the edge of the counter. It was bad enough knowing someone had my home address. But if that doll was loose in my mailbox, someone placed it in there.

Someone was *at* my home.

114

# CHAPTER 23

When the girls and I finally get back to the house after a busy afternoon, Jason's waiting there with a bouquet of spring flowers and a large bag filled with Chinese food. A lump forms in my throat when I see the flowers and food. He's so thoughtful. I don't deserve him.

"I figured after your crazy day, you wouldn't feel like cooking," he says, as he gives me the hug I so desperately need.

"And the flowers are for . . . ?"

"To remind you how much I love you . . . in case you forget."

I hug him again, and peer over his shoulder at my two daughters who are now both making kissy faces at each other.

"I see you two," I say, with a smile. "C'mon, time to get washed up. Who wants an egg roll?"

Dinner in the kitchen is lively, filled with laughter and stories from school. I try to join in, but after everything that happened today, I'm still not myself. Jason notices I'm more subdued than usual. I know this because he squeezes my arm several times during our meal.

"Everything all right?" he whispers later, leaning over to me when we're cleaning up the dishes.

"I'm just tired," I say. "After we get the girls to bed, I'm going to take a shower and go to sleep early."

Five hours later, in the middle of the night, I have another nightmare. It's a bad one, maybe my worst. When I finally wake up, my face is soaked with tears. Jason is next to me, with a terrified look on his face.

"Mom?" says Luna, from out in the hallway. "Are you okay?"

Jason and I turn our heads towards the doorway.

"Mom's all right," my husband says. "Go back to bed."

"Why does this always happen to you, Mommy?" says my older daughter. "Why do you have so many bad dreams?"

*That's a very good question, Luna. But I can't tell you the answer. If I do, I'll lose you forever.*

I know exactly why I had such an awful dream — those freakin' Russian dolls. Who the hell sent them to me? Someone out there knows the truth about what happened in Warwick, and they're playing some sick game. I have to find out who it is and what they want before things spiral out of control.

The next morning, Jason's off early for some presentation in Lower Manhattan. I drop the kids off at school on my way to an ECC meeting at the Eastport Library.

At 10 a.m., we'll begin planning our new initiatives for the fall season. That's when I'll give my update on the St. Vincent's nursing home program. As I enter the conference room, I wave to a few of the other women in the group. We've all worked on so many different projects together that I've become friends with many of them. They're nice women.

I'm dragging today after the rough night I had. The minute I put my things down, I go straight for the coffee set-up in the back of the room. While I'm pouring milk into my cup, Bianca sidles up next to me, holding her usual Diet Coke.

"You've got dark circles under your eyes," she says. "You need to get more sleep."

"Thank you," I reply, as I roll my tired eyes. "People don't enjoy it when you tell them they look tired. You know that, right?"

"That's what friends are for," she says, teasing, before moving onto the subject she really wants to talk about. "I still can't get over how rude that nurse at St. Vincent's was yesterday. From the minute I saw her . . ."

Bianca launches into a rant seconds before the chairwoman calls the meeting to order. We grab two seats next to each other at the large wooden conference table and settle in for the next two hours.

When the meeting adjourns at noon, Bianca and I walk out to the parking lot. Her car is parked several spots away from mine. I wave to her as I open my car door.

"We still need to brainstorm about what we're bringing for our next visit," I shout to my friend. "I was thinking about something with clay, so they can use their hands."

"I love that," she says with a smile. "Want to grab lunch?"

I'm hungry, so I follow her to the local diner, where they serve unlimited coffee for the price of a single cup. Since I'd been up half the night screaming at no one in particular, endless coffee is just what the doctor ordered.

We luck out and get a booth, which gives us room to spread out. I pull out my notebook containing lists of projects and ideas for St. Vincent's. We kick around a few concepts and ultimately decide on letter-writing to soldiers who are currently serving in our military overseas.

"The residents can dictate to us, and we'll write the letters in longhand," I say.

"When we finish, they can actually sign the letter themselves and stamp it," says Bianca. "That way they'll feel a part of it."

With our creative problem solved and not much prep to do for it, we dig into our lunch.

"So, what's the deal with that nurse?" says Bianca, just before she bites into her turkey sandwich. "Something's funny about her. I can feel it."

I roll my eyes. "She's polite, but I know what you mean. I try to avoid her whenever I can."

We spend the next twenty minutes coming up with and tossing out all sorts of outlandish theories regarding the relationship between the nurse and the priest.

"Maybe they're having an affair, and she's jealous of other women," my friend says. "Maybe she sees you as her rival."

I shake my head. "Father Cleary's in his nineties and not mentally home half the time. I doubt they're having an affair. The man can't even walk."

"Well," she says, "all I know is, something's not right."

*You can say that again, Bianca. Something's definitely not right.*

\*\*\*

Later in the week, Bianca and I both purchase some pretty stationery, envelopes and stamps for our military letter-writing exercise. I pick her up the morning of our visit to St. Vincent's and we drive out there together. With our regular routine down, we split up in the lobby agreeing to meet back at reception in two hours.

Today, I start with Ms. Gill, and she doesn't disappoint. She's dressed in an elaborate outfit involving many colors and textures. I suspect she may be wearing every item she owns all at the same time. I love her.

"The nurse told me you were coming today," says the old woman, smiling at me from her wheelchair. "I got all dolled up for your visit. Not bad for an old lady."

Ms. Gill's wearing a long green gown with dainty flat green satin slippers. She's got on a cream-colored cardigan sweater with little brown leather buttons. Her accessories include thick gold hoop earrings, and more bracelets and rings than I can count. Several different colored scarves are draped around her neck and over her shoulders. Her hair has been styled and poofed, and she's wearing an enormous amount of bright red lipstick that extends well beyond her lips.

In short, she's fantastic. I smile at her, feeling so honored she went to all that trouble for me.

"You look beautiful, Ms. Gill," I say, grinning from ear to ear. "You're like a cover girl."

I'm pretty sure I see the old woman blush as I sit down next to her. For the next fifteen minutes we compose her letter to a soldier. She dictates, making numerous changes while I write. When we're finished, she licks the envelope and puts the stamps on. I promise her I'll mail it when I leave the building.

As I move from room to room, the letter-writing exercise is well received. As always, I save Father Cleary for last, so I can take my time. Is it possible that he somehow sent the dolls? I shake my head. It couldn't be. Father Cleary needs help to do everything.

Arriving at the priest's room, I look around and breathe a sigh of relief when I see he's alone. Nurse Watchdog isn't guarding the gates this morning.

"Hello, Father. Beautiful day," I say. "How are you doing this morning?"

The old man, who'd been dozing in bed, looks up at me but says nothing.

"It's me, Father. Abigail Sterling. We're writing letters to soldiers today. Would you like to pick out the style of stationery you'd like to use?" I say holding up a few different colors. "You can dictate to me, and I'll write it for you. Then you can sign it. How does that sound?"

The priest's face breaks into a smile.

"It sounds like a marvelous idea, young lady. Did you think of it yourself?"

I nod as I pull a chair over next to his bed and sit.

"I used to write letters to soldiers all the time," he says. "My hands don't work so well anymore."

For the next several minutes, Father dictates and I write. When we're finished, we've created a beautiful letter for some far-away soldier. I finish the last sentence and hand the pen to him so he can sign it. His signature is shaky but legible. I read the letter back to him one more time before folding it and placing it inside the envelope.

"Those were lovely and comforting words, Father," I say, thinking how normal he is today, compared to some of the other times I've been here.

"You know, you look familiar to me, young lady," he says. "Have we met before?"

"We met here at St. Vincent's," I say, dying inside. "Don't you remember?"

Standing now with the letter in my hand, I walk across the room and look out the window. My back is to him as I begin to speak, choosing each word very carefully.

"Father, when you were in a parish, did you regularly say mass and hear confessions?"

He perks up right away. "For over fifty years, I did. Not only that, I officiated at weddings, funerals and communions, too."

"It must have been very gratifying to help so many people," I say.

"Parts of the job were very enjoyable, but not always. Many people came to me in a lot of pain, or in times of dire need. That's part of the job, too. The good and the bad; it comes with the territory."

I turn around and face him squarely.

"You must have been a great comfort to people at funerals and things like that," I say.

The priest is quiet for a moment before he answers. "Funerals were hard, especially if the person who died had been young. I never got used to that."

"I suppose you wouldn't."

"But it wasn't the funerals that were the most difficult. It was the tortured members of my flock, the ones who were burdened with guilt and remorse. They couldn't get away from their feelings. It followed them wherever they went. Those were the people who really suffered, the ones with nowhere to run, because their pain was coming from within."

I gulp. "And, did it help them . . . to talk to you?"

"Jesus forgives all those who confess, if their repentance is genuine. He can forgive, but he cannot remove someone's guilt. That forgiveness only comes from within the person themselves."

"Have I missed something?" A woman's voice rings out behind me. I don't have to turn around to know who it is. Happy days. Nurse Peggy must be back on duty, which means any further conversation with Father Cleary will have to wait.

"We were just chatting about Father's days working in a parish," I say gathering up my things.

I walk over to the door. Nurse Peggy takes her usual seat in the chair facing the priest.

"See you next week, Father," I say. "I enjoyed our talk today."

"Abigail," says the priest, pointing to his head, "I remember everything. It's all locked up in here, and that's where it will stay."

I walk out into the hallway feeling like someone just kicked me in the stomach. What did he mean, 'I remember everything'? Was he referring to what we talked about today? Or does he remember I told him I killed my mother?

# CHAPTER 24

The following week, I'm at home one morning, getting ready to leave for St. Vincent's, when Jason calls. One of his vendors has invited us to join them for dinner on Saturday night. My husband knows I hate those kinds of things and avoid them whenever possible.

"I know it's not your thing, but we're considering investing in this company, Abs," says my husband, starting his pitch. "They said they'll come up to Eastport for dinner, so we wouldn't have to travel anywhere. I promise, we'll be home by 9:30."

Jason tells me that the founder of this company is a real innovative guy, and that we'll be having dinner with him and his partner. Since my kids were already planning to do a sleepover at a friend's house on Saturday night, I have no good excuse to say no. Mildly curious about some of my husband's current investments, I agree to go.

I've been seeing Dr. Goldberg once a week, and my nightmares have slowly been decreasing in frequency and ferocity. I guess talking about the bad dreams in detail really does help. At least that's what Goldberg says when I tell him I haven't had any nightmares for a few days.

I pick up Bianca and we head off to St. Vincent's. Spending the morning with the residents, who I've come to love, keeps my mind occupied and leaves me no time to worry about all the other stuff. Since receiving the dolls, there's been no further communication from my unknown nemesis. But I'm not complacent. I know the person is still out there. I just don't know what they want.

Right after my mother was found dead, I was questioned extensively by the Warwick PD. Because I was only fifteen, tiny and an emotional wreck, the cops ruled me out pretty fast. A year later, while I was living in New Jersey, I overheard Aunt Eileen on the phone with my father. I could only hear her side of the conversation, but I gathered that people in Warwick were gossiping. It sounded like some of them thought I may have had something to do with my mother's death. I remember Aunt Eileen getting really mad at my dad. She was yelling that all those people were 'pathetic losers'.

Now, the question I keep asking myself is, why is someone making contact with me twenty years after the fact? What made this person pop up so many years later? And, the most important question: what kind of proof could they possibly have?

I turn the car onto the final leg to St. Vincent's.

"You got all the costumes?" I say, just to make small talk.

"I had a little trouble locating a diamond tiara," says Bianca. "But I found something that will work in an old Halloween costume box in my basement."

Today, we're doing a 'remember when' project with the residents. The last time we were there, we asked everyone if they could remember their thoughts from when they were five years old. The assignment: what did they want to be when they grew up? Today, they'll be dressing up as who they wanted to be when they were five.

We'll take lots of pictures of them in their outfits. Then, the photos will be displayed on the big screen TV in the dining room for a few weeks. Not only will it be fun for them to get dressed up, but it will also be a great conversation starter during their meals. Everyone, including the hospital adminis-trators, is participating.

We get to St. Vincent's and lug all of our costume par-aphernalia into the lobby. Today, Bianca and I will work together rather than splitting up. While one of us helps them put on their costumes and makeup, the other will pose the shot and take the photos. We do Bianca's Maple Wing first. I finally get to meet all the residents I've heard her talk about.

Our dress-up activities go well, and the pictures turn out great. One ninety-eight-year-old man had wanted to be a fireman; a ninety-five-year-old woman dreamed of being a princess. There were quite a few of those. The tiara Bianca brought gets a workout.

Halfway through the Birch Wing, we arrive at Ms. Gill's room. I ask her what she wanted to be when she was five and her answer surprises me. Since she's always in full hair and makeup, I assume she'll go for princess, ballerina or actress.

When she says cowgirl, I nearly fall out of my chair. Laughing to myself, I dig through the costume bag for the cowboy hat. Seconds later, Ms. Gill is transformed into Annie Oakley, assuming the famous cowgirl wore red lipstick and gold hoop earrings. Regardless, Ms. Gill looks fantastic.

Saving Father Cleary for last, Bianca and I push our cart to his room and knock on the molding of the doorway. The priest is seated in his wheelchair. Nurse Peggy is next to him whispering into his ear while patting his forearm. She looks up at us when we enter the room.

"Oh, it's you," she says, with the face of someone who's just smelled something unpleasant. "I'm afraid Father isn't feeling too well today. He's not himself and a bit confused. He thinks he's in a Korean hospital. He was a young chaplain in the army back in the fifties, you know."

Bianca and I look at each other, not sure what to do.

"We can try doing this another day, when he's feeling better," I say. "Has he been like this long?"

"For the past few days, he's been hearing confessions," says the nurse.

"People come here to St. Vincent's to give their confession?" I say, totally surprised.

Nurse Peggy locks eyes with me, stands and comes towards me and leans in.

"No one comes here for confession," she whispers, standing far too deep inside my personal space. I try to step back, but she follows me. "Father is reliving confessions he heard years ago. It's amazing, really. The man remembers every detail as if it were yesterday. It's quite extraordinary given his condition."

Bianca looks at me from behind the nurse's back and mouths, "What the hell?"

"I try not to listen to what he's saying, because I know it's sacred," says the nurse, as if she and I were confidants. "But sometimes he gets so loud. I've heard some of the confessions. They're terrible things that I shouldn't hear. They're meant to be kept under the Seal of Confession. Do you understand what I'm saying?"

I nod and look at Bianca. Her eyes are about to bug out of her head. She's not good at playing possum.

"But," says Nurse Peggy, in a voice barely above a whisper, "once a bell's rung, you can't unring it. I know what I've heard. Some of them were crimes. Now, I have to decide what to do."

I feel myself getting hot all over and not in a good way.

"How do you know what he's saying is for real?" says Bianca. "If he's that confused and thinks he's in Korea, maybe his dementia is affecting his imagination. Maybe it's all a fantasy."

"Maybe," says the nurse, as she turns and takes her seat next to the priest again. "But maybe not. That's for me to figure out."

I look over at Bianca.

"We'd better go," I say, as I move my friend towards the door. "I hope Father feels better. We'll try doing the costumes next time we come."

Bianca and I don't say a word until we get into the lobby.

"That was seriously weird," she says, grabbing my arm. "That woman is so bizarre. What's her story?"

The entire drive home Bianca talks only about the retired nun.

"And she's always there?" she says. "Every single time?"

"Seems like it."

"She's scary," says Bianca, rambling on, speculating about the weirdness of Nurse Peggy.

My question — is that weird nurse going report what she's learned to the police? And, is what she learned about me?

# CHAPTER 25

*Three months earlier*

*Christian Wendt*

As the 6 train bumps along the subway tracks heading to Downtown Manhattan, I go over the key selling points for my big sales pitch today. I've got to be on top of my game this afternoon . . . no mistakes. Two and a half hours from now, I'll get my one big shot. I've got to give the performance of a lifetime.

After months of chasing down different investment groups, I finally secured a meeting with a couple of junior members of the Halo Group. They're a premier boutique investment organization that sprinkles seed money into start-ups. One of Halo's big areas of interest is in slowing down climate change. That's exactly what my company does. My intention today is to get them to consider putting a substantial amount of their capital into my clean energy solution, Renewable Dairy Ventures, aka RDV. Halo has tons of cash and I think their managing director, Jason Sterling, will get behind our mission and invest.

Basically, my company has developed a new design and methodology of anaerobic digesters that convert energy. In layman's terms, our technology and equipment takes methane gas from dairy cows and turns it into usable energy — for only pennies. I've set up a network of dairies across the country that are already on board and participating in the program. My company is right in the Halo Group's sweet spot. They're on the lookout for green energy solutions, and that's what I'm selling. The best part for them, RDV is one hundred percent turnkey; it's up and running in over eighteen western states.

Once they see all the construction schedules, invoices and power generation reports along with photos of the different dairy sites, I'm confident they'll bite. We've got ads running in all the energy trade publications. This past winter, I spoke at a green energy conference in Arizona and got a great response. Today, I'm going to do more of the same. I'm going nail it.

My partner thinks I'm overly confident. Why shouldn't I be? My business proposition is airtight and right in line with the government subsidies available for addressing climate change. The people I'm meeting with today are angel investors with a mandate to save the planet while also making a return on their investment. The Halo Group calls themselves the 'investment group who does good'. Why do I want to work with them? Because everything Jason Sterling touches turns to gold.

With their investment of just ten or fifteen million to start, my company could triple their money in six months. I've already got a few small investors on board, but they're small change, not nearly enough to sustain our program. At this point, I need a big cash infusion. Halo's got that kind of money.

The subway stops and the doors open. As I watch the other passengers get on and off, I notice almost everyone is wearing earbuds and playing with their phones. Each person's in their own world, unaware of their surroundings. That's not smart. I like to know exactly what's going on around me. I don't like surprises.

The train moves forward, and I go back to my notes. Everything I've worked on for over a year is riding on today's presentation coming off without a hitch. Halo's been on my target list from the beginning. It took me six months of continuous emails and phone calls before any of the junior partners agreed to meet.

But I don't want to get ahead of myself. Even if it goes well today, it's only the first step. Halo Group deals only get done when their top dog, Jason Sterling, signs off on them. He's my next hurdle, if I get through today. As always, in case things don't go as I think they will, I've got a Plan B. I learned early in life that you always have to be ready with other options, because things can always go wrong. One way or another, I'm going to make this deal happen.

When the subway doors open at Canal Street, I leap out of the car and run up the battered, uneven steps to the surface. It's a warm, sunny day, and very bright when I get out onto the street. My eyes take a moment to adjust. Squinting, I slip on a pair of Ray-Ban Wayfarer sunglasses and look around to get my bearings.

Briskly walking down Canal Street, I look in all the store windows. There are two things I need to buy here before my big presentation today. Stopping at a small market, I make my first purchase — a scratch-off lottery ticket. I always get one or two before any important meeting, to bring me luck.

As I reach for the door of the small market, I catch a glimpse of my reflection in the glass plate window. I assess my appearance and straighten my collar. I look good, professional and successful, the exact image I wanted to project. In my new gray wool suit, expensive Egyptian cotton white shirt and lucky cufflinks, I look every bit the part of a successful entrepreneur. I even got a haircut and had my beard trimmed yesterday.

Adjusting the sunglasses on the bridge of my nose, I run my fingers through my dark-brown hair to smooth it out. I've come a long way. After spending my twenties finding myself, my thirties have been all about setting myself up for the future. With forty just around the corner, it's now all about making things happen fast. *Carpe diem* is my single mantra.

I get my lucky lottery ticket and put it in my pocket for later. Now, I've got one more purchase to make — the main reason I've come to Chinatown. Today, I'm in the market for a really good knock-off watch. In this neighborhood, you can find world-class fakes if you know the right places to look. You've got to time it right, though. Every few months, the NYPD cracks down on all the counterfeit handbag, clothing and jewelry vendors. Everything is carted out, but within a few days of the raid, the same vendors are back, merchandise is restocked and they're open for business again. This cat-and-mouse game has been going on for decades. I don't know why the cops waste their time. Chinatown fakes are a New York City institution.

As I stroll through a number of shops, the salespeople try to interest me in ladies' designer handbags for my 'girlfriend or wife'. If I was so inclined, I could pick up a Prada, Louis Vuitton or Chanel bag for next to nothing. But that's not what I'm after. Today, I'm on the hunt for a men's Rolex watch to round out my look.

A few months ago, I bought a pair of faux-gold Hermes cufflinks right here on this same street. Whenever I wear them, people always notice. They're excellent copies. You couldn't tell they're fake unless you had a magnifying glass. Even then, you'd really have to know the product well to spot the subtle differences. They're practically flawless. Naturally, I'm wearing them today . . . for luck.

Walking down the aisle of a long, narrow shop, I shake my head at the persistent saleswoman hovering around me like a hummingbird. She shoves several phony Bottega Veneta bags at me as I head to the back of the store. On the back wall, behind a dingy gray curtain, a hidden door opens into another smaller, more 'exclusive' boutique. Only people in the know have any idea it's there. That's where they keep the good stuff. It's the only place I do my shopping.

"How you doing, Mr. Chen? Remember me? Christian Wendt," I say as I greet the owner and lift up my sleeve to show him the cufflinks I'd bought there. "You sold me these beauties a couple of months ago. You drive a hard bargain, you know that?"

Fully aware that the older Chinese man has no idea who I am, I keep the conversation going and he plays along, smiling as if we're old friends.

"Oh yes, of course, Mr. Wendt. You're one of my favorite customers. You got a very good deal on those cufflinks. Make you look like a very important man. What can I help you find today? You looking for a Chanel bag for your wife, maybe?"

"I don't have a wife, Mr. Chen."

"No wife? Why not? How old are you?"

"Thirty-nine."

"You should have a wife by now."

"Mr. Chen, I've got a very important meeting today. It's absolutely critical that I look successful. I'm thinking of a Rolex. Nothing too flashy, something elegant and understated. Got anything like that?"

The old man nods, smiles knowingly, bends over and opens a drawer. He wags a finger. "I have something very special, but only for my best customers like you."

Seconds later, he extracts a tray from the drawer filled with all sorts of fake men's Rolex and Patek Phillipe watches. They are so much better than the knockoffs sitting out on tables on the street. I can spot a fake a mile away. But the watches Mr. Chen sells are practically perfect.

I try on a few and decide on one that's sleek and subtle and not ostentatious. This afternoon, I'm going to be asking wealthy people to invest a substantial amount of money in my company. I need to look like a winner. At the same time, I don't want it to appear like I spend money frivolously.

For the next few minutes, Mr. Chen and I do a little haggle dance over the price before finally arriving at a number that makes us both happy. I give him seventy-five dollars, and slip on a watch that would normally retail for over nine thousand. Who cares if it's fake? It looks like the real thing; that's all that matters.

With still an hour to go until my meeting, I take my time walking over to the Halo offices reviewing the elements of my pitch. Passing a Starbucks, I check the time on my new watch. I've got a few minutes to kill, and stop in for a quick hit of espresso. Fifteen minutes later, when I walk through the front doors of the tall brick building in Lower Manhattan, my entire body is one giant vibrating nerve. That's when it occurs to me that I probably didn't need that extra shot of caffeine.

I do a few breathing and meditation exercises to prepare for what comes next. In a few minutes, I'll be standing in front of a roomful of people who could make or break me. If I don't capture their attention within the first few seconds, they won't send me on to meet their top person. He's the one who counts. Jason Sterling makes all the final decisions. If I don't win him over, I don't win.

I take three deep breaths and blow them out. Everything I've been working towards for over a year is riding on my presentation today. There's no second chances. I've got to nail this one.

Approaching the security desk, I provide the uniformed guard with my ID. He's an older man with a white mustache who studies my driver's license as if he were preparing for an exam. When he finally looks up, he peers at me but says nothing.

"Is there a problem?" I ask, as I look at my watch impatiently. I can't be late today.

He cocks his head to one side, possibly because I've challenged his authority. He's clearly not having any of that.

"Doing my job, sir," he says, as he takes another look at my license. "There's all sorts of crazies in this city. You can never be too careful."

I figure this is his only chance to throw his weight around, so I smile and nod. Eventually, he gives me a building pass and directs me to the back elevator bank. As I'm riding up to the twelfth floor, a tiny creep of insecurity starts crawling around in my brain.

*What if they don't get my concept? I need to be the velvet hammer that they don't see coming until they feel it hit. Don't sweat it . . . there's always Plan B.*

'You gotta keep a lot of pots on the stove, kid. One or two of 'em will eventually boil over.' That's what my old man used to say. Of course, he was always drunk and rarely coherent. But occasionally, he said something that made sense. That was one of them.

The elevator bell rings and the doors open. In front of me is a wall of glass with two glass doors in the center. The black and silver lettering on the wall says *Halo Group*. A very attractive young woman with red hair sits on the other side of the glass at a reception desk. I take a deep breath and walk through one of the doors.

"Good afternoon. I've got a meeting with Steven Cox and Peter Kaminski," I say, with a warm smile. "I'm Christian Wendt."

# CHAPTER 26

Ninety minutes later, I walk out of the Halo Group offices with a big smile on my face. The presentation was a huge success. Those two junior partners were totally on board with everything I said. This is going to happen; I can feel it. When I walked them through the schemata and showed them how much energy my dairy network is able to convert, they went nuts.

"This is extremely impressive," says Kaminski.

"I couldn't agree more," says Cox. "It's a brilliant idea. Exactly the kind of energy innovation we're looking to support."

I smile sheepishly at them for effect.

"How did we not hear about RDV before today?"

I look at them both and grin. They're hooked. Now, all I have to do is reel them in.

"I'm just a simple engineer, not a salesman," I say, my palms turned up and outstretched. "I've worked hard, kept my head down and tried to build the best damn renewable energy solution possible."

"You've nailed it, man. We love it," says Kaminski, looking at his colleague.

I smile again. "I'm at a point with my company where I need to expand. With Halo Group's muscle, connections and money behind me, think what we could do together and where we could take this. It could be a climate game changer."

I know I've hooked them. Of course, the senior partners will be tougher. They'll ask harder questions and require a lot more documentation. But I'm so ready for it. I was *born* ready for it.

The two junior partners tell me they'll hook me up for a meeting with the top guys. I remind them that I'm talking to other investor groups and drop a few strategic names that they'd know.

The truth is, I'm not talking to anyone else. I couldn't get my foot in the door at the other firms, but Halo Group doesn't know that. Angel investing is a very secretive business. No one wants anyone else to know what they're doing. I use that cloak and dagger mentality to my advantage. Cox and Kaminski ask me to send them our most recent revenue numbers. They've also promised to set up the big meeting with their managing partner.

I leave the building walking on air and head uptown. After a few blocks, I pass a bar and duck in to treat myself to a beer for a job well done. Sure, it's only three o'clock, but what the hell, today's a big day. As the bartender places a pint of IPA in front of me, I whip out the scratch-off lottery card I'd stashed in my wallet.

Using a quarter laying on the bar, I methodically scratch off the silver covering on the ticket. I smile when I see I've won five dollars with three matching numbers.

My day keeps getting better and better.

* * *

Three weeks later after providing the Halo Group with a mountain of documents, they give me a date for the big meeting — it will be in a few weeks on a Tuesday morning at 10 a.m.

To prepare for the important meeting with Jason Sterling, I reach out to an associate who's been working with me on the

RDV project — Sophie Boyd, the consummate pro. Sophie's in her early forties and solid as a rock. She exudes confidence, especially during a pitch. We've partnered up before on a number of other ventures over the past six or seven years. I'll need her in the Sterling meeting. With her by my side, we'll be able to land this plane. After all, renewable energy *is* the way of the future.

For the next couple of weeks, Sophie and I meet daily in my New York City apartment to plan our strategy and general attack for the pitch.

"We've got only one shot here. We can't screw it up," I tell her.

"Relax," she says. "From what you've told me, Halo is salivating for something like this for their portfolio."

I hand her a beer. "The younger associates are on board. But they're green and only thinking about making their mark. The top dogs like Sterling and a few others, they're going to be much more of a challenge and put us through our paces."

"But they've given you a meeting. That's half the battle. It means they're interested."

"Yeah, but it's still ours to lose. Remember, never be too complacent."

A few weeks later, Sophie and I head downtown to Halo's offices. I'm wearing a brand-new navy suit that fits me like a glove. For added pizzazz, I'm sporting my lucky Hermes cufflinks and my new Rolex watch, compliments of Mr. Chen.

I hold open the inside door of the building for Sophie and admire her appearance as she passes. First impressions count, and Sophie's got the right look. With her brown, shoulder-length, no-nonsense bob and three-inch heels, she projects the right image. Her look says, *I'm feminine but not too sexy. I'm attractive, but not so pretty as to be a distraction.* She's perfect. I want those investors focused on what we say, not on Sophie's legs. People trust her. In no time, she'll have them eating out of her hand. I've seen her do it before. She's amazing.

We approach that suspicious security guard in the lobby. He takes his sweet time analyzing the information on our IDs.

I remain calm and pleasant, because I don't want any bad karma coming my way. If it's not important, I let it roll off my back. Everything has to go smoothly today. *Namaste.*

We arrive in Halo Group's reception area and are ushered into a large sleek gray conference room with floor-to-ceiling windows and amazing views. Scoping out the room, we take seats next to each other on the same side of the table. Then we wait for the others to arrive.

As each minute passes, I feel my nerves banging against each other under my skin. This is what I've been working towards for the longest time. Today is everything; I need to be on top of my game.

Suddenly, the conference room door opens. Peter Kaminski and Steven Cox enter first and shake our hands. They're soon followed by nine other investors, all men. The last one to enter the room is the key decision maker, Jason Sterling. If he doesn't take a bite out of what I'm selling, regardless of the others, the deal's dead.

I'm asking for fifteen million dollars, with hopes of getting ten. Ten million is chump change for this group. Still, they're not going to throw money away. Our presentation has to be flawless.

"Christian," says Jason Sterling, extending his hand. "I've heard a lot of good things about you and reviewed the notes on your company. You have a very compelling and potentially game-changing proposition. A few of my colleagues here are very impressed. I'm hoping you dazzle me as well. I will say that what you're doing seems to be a fit with our mission and could round out our portfolio."

Everyone takes a seat and it's show time. Sophie and I play a short video that shows our network of dairies and our anaerobic digesters at work. From there, we take the group through each phase of our operation. We show them our growth to date and where we expect to be in three years. I'm not going to lie; our numbers look fantastic. Judging from the nods and smiles in the room, they think so, too.

Why do our numbers look so amazing? Because I made them up. Every piece of data we're showing these people came out of my noggin. The diagrams, the pictures, the videos, the anaerobic digesters, the dairy network and, of course, the spectacular revenue. It's all part of the game. The whole thing is a scam, a con. None of it actually exists or works. There is no Renewable Dairy Ventures. It's a carefully crafted mirage.

But if things go the way I hope, I'll be long gone with my millions before anybody realizes they've been taken. That's how the game's played. Go in hard, get out fast . . . real fast, and have your passport up-to-date at all times.

Standing in front of the roomful of men explaining the ins and outs of our technology, I watch Sophie expertly work the room. She's totally on point today. I know everything she's saying is bullshit, but she's so good, even I'd buy from her. When she's finished, I get up to tell them what they really want to know . . . the bottom line. What kind of return are they going to get on their investment? That's what they care about.

"What I can tell you," I say, wrapping up the pitch, "is that RDV's proprietary technology is on the cutting edge of renewable energy. We don't approach the dairies anymore; the dairies are coming to us because it's a moneymaker and costs them nothing. We're signing up new farms every week. Your fifteen-million-dollar investment today will turn into fifty million by the end of next year. And the best part is, we all make money while cleaning up the environment and slowing down climate change. What's better than that?"

After the room breaks out in enthusiastic applause, I give Sophie a nod. Everyone stands, smiles and shakes hands. We've pulled it off. Before anyone leaves, I wade through the crowd to get to Sterling.

"Jason," I say, "I really appreciate the positive response from your team. What else do I need to show you to secure your investment in RDV?"

There's a twinkle in Sterling's eye and he smiles. I take it as a good sign.

"We're not quite there yet," he says, holding up both hands. "So far, I like what I see. But we invest in a lot of projects, and it's our policy to take our time. Since we're investing our own money, we have to be one hundred percent certain about a project before we release any funds. We need to do a little more due diligence on your proposal before we'd consider giving it a green light."

I can live with that . . . for now.

# CHAPTER 27

After the Halo Group meeting, Sophie and I leave the building without saying a word. We have a hard and fast rule. Never discuss anything regarding a presentation until we're far away from the site and in a place where no one can hear us. I got burned once and will never do that again.

We head to a small Manhattan park and sit on an empty bench to discuss next steps.

"Overall," says Sophie, "they seem extremely interested, don't you think?"

I pop a piece of gum in my mouth. "Sterling's not sold yet."

"Based on their questions," says Sophie, "most of them appeared to be on board."

"Only one person matters, Sterling. Without him, it's not going to happen. We've got to grease the wheels and make it easier for him to say yes."

"And how are we going to do that?"

"Sterling is a people guy. Relationships matter to him. I'm going to invite him out to dinner so he can get to know me better. I'll lay it on thick and present him with even more impressive data. I'll show him new and even better revenue numbers that will make him salivate."

"And where are you going to get those from?" says Sophie, her eyebrow raised.

"From here," I say, tapping my head.

A week later, I'm sitting across from Jason Sterling in a steakhouse in Midtown Manhattan. He requested an early dinner so he could get home to see his kids before they go to bed. Naturally, I agreed and applauded him for putting family first.

"You never get those early years back," I say, when Jason tells me he needs to catch the 7:37 p.m. train out of Grand Central.

"You have any kids, Christian?" he says, as he takes a sip of his red wine.

"Not yet," I say, furrowing my brow to appear sad about that fact. "Honestly, my business has taken over my life. You know how it is. Haven't had much time for a personal life. I've been on the road fundraising 24/7. But after we get the next cash infusion, I can relax a little and smell the roses."

"I know how you feel. When I started my first company, I worked non-stop, days, nights and weekends. I didn't date. Like you, I didn't do anything but work. Luckily, my wife, Abbie, came in to do bookkeeping for us. We hit if off immediately and the rest is history."

"That's an encouraging story," I say, taking my first sip of wine. I only sip it for social reasons and will only finish half of a glass. I don't want anything impeding my thoughts while I'm doing business. Every word counts; alcohol makes one's thoughts too loose. One wrong word can sink a deal. I can't afford that.

I order exactly what he orders — ribeye steak, baked potato and creamed spinach. It's called mirroring, a form of subliminal flattery. The mark is totally unaware of what you're doing, and you score points.

While we wait for our food, we chat about some of the initiatives the Halo Group has invested in over the years. I'll wait until the food arrives, before going into my hard pitch.

Once I'm on a roll, I don't want any interruptions from waiters. I want Jason's full and undivided attention.

As the waiter serves us our meals, I ask Jason if he needs any additional sauces for his steak or toppings for his potato. I don't want any distractions while I'm closing him.

With our dinner underway, I begin my pitch. First, I tell him how impressed I am with his group and their illustrious history of savvy investments.

"Given your existing portfolio in renewables, the way I see it," I say, "is that my company rounds you out. There's a lot of symmetry with RDV and your other investments. There might even be an opportunity for joint ventures."

Jason dips his meat into some steak sauce and puts it into his mouth.

"Great minds think alike," he says, chewing slowly. "We do look for potential overlap with our other investments when deciding on a new venture."

I'm getting good signals from Jason. It's time to pull out the new set of data Sophie and I put together this morning.

"I hate to do this during dinner, but can I show you something?" I say, holding up my phone so he can see the screen. "Since you have a hard stop to catch your train, I'd be remiss if I didn't show you the new numbers that came in this afternoon. They'll blow your mind."

Jason puts down his fork and takes the phone from my hand.

"Wow," he says reading the made-up data. "You're seriously rocking it. Can you send me a copy of this, so I can show it to the others?"

I nod. "This is rough right now. I'll lay it out on a chart tonight and you'll have it first thing in the morning."

At seven, Jason thanks me for dinner and leaves to catch his train. I'm feeling fantastic. The new numbers Sophie and I dreamed up may have just clinched the deal. I definitely moved the needle tonight, but did I move it far enough? Time will tell.

Out on the street alone, I call Sophie.

"How did it go?" she says.

"We're close, very close. After he has a chance to show the group our new revenue numbers, I think he'll move forward."

The next morning, Sophie sends Jason the fictional numbers, as well as a couple of newly written testimonial letters from two of our dairies. I wrote them myself, and they're glowing.

Things are moving in the right direction. I can already taste the lime in my margaritas on a remote beach in Mexico. I think I'll rent a house in Baja for six months while planning my next business venture. Obviously, I'll have to steer clear of the USA for a few years. Once Jason figures out I've sold him a bunch of crap and some empty cow stalls, he's not going to be very happy.

Will he call in the feds? Maybe, but probably not. He won't want the financial community to get wind that his Halo Group got taken so badly. That would make them look like amateurs. I'm counting on him just writing off the money and licking his wounds in silence. For these investment groups, appearance is everything.

I give Jason another day to digest the glorious new numbers before I call him.

"If you're looking for an answer right now," he says, when I try to close him again, "I'm afraid I can't give you one."

"Is there something that's holding you back? Can I provide you with additional data?"

"Let me be clear, Christian. I like what you're doing, but I don't rush into these things. You and Sophie have been great, and everything seems to check out. But I'm not ready to make a commitment yet. I like to take my time when I'm investing millions in anything."

Is Jason signaling that the deal might not happen? I didn't want to go there, but Plan B may end up being my only option.

"I want you to be one hundred percent comfortable with me and my company," I say to him. "We can certainly take things slower."

"What about the other investors?" he says. "I thought there was some urgency."

"I can slow the other investors down. Sophie and I want to work with the Halo Group."

"Ok. If you're not in a rush," says Jason, "let's keep our conversations going."

Anger and frustration bubble up inside me, but I don't let it show. My face remains calm, serene and amiable. I smile.

"I couldn't agree more," I say. "No reason to race to the finish line. Let's get to know each other better. In fact, I have an idea. How about Sophie and I take you and your wife out to dinner this Saturday night? We'll make it easy for you and meet somewhere near your home in Connecticut. You pick the place and we'll be there."

# CHAPTER 28

*Abbie*

At 6:30 tonight, I'm supposed to meet my husband and a couple of his business associates for dinner at our favorite restaurant in Eastport, Audrey's Kitchen. I already had a 4:45 p.m. hair appointment scheduled for highlights and blow-out at my salon. I have no intention of missing it, not with our big party happening next weekend.

We're hosting our annual Memorial Day barbecue for over hundred people, and I want to look good. Not knowing how long the salon will take, I told Jason I'd meet him at the restaurant and to start without me if I'm a little late.

I don't often attend these business things. Usually, I find them so dull. But when Jason told me the people he's having dinner with have an innovative and game-changing method for tackling climate change using cows, it piqued my curiosity. I've been really involved in local environmental issues through my community group. I also run all the Earth Day activities for the schools every spring. So when my husband asked me to go to dinner, I surprised him and said yes.

I arrive at my hair salon early hoping that they might be able to take me sooner. Wishful thinking on my part, because the minute I walk in, my colorist informs me that she's running twenty minutes late. I text my husband to let him know there could be a delay, and settle in to watch some Instagram videos and catch up on email until they're ready for me.

At 5:05 p.m., as one of the assistants is getting me prepped in a chair, my colorist sails by. I call out to tell her I've got a dinner reservation and need to be out of the salon by 6:15. She rolls her eyes but keeps moving.

"You can't rush color, Abbie," she shouts back, over her shoulder. "It's gotta sit on your head for a certain amount of time."

When she finally starts to work on me, she does her best to speed up the whole process. By the time she finishes my blow-dry, it's nearly 6:45. Since it will take me at least ten minutes to get over to the restaurant, I text Jason again to let him know I'm on my way.

Audrey's Kitchen is a large, busy, open-concept bistro with high ceilings. It overlooks a pond, and when the weather's nice, there's additional seating outside on a large patio. The air is cool tonight, so most people are inside. Before I get out of the car, I run my fingers through my newly highlighted hair and swipe some pink gloss across my lips.

Approaching the maitre'd, I look around for my husband. The restaurant is full, with a dozen more people standing by the front door waiting for a table.

"I'm meeting some people here," I say to the hostess, while scanning the expansive dining room. A hand shoots up midway across the room and waves to me. It's Jason. I smile at him and tell the hostess that I've found my party.

Sidestepping through the main dining room, I approach the table, but can only see the backs of the two people Jason is sitting with. One is a woman with shoulder-length brown hair. Seated next to her is a man with a beard. I walk directly over to my husband, lean in and give him a kiss.

"Sorry I'm so late," I say, looking into his beautiful brown eyes. "They were backed up at the salon. You know how it is."

146

He laughs. "Actually, babe, I don't. But you look great, anyway."

I smile, sit down and place my bag underneath the table before turning to greet Jason's two dinner companions. My eyes land on the woman first. She's very attractive and confident.

"Sophie, this is my amazing wife, Abbie," says Jason. "Honey, I'd like you to meet Sophie Boyd."

Sophie smiles as she half stands and reaches across the table to shake my hand.

"And, last but not least," says Jason, "the founder of RDV, Christian Wendt. These are the two masterminds behind that renewable energy project using dairies that I told you about. They have a method of converting gas from cows into energy."

A strong male voice rings out, summoning my attention.

"I've heard so much about you, Abbie," says the handsome bearded man with light-brown hair. "Jason told us about all the public service work you do, including the local environmental programs you run. That's fantastic."

I barely hear what he says, because there's something eerily familiar about him, but I can't put my finger on it. As his mouth moves, I look into his eyes. They're black and intense. I can't stop looking at them, but at the same time, they make me nervous and I want to look away. The man keeps talking while I rack my brain for exactly why I feel like I know him. After a few seconds, I'm overcome by high-pitched ringing in my ears. What's happening to me?

". . . and I'm sure you know that your husband's a stickler for details," the man with the beard says to me, with a little laugh. "That's probably why he's so successful. Weren't you listed in *Tech Entrepreneur's* "Top 100 To Watch" this year, Jason?"

"Guilty," says my husband, enjoying their admiration. "Last year, too."

"Impressive," Christian says, with smile. "Abbie, you must have been very proud of your husband when that list came out."

My mouth is fixed at half open. I feel unsettled, confused and anxious. For some reason that I can't pinpoint, I sense overwhelming danger. But of what? Him? Her? We've all just met. I don't even know them. *What's wrong with me? Get it together.*

"Abbie?" says Jason, leaning over and whispering in my ear. "Are you all right?"

I jump back in my seat as if I'd been bitten by a snake. I'm not sure how long I've come across as dumbstruck, but clearly long enough for my husband to be alarmed.

I shake my head, as if to clear some brain fog that's overtaken me.

"I'm sorry. I guess I'm a little worn out," I say, trying to look anywhere but at the man and woman I just met. "I did a lot of running around today, getting ready for our barbecue this weekend."

Christian leans forward, giving me a chance to further examine his face. There's something about him. It takes me a minute. Then it hits me like a ton of bricks. It's his eyes. Christian has black eyes that remind me of Travis — dark, shiny and intense.

But that's where the similarity ends. His nose is completely different. Travis broke his nose when he was a kid. When I knew him, it was slightly crooked. I thought it made him look cool, sexy and edgy. Christian's nose is perfectly straight.

"Your husband was just telling us about your upcoming Memorial Day bash," says Christian, dipping a piece of bread into some olive oil. "It must be a lot of work pulling off a big extravaganza like that."

"Abbie's amazing when it comes to entertaining," says my husband. "She makes it look effortless."

I smile at my husband, but my mind is focused on the strange man sitting across from me. I don't know why he reminds me of Travis, because other than his eyes, he really looks nothing like him. His forehead is less prominent, and his cheekbones aren't as high as Travis' were. His hair is different, and his face is much fuller. The more I think about it, it's only the eyes that are the same. Did Travis have a brother?

"Sophie and I appreciate you making time to join us tonight, Abbie," says Christian. "Hopefully, this dinner is the first of many."

"There's so much synergy between our two organizations," says Sophie, shifting the conversation back to business. "We all want to stop climate change, don't we?"

"Hear, hear," says Christian, raising his wine glass.

Jason picks up a full glass of white wine that's sitting on the table and hands it to me.

"I ordered you a Chablis. I hope that's all right," he says.

Still unnerved, I gratefully take the full glass from him. What I could really use is a few shots of tequila right now, but the wine will do. We all clink glasses as Jason gives a toast. As soon as I get the rim of the glass to my lips, I suck down half of it in one large gulp. Jason shoots me a quizzical look, but soon goes back to the group conversation.

While the three of them chat about energy and saving the planet, normally something I'd be interested in, I use the time to unpack exactly what's happening. I've met plenty of men with dark eyes before. So, why do Christian's eyes unnerve me?

I listen carefully to the timbre of his voice, and try to remember what Travis' voice sounded like. I can't get a read on it, because it's been so long. There's something similar in the overall tone of his voice, but maybe it's my imagination. I home in on Christian's vocabulary choices, to see if maybe they ring a bell. They don't. This man's speaking rhythm is different from what I remember of my old boyfriend. But it's been twenty years since I've seen Travis, so it's not surprising I can't recall the tiny details. Plus, we were high most of the time. I don't know why I'm working myself up over this. Travis is dead anyway, so what does it matter?

# CHAPTER 29

The evening continues, and I try to engage in the conversation at the table, but barely get out two sentences. I'm usually a chatty person, so my husband keeps looking at me clearly wondering what the hell is wrong. Despite Christian's friendly demeanor at the table, I still can't shake the weird feeling I have. Then he says something that sends me deeper into orbit.

"I'd like to order something special to help celebrate this wonderful evening," says Christian. "How about I get us all some champagne? Nothing says success like a little champagne."

*What did he just say?*

Travis always talked about champagne being the sign of ultimate success. Gripping the edge of the table with my fingertips to steady myself, I take a deep breath as the waiter approaches to take our order. I'm so out of sorts at this point that I randomly choose the first dinner item on the menu.

My husband notices I'm acting weird, because he leans over to me again.

"What's wrong?" he whispers into my ear. "You ordered fish. You hate fish."

I force a smile. "I'm trying something new. Getting out of my rut. I'm fine . . . really."

He turns back to the other two, and the three of them continue talking about energy while I try to make some sense of this seemingly surreal coincidence. By the time our waiter brings our dinner, I'm heading into an emotional tailspin.

"Abbie, you want another glass of wine?" Jason says, trying to get my attention while the waiter waits for my reply.

I look up from my trance and nod as the waiter disappears.

"Believe it or not, having grown up in the Midwest," says Christian, "I've never been to this part of Connecticut before. It's beautiful. Sophie and I got up here early today and had a chance to drive around town. Eastport is a pretty little town and a reasonable commute to Manhattan. You picked a great spot to raise your family."

I continue examining this stranger with the beard, who doesn't seem to notice my scrutiny or doesn't care. Jason nudges me under the table with his knee and gives me a 'what's going on?' look.

"We love it here," my husband says, moments later, while squeezing my hand and giving me a nod.

"It's a great place to raise kids," I say, jumping into the conversation while polishing off the remainder of my Chablis.

"Sophie and I got a good vibe the minute we pulled into town," says Christian. "It's country-ish, but still has a bustling downtown. You don't feel like you're out in the sticks at all. I heard you have great schools, too. We might consider moving here when we have kids."

"You're married?" my husband says, clearly surprised. "I didn't realize you two were a . . ."

Christian raises up both of his hands with great flourish. "Sophie came to work at RDV about two and a half years ago. She's been an amazing contributor to the success of the company. We couldn't have done it without her. All those long hours working together and traveling to dairies around the country, and something finally clicked."

"Sounds just like Abbie and me. When's the wedding?" says my husband with a grin.

"Next year, sometime," says Sophie sheepishly. "We've been so busy with the business that there hasn't been time to plan one. Christian and I agreed that once we secured all the financing, we'd take a breath and get things rolling."

Jason leans forward and holds up his glass.

"Congratulations to you both," he says. "To be honest, knowing you're planning a family makes me view you and your company in a somewhat different light."

"In what way?" says Christian as he pours us all a glass of champagne with tremendous flourish.

"It may sound stupid and old-fashioned," says my husband, "but I guess I trust a man with a wife and kids more than someone who's single."

"I'm glad we put you at ease, then," says a smiling Christian before turning to me. "Jason tells me you have two beautiful little girls. It's Luna and Grace, right?"

I nod, still not sure who or what I'm dealing with or if I'm simply losing my mind.

For the rest of the dinner I barely say a word. A good portion of the meal is spent talking about energy, government regulations and cows. I half listen as Christian gives my husband the hard sell and look over at my husband's face. I know Jason. He's not buying everything that Christian's selling tonight, that's for sure.

When the check arrives, Christian ceremoniously sweeps his arm down and grabs it with a little too much fanfare. Travis was the same way, always putting on a show. I liked it when I was fifteen, but now gestures like that just look pretentious.

After he pays the bill, Christian suggests we all move to the bar for a nightcap. Over my initial shock, I start to wonder if I've pegged this man completely wrong. He has a different name and face and hasn't shown any indication that he's ever met me before. Lots of people like champagne, including me. Still, those eyes . . . something's not right.

I try to take in a breath and can't. I'm having a panic attack and need to get out of here right now. Standing up abruptly, I nearly knock over my chair.

"I'm sorry, everyone. I don't feel well. Jason, I'll meet you at home," I say as I turn and race from the table towards the exit.

Once outside, I walk quickly to my car allowing the cool night air to fill my empty lungs. As I get closer to my vehicle, I hear a voice call out.

"Abbie, are you okay?" shouts my husband running up behind me.

A bead of sweat runs down my spine as I turn around.

"I feel nauseous," I say, as I open my car door. "I'll see you back at the house."

He asks a few more questions about my health, shrugs and goes back into the restaurant. I start the engine and get out of that parking lot as fast as possible.

As I drive, it occurs to me that Jason is going to have a lot of questions when he gets home. Ordering fish and running out of a public place is not my typical behavior. The shock of meeting someone who reminded me so much of Travis caught me by surprise. Still, Christian and Sophie seemed so normal. Am I inventing drama where there is none?

*Get it together, Abbie.*

Pulling into our garage, I remember the girls are away at a sleepover. Exhausted, and not in the mood to answer Jason's questions about my strange behavior tonight, I get changed and into bed as fast possible. I'll pretend to be asleep when he gets home. Any questions he may have will have to wait until morning. That will give me time to come up with some plausible reasons for my clearly odd behavior.

Within five minutes, I brush my teeth and get into bed. There's no way I'll be asleep when Jason gets home, but he won't know that.

Thirty minutes later, our bedroom door opens slowly. I keep my eyes closed tight as my husband walks past our bed and goes directly into the bathroom.

I'm safe from an inquisition for tonight, but a little voice in my head keeps telling me something's not right.

# CHAPTER 30

When I wake up the next morning, Jason's not in bed. I figure he went out for a run, his usual weekend routine. Him being gone gives me more time to come up with some good answers to the questions I know he'll ask.

While my husband slept soundly, I was awake half the night trying to talk myself down. I can't shake the feeling that I once knew that man. He's not Travis, but somehow, I know him . . . I think.

At 9:30 a.m., I get out of bed and head down to the kitchen for a much-needed coffee. After my sleepless night, I'll be living on caffeine today. We're supposed to pick up the girls from their sleepover at noon. I'll talk to Jason about last night as soon as he gets back from his run. It's better if he and I have our discussion and clear the air before the kids come home.

Fifteen minutes later, Jason's footsteps bang up the stairs of the back deck. I'm sitting at the kitchen table sipping my second coffee when he comes in through the back door. Covered in sweat, he walks directly to the sink, fills a glass with water and downs it without saying a word.

"Good run?" I say, looking over at him, a cheery smile on my face.

"I was moving slow today," he says, examining the data on his sports watch and making a face. "It's not surprising, given all the wine and champagne I had last night."

And there it was. My husband's not-so-subtle segue into the events of the previous night. I decide to get ahead of it.

"About last night," I say, "I didn't tell you the full story of what happened."

Jason fills his glass again and looks at me. "There's a story?"

"The real reason I was late was because I got really sick at the salon. I threw up in their bathroom . . . twice. I think it was the chicken salad sandwich I had for lunch. I almost didn't make it to the restaurant."

Jason places his glass on the counter and comes over to the table.

"Babe, why didn't you just tell me?" he says sitting next to me.

"I didn't want to ruin the evening. I thought I'd be okay. But once I got inside that crowded restaurant, another wave of nausea hit me hard. That's why I barely said anything."

"You should have gone home," he says, rubbing my arm. "Everyone would have understood."

"I know; it was stupid. I thought the sick feeling would pass, but it didn't. It got worse. I'm so sorry. I must have looked like an idiot in front of those people."

Jason weaves his fingers through mine and gives my hand a squeeze.

"I don't give a shit about them. You know that. You and the kids are the only things that matter to me."

"I love you," I say, making a frownie face. "I'm fine now."

"No more secrets, okay?"

I nod. "Promise."

My lies seem to be flowing out of me like running water. At the same time, I hate myself for not being truthful with the one person who loves me the most. But what choice do I have? I can't tell him the truth.

"I wish you'd stayed, though. I wanted you to hear the whole background on Christian's energy business. You know how much I value your opinion, especially when it comes to climate things. I think they've really got something there."

"You're going to invest in their company?" I say, trying to control the disturbed look I feel creeping across my face.

"Not sure yet, but I'm warming to the idea."

Hearing my husband say that has made things go from bad to worse. I'm not a hundred percent sure about the identity of the man calling himself Christian. Until I know for sure, Jason absolutely cannot go into business with him.

I get up from the table and put my cup in the dishwasher, trying to think of a rational reason Jason shouldn't get involved with Christian. Nothing remotely comes to mind, so I resort to 'a gut feeling'. I've heard Jason use that phrase a million times. Sometimes, I think he trusts his gut more than me.

"To be honest," I say, with my back to him, so he can't read my terrible poker face, "I didn't get a great feeling from those two people last night."

"Of course not. You were as sick as a dog."

I spin around and go for it. "I was sick to my stomach last night, but my brain was working just fine. Something about them felt off. I can't explain it. He struck me as . . . a little disingenuous. It's a *gut* thing."

"I didn't get that at all," says Jason. "But the good news is that your gut will have another chance to evaluate them. They're coming to our Memorial Day barbecue next week."

It was like someone hit me over the head with a bowling ball. "Those two are coming to our house?" I say.

"They're thinking of moving to Connecticut," says my husband nonchalantly. "I thought inviting them up here would help them get a better feel for Eastport. Also, I could spend a little more time with them, get to know them better outside of the office."

"But I don't know if we . . ."

"You'll have time to talk to them at the party. See if you still feel the same way," he says, as he heads towards the stairs to take a shower. "Once you get to know them, I'll bet you'll have a change of heart."

After staring out the kitchen window looking for a solution and finding none, I go into the family room. Opening my computer, I do a Google search for a Christian Wendt.

Not much comes up beyond one or two links related to his company, RDV. Everything I find is about dairies and energy, so that checks out. I can't find him anywhere on Facebook, Instagram or Twitter. While I locate several other Christian Wendts, there's no social media account for the man I met last night. I know it's pointless but then I do a search for Travis Ritter. Nothing pops there, either.

*Am I totally wrong? It's been a really long time since I've seen Travis.*

As I second-guess myself over Christian's identity, a single nagging thought runs repeatedly through my mind. If that man is somehow connected to Travis, he's not here by accident. My world could come crashing down at any moment.

# CHAPTER 31

Monday morning, I have an emergency appointment with Dr. Goldberg at 10:30 a.m. After my confusing encounter with Christian at the restaurant Friday evening, I had a whopper of a nightmare on Saturday night. Fortunately, the kids slept through it, but my poor husband wasn't as lucky.

"I thought your sessions with Goldberg were helping," Jason said while holding me quivering in our bed. "This one tonight was worse than the others. Maybe we should try a different therapist?"

I wanted to tell him that it wouldn't matter what doctor I went to. I could see every therapist in the state of Connecticut and none of them would be able to help. What's happening to me is a result of my overwhelming guilt and bone-crushing remorse for ending my mother's life and never taking responsibility for it. Right now, there's someone out there who knows what really happened, and possibly, more than one person. How would my husband react if he knew that his wife, his children's mother, the Eastport Volunteer of the Year, is also a cold-blooded killer? That's the reason she screams night after night.

But I can't tell him, or anyone else. I have to protect my family. I'll do what I always do. I'll keep swimming upstream, against the current, trying to keep my head above water.

"I like my therapist," I had said. "I don't want to change doctors. I am making progress. You even said that the frequency of my nightmares has diminished."

"But this last one was really bad," he said. "I was scared."

"I just need a little more time. Dr. Goldberg will know what to do."

Jason turned me on my side and curled his body around mine as if to protect me from the world. I lay there next to him wondering how I'd ever survive without him. He and the girls are the best things that ever happened to me. If I lost them, I wouldn't want to go on.

I drive to Goldberg's office in the morning wondering if there's some kind of medication that could help me. At this point, I'll try anything to get some relief.

"So, tell me what's going on," Goldberg says, as we take our seats in his office. "You sounded pretty upset on your voicemail yesterday."

"I was holding it together until this past Saturday night. That's when I had a nightmare tsunami. It was awful, and my husband got pretty freaked out."

"The same dream you always have?"

I nod. "But more violent and with more blood. According to Jason, my screaming was much louder than before, and it took him longer to wake me up."

An audible rush of air escapes from Goldberg's parted lips. He presses them together and looks up at the ceiling.

"Are you open to trying something else?" he says.

I emphatically nod my head.

"I'll do anything. This has to stop. I can't do it anymore."

"Ok. I think we should try hypnotherapy. I'm licensed and trained in it. I've used hypnosis very effectively with some of my patients. You'd be a good candidate. Want to give it a try?"

I look out the window. *What if I say something to him when I'm under that I shouldn't?*

"I can tell by the look on your face that you're not sold," Goldberg says. "I promise you, it's very relaxing. You'll be in control the whole time, and I'll be right here with you. The idea is to get into your subconscious and access the source of your nightmares. Going forward, it should help you re-imagine the dream scene differently and diminish the fears."

"But how? The dream is of my mother dying. My mother *did* die. How do I re-imagine that differently? It actually happened."

"Leave that to me."

"But what if . . ."

"It might involve changing the ending of the dream or removing some of the frightening elements. We'll replace them with calming visuals to give you a sense of control."

"Is there a downside?" I say.

He smiles. "No. People tend to be afraid of hypnotherapy because of things they've seen in movies. I promise, you will not walk out of here clucking like a chicken or barking like a dog."

I grin. "Ok. Let's do it."

"All right," he says, standing up. "Why don't you sit over there in the big brown chair with the ottoman and put your feet up."

I move over to the brown chair. It's soft and plush and instantly feels cozy. I settle in.

"Are you comfortable?" he says, pulling up another chair so he's only a few feet from me.

"Yes," I say.

"Let's get started. Close your eyes. Take a deep breath and let it out. I want you to think about the top of your head. Now, the skin on your scalp. Imagine the muscles on your face and let them all relax and go slack."

I try to do as he says.

"Feel your eyebrows, your eyelids. Now your cheeks, mouth and chin. Slowly, you should feel your face settling down. Your mouth may be slightly open. Unclench your teeth and relax your tongue, so you can mentally switch everything off."

As I listen to his reassuring voice, I'm surprised: I do feel more relaxed.

"You may notice different sounds around you, some inside this room and some outside," he says. "Every sound you hear allows you to relax even more. But I want you to continue to focus on my voice."

My body follows his commands as I sink deeper into the oversized chair.

"As you begin to relax, remember that nobody wants anything from you right now," he says softly. "This is your time, Abbie. The only thing you need to do is let everything go. Allow your mind to drift wherever it wants."

After several more minutes of relaxation talk, he directs me to my dreams.

"Your dreams always start with you in your mother's bedroom sitting at her vanity table. She walks in and you ask her if you can try on some of her things. I want you to imagine that you don't ask her that question. Instead, when you see her, you get up from the vanity, walk over to her and give her a hug. Then, I want you to go directly downstairs."

In my mind, I visualize doing exactly as he says.

"Have you gone downstairs yet?" he asks.

"Yes."

"Good. Now, I want to make a positive suggestion to you. Repeat this after me. I have peaceful and calming dreams. I sleep soundly at night."

I parrot his words. "I have peaceful and calming dreams. I sleep soundly at night."

He asks me to repeat it several times and helps me create other positive changes to my recurring dream before he gently gives me cues to wake up. When I open my eyes, I feel refreshed, like I've taken a restorative nap.

"How do you feel?" he says, leaning towards me.

"Good," I say, smiling as I sit up straight. "I feel relaxed; my jitters are gone. Do you really think what we did here will help when I go to sleep tonight?"

Dr. Goldberg stands, a signal that our session is about to conclude. I follow his lead.

"I've used hypnotherapy with many other patients and have had good results. I can't guarantee it will stop all the nightmares right away, but over time, it should give you some relief. We'll reinforce what we did today in our future sessions. Next time, we'll also record it, so you can listen before you go to bed at night."

Walking to my car, I ask myself the million-dollar question: does hypnotherapy still work when you lie to your therapist?

# CHAPTER 32

Saturday morning, I get ready for our big Memorial Day party. After the awful scene the other day with Father Cleary and Nurse Peggy, preparing for our annual barbecue is a welcome distraction. We've hosted this early summer bash every year since moving to Eastport. This time, it's going to be bigger than ever before. Last count, we're expecting a hundred and twenty people. Most of our guests are friends and neighbors, but Jason has also invited a handful of business associates.

Because of the large crowd coming, I've hired plenty of help. The caterer is bringing three grill masters with oversized grills whose sole job is to cook burgers, dogs, shrimp, chicken and ribs. There will also be six waitresses, three bartenders and a head chef to keep things running smoothly.

The Connecticut weather at the end of May can be unpredictable. This year we're lucky. According to the forecast, today is supposed to be perfect for an outdoor event. It will be sunny, but not too hot, with a warm breeze.

The crew from the party rental place arrived at eight this morning to set up everything. I walk around the flagstone patio counting the rented white tables and chairs. I want to make sure everything is in the right place and nothing is missing. Wandering through my yard, I check the positions of the small food station tables and count the chairs.

Over my left shoulder, men on ladders are stringing hundreds of little white lights around the patio. Two others are securing a giant American flag to the side of our house. Everything's shaping up beautifully. When it's done, the place will look amazing.

The big surprise for our guests comes after dark. We've hired a professional pyro-technician to set off fireworks. If everything goes as planned, it should be quite a night. Getting ready for this party has mercifully taken my mind off all the other crap that's been going on. I've become very good at compartmentalizing when I need to. If only I could do it when I'm sleeping.

* * *

At a little before 3:00 p.m., I'm sitting at the vanity table in my bedroom putting on my last dab of lip gloss when Jason calls to me from downstairs.

"Abbie, let's go. The first guests just pulled into the driveway."

After one last look in the mirror, I take a deep breath. For days I've been agonizing over Christian's black eyes and wonder if I'm blowing the whole thing out of proportion. My fears are solely based on his eye color and the fact that he ordered champagne. When I think about it now, it sounds ridiculous. They are not the same person.

The Travis I knew was lanky and thin with long, dark-brown hair and clean-shaven. He was usually disheveled and grungy and didn't care about appearances. Christian is well groomed, and wears expensive designer clothes. He has short, lighter brown hair, a cropped beard and glasses.

You can tell Christian works out a lot, too. Travis never did. He said exercise was a waste of time, because it was all about genetics in the end. Christian's very polished, nothing like the Travis I knew . . . except for those eyes. But if there's really no other similarity between them, why am I so unnerved?

All morning, I've been worrying about seeing Christian at our barbecue. I've run a million possibilities through my mind and there's only one that makes any rational sense — I'm clearly mistaken and need to get a grip on reality. And, if that doesn't do it, I remind myself . . . Travis is dead.

"Abbie, are you coming down?" my husband shouts a second time, from the foot of the stairs. "People are here."

I run a comb through my long brown hair, stand up, throw my shoulders back and walk down the stairs to greet my hundred-plus guests.

Twenty minutes later, my house and yard are filled with people. Red and white wine has been uncorked and the appetizers are being passed around by pretty young girls in black uniforms. As I greet my guests, the exchanges of smiles, quips and laughter momentarily take my mind off my worries. Although I still have no idea what to say to Christian when I see him.

Our beautiful, green, freshly mowed lawn looks so inviting and dewy. At the far end of our property, a bunch of kids are playing on the swing set. Across the grass, more kids are kicking a soccer ball around. Over in the pool, at least a dozen others are splashing and making a racket. From their squeals, it's apparent they're having wonderful time. I smile as I watch my two daughters laugh together just before they do simultaneous cannonballs into the deep end of the water.

Seeing my kids so happy and innocent only underscores my unsubstantiated fears and triggers my anxiety. I can't shake this overwhelming feeling of dread that some danger is lurking around the next corner for me and my family. It's amazing what one's imagination can serve up when you're scared. It's like I'm waiting for every possible catastrophe in the world to happen. All I know is, my husband and kids know nothing about my past and I want it to stay that way.

Thankfully, as soon as school lets out, the kids will be leaving for summer camp. With them safely out of the house,

I'll breathe much easier as I sort through this situation. Still, it feels like things are coming at me from all directions. First, there was discovering Father Cleary, followed by the note on my car, then those dolls, and now Christian, a man who kind of reminds me of Travis. All of these things independently don't add up to much. But together, they look like a whole lot of trouble.

Looking across the yard in the other direction, I see Jason chatting with a few neighbors. I can't hear what he's saying, but based on his body language, he's telling a story. Jason's a wonderful storyteller, and often gets animated when he's in front of a crowd. Suddenly, he turns his head and waves enthusiastically to someone. I follow his gaze and feel sick to my stomach. Christian and Sophie have just walked into our backyard.

Christian's got a bottle of wine in each hand and Sophie's holding a small white bakery box. I should walk right over to greet them, but I'm not ready to interact with *him* yet. I've accepted that my imagination went haywire when I met him, but it's going to take me a little time to get past that feeling. I take the coward's way out and go into the house to check on the catering staff.

Inside the kitchen, everything is running smoothly, requiring no help from me. The caterer tells me she's 'got everything under control' and that I should 'go enjoy your party'. I want to tell her that enjoying my party is sadly not in the cards for me. I'm too rattled, even though my common sense keeps telling me I'm imagining things.

Returning to the backyard, I look around for Bianca. She was supposed to pick up the big cake from the bakery for me. Granted, she's always late, but she should have been here by now. I text her. All I get back is a text saying, *on my way*.

I find a quiet spot away from the crowd under a tree and try to relax. From my perch, I can watch my kids playing in the pool while simultaneously surveilling Christian. He's by the tennis court chatting with our next-door neighbor.

A waitress comes over to me carrying a tray of freshly filled wine glasses. I pick up a glass of white. After taking a few sips for fortitude, I breathe deeply several times and walk towards Christian. Halfway across the lawn, I'm accosted by some of our neighbors. Soon, I'm surrounded and unable to get away without seeming rude. I chat with the small crowd for a few minutes before breaking free and look around for Christian again. I don't see him anywhere. Sophie's now over by the tennis court talking with my husband and a few of our other guests, but no Christian.

Where the hell is he? That icky feeling starts to rise up again. I force myself to squash it down as two friends from my committee grab me to discuss teacher appreciation day at the school in the fall.

# CHAPTER 33

*Christian*

I nearly fell over when I saw the magnificence of Jason Sterling's home and property. Talk about living the good life. Most barbecues I get invited to involve coolers of beer and cheap hot dogs. This party is in a class of its own. After finishing my glass of expensive wine, I slip away from the party to get a better look at the other side of the house and the grounds.

Casually strolling under the trees, I notice everything is perfect. The gardens and lawn look more like what you'd see at a botanical garden than a private home. Everything is meticulously cared for. The Sterlings have all the toys — a pool with a spa and pool house, a tennis court, a pickleball court, a putting green and a dock on the water with a boat that looks like it could sleep at least six. This is the life I want. And if I play my cards right, I'll get it.

Who would have ever guessed little meek Abbie Lester would have done so well for herself? Not me. Looks like marrying Jason Sterling was her golden ticket. Hopefully, it will also be mine. I've studied Jason for a long time. Everything came so easily to him. He never struggled like I've had to.

That's what happens when you have an Ivy League education. It opens doors that would never open for me.

One thing's for sure, Abbie hit the jackpot when she married Sterling. The guy is good-looking, smart, successful and made millions before he turned thirty. That bitch is set for life, and I'm here to collect.

When we were a thing back in Warwick, she was a naive and insecure little girl. She was so fucking easy to manipulate, especially after a couple of lines or a few cocktails. As I recall, she was scared of her own shadow and used to apologize for everything. That used to grate on my nerves.

Sure, I was the ringmaster of all those Warwick kids then, but I didn't *make* her do anything. She told me that I was the great love of her fifteen-year-old life. I was just killing time until I had enough money to get the hell out of that town.

Everything would have been fine, until her mother died. That changed all my plans. Right away, the town was crawling with cops and press asking a million questions. When the police finally finished grilling me, I knew it was time for me to get as far away from Warwick as possible. My family didn't give a shit what I did, so I took off.

More cars pull on to the Sterling property, and I go around to the front of the house trying to guess the square footage of their home. They have a two-story, six-column entryway with a large portico and a five-car garage. I'm thinking the place is ten or twelve thousand square feet. According to Zillow, they paid thirteen million for this place when they bought it.

I'm looking up at the roofline in the front of the house, when I hear a groan behind me. An attractive woman in very high heels with long, almost-black hair is attempting to carry too many things from her car into the house. She's got a very large white box and four or five full shopping bags clenched in her hands. When I see her nearly trip and almost drop everything, I run over to help.

"Let me take some of that from you," I say, reaching for the big box.

She lets out a sigh. "Thank you so much," she says, as she passes the box to me. "It's the cake for the party. It almost smashed on the ground. Abbie would have killed me."

"We wouldn't want that to happen," I say, noticing her short skirt and long legs. "I'm Christian."

She feels my eyes on her and blushes. "Bianca. I'm a friend of Abbie's. How do you know the Sterlings?"

"Jason and I are doing some business together," I say, as we walk towards the front door. "They have quite a place here."

She nods as we approach the front door. It's locked.

"I guess we'll have to walk all this stuff around to the back of the house," I say.

She smiles. "I know the code," she says, as she punches some numbers into the keypad on the door. Seconds later, it opens and we enter into the Sterling's large two-story foyer, a grand staircase in front of us. Carrying the cake box, I follow Bianca into the kitchen and place it on the table.

She explains everything to the catering staff, and we each grab a glass of wine before heading out the back door to join the party. As we step onto the patio, a waiter passes us holding a jumbo shrimp cocktail platter. We both take one.

"How long have you known Jason?" she says, popping the shrimp into her mouth.

"A few months. I started a renewable energy company. Jason and I are working on a deal together. He's a great guy."

"Jason's the best. Did you say renewable energy? My husband would have loved to meet you. He's fascinated by that kind of stuff. Unfortunately, his mother isn't well, and he had to fly down to Florida to be with her for a few days."

"Maybe another time," I say, as we approach Abbie and some other guests.

"Sorry I'm late," says Bianca, tapping Abbie on the shoulder. "I almost dropped your cake on the front walk. Thankfully, your friend Christian saved the day."

"Glad to have been of service," I say, bowing slightly, trying to appear gallant.

"He's not my friend," says Abbie, a little too quickly. She checks herself, but I heard it.

"I mean, we just met each other," she says. "Jason knows him through his work with the Halo Group. Christian and I have only just met."

"That may be so, Abbie," I say, taking a sip of my wine and tipping my head in deference. "But hopefully one day, you and I *will* call each other friends."

She gives me a look. It's a mix of fear and confusion. I know that look. In my line of work, I get that and more all the time. It doesn't faze me. Comes with the territory. If she's afraid of me now, she'll really be terrified when I let her in on Plan B.

# CHAPTER 34

*Abbie*

With the barbecue in full swing, everyone is having a great time, except for me. Christian's standing next to me while sucking up to Bianca; and that's all I can focus on. I still have that same weird feeling about him no matter how I try to talk myself out of it. It has to mean something.

I'm dying to pull Bianca aside and tell her to stay away from him, when she suddenly dashes off to greet some of our mutual friends. That saves me from having to share my half-baked suspicions with her, which would only make me sound nuts.

With Bianca gone, Christian and I are left standing alone together. Still debating what to say, I decide to play nice, since my fears are based on nothing concrete.

I look up into his dark eyes. I feel a chill, but force a smile.

"I'd like to apologize for my behavior last week at the restaurant," I say, piling on the fake sincerity. "You must have thought I was so rude when I ran out of that place. I ate something for lunch that day that didn't agree with me. Please accept my apology."

"None needed," he says. "We've all been there."

"I must have seemed so stand-offish to you and Sophie. That wasn't my intention."

"Not at all."

I look around the party. There's no one in our vicinity or within earshot. It's now or never, so I go for it.

'Something's been puzzling me since that night," I say, looking out at the crowd and not at him.

"Oh?"

"You look so familiar to me. Have we ever met before?"

He takes a sip of his white wine and looks up at the sky as if he's scrolling through his memory banks for a past encounter. That's when it happens, and my heart nearly stops. He reaches his right hand up and scratches himself three times behind his right ear. I know that move. I've seen it before. Travis used to do the exact same scratch whenever he was stressed out. It was totally involuntary. He wasn't aware he did it.

It was always the same. He'd scratch himself with his right index finger, three times behind his right ear. I used to tease him about it. My fifteen-year-old brain thought it was adorable. I told him he'd never be a good poker player, because that little tick would give him away every time. I'd forgotten about that until right now.

He takes a second sip of wine, clearly unaware of what he just did, and examines every inch of my face. I feel myself getting warm and start to squirm.

"No, I don't think we've met before," he finally says, shaking his head with what appears to be sadness. "I'd remember someone as attractive as you."

*That sounded exactly like something Travis would have said.*

Back in Warwick, Travis used to dole out the compliments to all the girls like a farmer spreading chicken feed. I was a teenager, vulnerable, mixed-up and desperate to be a woman. He used lines like that on me all the time and I fell for it.

When I was fifteen, I was drinking, and using and selling drugs. I did whatever Travis told me to do. It was like I had no will of my own. If he wanted me to steal something, I did it, no questions asked. That's what scares me now. It was a long time ago, but I still remember the incredible hold he had over me.

I take a sip of my wine and look again into Christian's eyes. "You remind me of someone I knew when I was kid," I say, evaluating the expression on his face as my words land.

"Someone you liked, I hope," he says with a big smile, showing all of his teeth like a wolf. "I'm sorry, but I don't recall meeting you before."

I smile back and keep fishing. "I guess so. You said at the restaurant that you'd never been to this part of Connecticut before. The person I was thinking of grew up not far from here. I must be mistaken."

"It happens," he says, as he looks out at all the guests milling around the yard. "Great party. The food is amazing."

I face him squarely. "It's just that you remind me so much of this person," I say.

"Maybe I have a doppelganger."

I stare at him. "You're not dead ringers at all. It's more like your essence is the same."

"My essence? Hmm," he says, with a smile. "That's a new one."

*He's smooth. Travis was like that. After I shot my mother, he convinced all those cops that it was a random home invasion. Travis never blinked once.*

"May I ask you something?" Christian says, leaning towards me and dropping his voice down to a loud whisper. "I'm wondering if you can help me out with your marvelous husband."

I cock my head. "In what way?"

"Jason and I have been carving out a deal for Halo Group to potentially invest in my start-up. I think he's still on the fence about RDV. Maybe you could put in a good word? It's pretty clear any endorsement from you goes a long way."

My mouth involuntarily opens. I'm literally stunned by this man's audacity, and convinced even more that he's up to no good. That's how Travis operated, too, silky smooth, using suggestions and innuendo to get what he wanted. That's how he hooked me and got me into drugs and so much more.

I collect my thoughts before I respond. My answer has to be perfect, loud and clear.

"I'm sorry, but that won't be possible," I say. "I never get involved in Jason's business. I'm not equipped to weigh in on something like a renewable energy initiative. That's his department."

"Surely, you're in favor of cheaper and cleaner energy?"

I let out a little fake laugh as I continue to play along.

"Of course," I say. "But I never interfere with my husband's business . . . ever."

"That's too bad. A positive vote from you would go a long way. I'd be eternally grateful. If, let's say, one day you needed a favor from me, all you'd have to do is ask."

I'm considering my response when one of my neighbors interrupts us, giving me an out. I break free and move away through the crowd. Minutes later on the other side of the party, I'm talking with several women from my community group and notice my heart is still racing. I look over my shoulder at Christian. He's by the pool now talking with a few of our guests. He must sense I'm looking at him because he suddenly looks up and smiles and nods at me.

A cold shiver goes down my spine. I don't know who he is or what he's after, but something's not right. That ear scratch may be a massive coincidence, but I still don't trust him.

# CHAPTER 35

With the school year winding down for summer break, the following Saturday is the Girls All County Soccer Jamboree. Teams from all over the area play simultaneous matches throughout the day. When it's over, one team will be the champion for each age group. Naturally, my two competitive little girls have full intention of being victorious.

As we prepare for a full day at the soccer matches, I'm at the kitchen counter packing snacks and drinks for the event. My daughters are on the floor putting on their shin guards.

"The coach says we could win if we try hard enough," says Luna, as she puts on her cleats.

"Win or lose, the main thing is that you have fun," I say, my mind a million miles away obsessing about the stranger who appeared at my barbecue.

"But winning is better," says my nine-year-old.

I roll my eyes. "Luna, life is about the journey, not the destination."

My daughter looks at me like I have two heads. I'm not sure if she understands my comment, or if her competitive little brain simply can't comprehend the idea of losing. She gets that from her father. Jason is very competitive . . . but in a good and healthy way.

I look down at my daughter. "It would be lovely if your team won, honey, but the main thing is to enjoy yourself and play fair."

"I want to win, too," says my seven-year-old, sitting on the floor next to her sister.

I give up. They're both too revved up for lessons on altruism today. "Go get your father, Grace. It's time to leave for the games."

Thirty minutes later, we're seated on bleachers on one side of an enormous county field at the north end of Eastport. The place is packed. There must be a thousand kids and double the number of parents attending the tournament.

By 9:45 a.m., it's already hot, and I realize I've left my hat in the car. As the games progress throughout the day, we'll move to other locations on the field if our girls' teams move forward in the rotation. I settle in for a long, hot day.

Since Luna and Grace are both competing in different games, Jason and I have to split up. I go to watch Grace's team and he goes to Luna's. By 2 p.m., it's getting really hot out and there's no shade. Grace's team has been defeated, but Luna's is still in the hunt and has one more match. Jason and I are sitting together on the bleachers waiting for the start of Luna's last game.

"They both played well today," Jason says, his eyes on the field as the horn sounds, signaling the start of the game. "Is Gracie is upset her team was eliminated?"

I look over at my younger daughter standing with a few of her teammates under a tree. They're laughing and poking each other while bouncing soccer balls on their knees.

"She'll be fine," I say, tipping my head towards my daughter. Jason follows my gaze and smiles. "Besides, the girls have to learn that you don't *always* win in life."

"Says who?" my husband says, stifling a laugh. "Who made up that stupid rule?"

I shake my head and turn my attention back to the game. Minutes later, I hear my name.

"Abbie? Jason?" says a male voice.

I turn. Christian and Sophie are walking towards us across one of the lower empty bleachers.

*What the hell are they doing here?*

"I thought that was you," says Christian, smiling and extending his hand to my husband.

"What are you doing here?" I say, no warmth in my voice.

Sophie steps forward. "We just fell in love with the area when we came up here for your holiday barbecue," she says, sitting down on the bleachers next to me. "The weather was so nice today that Christian and I decided to come up and look at houses. So, here we are."

*This isn't happening.*

"We've been out with an agent all day looking at homes," she says, with a smile. "It's so pretty up here."

"We love it. Eastport's a great town," says Jason, his eyes still on the field watching our daughter make a pass.

"I couldn't agree more," says Christian, taking a seat. "We were blown away by the beauty of this area. After meeting all the warm and wonderful people at your party, I told Sophie we should take a more serious look at Eastport."

"We're sold," Sophie chimes in. "It's idyllic."

"Yes, it's a great town. But, why are you *here*, at the soccer jamboree?" I say, losing my patience.

"We told the real estate agent we plan to have kids. She said it's a great town for families," says Christian. "When we finished house-hunting, she mentioned there was this big soccer event going on today."

"We thought we'd stop by and have a look while we were up here," says Sophie, all smiles. "You know, to get a better feel for the community. Maybe our kids will play soccer, too."

"While we were walking through the crowd, I suddenly remembered your daughters play soccer," says Christian, a look of astonished surprise on his face.

"We kept our eyes open for you as we walked around," says Sophie, "and here you are."

"Small world," says Christian, grinning at me like a hyena.

"Incredibly small," I mutter.

"See any houses you liked?" says my husband, his eyes glued to the field.

"A few, but it's early days," says Christian. "We wanted to get the lay of the land first. I'm not going to lie, we like what we see. Who knows, Jason? You and I might end up business partners *and* neighbors one day."

When it's halftime in Luna's game, Jason's hungry and takes off to get a hot dog from a food truck, leaving me alone with *them*. We make small talk about the school system and the parks in town until my husband returns.

Thankfully, by 3:15 p.m., Luna's team is eliminated from the competition, and we can finally leave. The girls go off with their friends' parents for an ice cream stop. We walk towards the parking lot with Christian and Sophie.

"That was a great goal your daughter scored in the second half," says Christian, as we arrive at our car.

"Her team still lost," says my husband, the ultimate competitor.

"I hear you," says Christian. "Winning is better."

Leaning over to Jason, I whisper into his ear. "Do not invite them over. I'm not up for it."

Jason nods. We say goodbye to the interlopers and get into our car.

"Talk soon," shouts Christian, as he and Sophie wave to us.

While we wait in a line of cars to get out of the lot, I turn to my husband.

"Are you going to do a business deal with him?"

"Who?"

I roll my eyes. For a sharp guy, sometimes my husband can be so dense. "Christian."

"Don't know," he says. "Everybody in the group likes what he's doing. But we haven't decided."

"There's something . . . odd about him."

"Odd? I don't see that. He's super focused and committed to his work. His company's doing something potentially game-changing in the environmental space."

I sigh. "Don't you think it's a little strange that in a very short period of time, Christian has inserted himself into our lives?"

My husband laughs as he pulls out of the lot. "You're exaggerating. He's been up here three times."

"Exactly my point. Three times in a couple of months. I don't see my own friends that often."

Jason laughs again. "I love you, but I think you've been watching too many thrillers."

The girls arrive home thirty minutes after we do and head directly upstairs to take showers. Jason and I look at a Chinese takeout menu for dinner. There's a pit in my stomach that I can't shake, along with an overwhelming feeling that something bad is about to happen. I'm positive Christian *accidentally* running into us today was deliberate and had nothing to do with house-hunting. He's after something, but what?

# CHAPTER 36

*Christian*

After the long hot afternoon at that soccer jamboree, Sophie and I get on the Merritt Parkway heading back to the city. The last place in the world that I'd ever live is Eastport. It's too quiet and pretentious for me. I need the energy and vibe you get in New York City, Boston or LA. That's where things happen.

Our accidental-on-purpose meeting at the tournament today didn't land the way I'd hoped. Jason was friendly, but more aloof than the last time I saw him. He's also been taking too long to make a decision about his investment in RDV. I don't have a good feeling.

At the same time, my gut tells me Abbie's trying to undermine any progress in our deal. I sensed negativity from her today, and it was directed straight at me. I've been trying to be gentlemanly and pleasant with her. She's not taking the bait. I think it's time I get to the point.

I'd hoped my presence alone would be enough incentive for her to play ball. After all, she's got the most to lose. Maybe she doesn't understand that one word from me and her

181

entire life goes up in smoke. All I have to do is snap my fingers and her marriage, kids, home, community, friends . . . *everything* disappears. She'll go off to prison for a very long time.

Clearly, she's got an inkling of who I am, even though I'm older and look significantly different. When I stole that car from the dealership and headed down the service road, I made a clean turn. Who knew there'd be a semi-truck coming around in my blind spot. They told me later they needed a six-man emergency rescue crew to pry me out of the wreck. My buddy Christian wasn't as lucky.

I met Christian Wendt in rehab. He was someone who had everything to live for. He didn't come from money, but he was smart and landed a scholarship to Stanford majoring in engineering. He'd probably be running a Fortune 500 company today if it wasn't for his little meth problem. Instead, he got a body bag and I got his wallet, ID and reconstructive surgery. I thought I was a pretty handsome guy before, but that plastic surgeon knew his shit. They used pictures the real Christian had posted on Facebook to do my reconstruction. I came out looking better than when I went in. And I had a new Stanford University identity that gave me street cred. Being Christian Wendt made it easier to float amongst the upper echelons.

Now after all this time, I need a little favor from old friend. Technically, Abbie owes me. After what I did for her with the cops in Warwick, all she has to do is put in a good word for me with her husband. Convincing Jason to invest a paltry ten million dollars in my business is a small price to pay for my silence and her peace of mind. Jason's net worth is more than ten times that. He won't even miss the money when it ultimately disappears.

I've tried to play nice, but it's probably time to have a private in-depth conversation with Mrs. Sterling. Once I put all my cards on the table, she'll understand who's running this show. I can tell you one thing, it's not her.

"You're awfully quiet," Sophie says, as I ease the car onto the FDR Drive heading to Downtown Manhattan. "That's so unlike you."

I weave in and out of traffic, find a clear lane and step on the accelerator.

"I'm thinking about our next move," I say.

"There is no next move. Let's be honest. This deal's going nowhere," she says, rummaging through her bag. "We've been working this game for months now. In case you haven't noticed, the needle's not moving."

"Give it a little more time."

"This isn't my first time at the rodeo," she says, bristling. "It's pretty clear Sterling's not sold. He's taking too long. The longer we stay in the game, we leave ourselves open."

"Trust me. I still have one more card to play."

"From where I sit, you got nothing."

"Abbie Sterling and I go way back," I say, turning onto Delancey Street a few blocks from Sophie's apartment.

"And what does that buy us? I don't recall her skipping down memory lane with you when we got together."

"Let's just say our history isn't all happy times. I know something she did a long time ago. It's something she wouldn't want anyone to know about, especially not her husband."

I pull up in front of Sophie's building and stop the car. She makes no move to get out, but instead turns in her seat and faces me.

"Is this *thing* you know about Abbie Sterling big and bad enough that she'll get her husband to give us ten plus million dollars to keep it under wraps?" she says.

"She'd probably pay more than that, but I'm not a greedy man. Bottom line, if Abbie doesn't want her life to implode, she'll convince her husband to invest in RDV."

Sophie sits back, and stares straight ahead. "I got a call for another job. I'm thinking about it."

"You can't bail on me now, when we're so close to clinching this. I need you."

"We're not so close. And, this is a sure thing up in Boston. It's an easy bait and switch. I get in and get out with my money. I know the guy running it; he's reliable. He says I'll have all my cash in a month."

I snort for effect and shake my head to register my disappointment.

"Let's be honest," she continues, as she gets out of the car, "we've been working this thing with Sterling for nearly a year. It's not going anywhere."

Standing on the curb, she closes the car door and leans down into the open passenger window. "I'll give you another two weeks, but after that, I'm going to do the job in Boston."

I stare at my partner in crime for a few seconds. From the look on her face, she means what she says. She can't walk away now. Losing her will screw up the entire deal, and I can't afford that on so many levels. I've got creditors to pay who won't be inclined to give me a loan extension. Sophie needs to be a part of this deal until we close. If she takes off, it will spook Jason and I'm screwed.

"Do you want your five hundred thousand or not?" I say. "It won't be that much longer. You've gotta trust me."

"Who said I didn't want the money?" Sophie says, biting her bottom lip. "You know I've got a kid to feed and boarding school tuition to pay. I want to change my terms. Why is my cut only five hundred? Since we started this thing with Sterling, I've watched you float the take up to fifteen million. If that's the case, I want a bigger cut."

"A deal's a deal. Besides, your cut is generous."

"That's not how it looks from where I sit," she says. "I want another five hundred thousand."

*Shit. I can't lose her now. It will look bad.*

"I'll give you another two-fifty, but that's all. I've got other people to pay."

"Yeah, sure."

"Where do you think I got all the money to start this whole thing? That has to be repaid first."

"Not my problem," she says. "Out of curiosity, who lent you money for cow farts anyway?"

I swallow. "Kenny Wong."

She turns and faces me. "Are you kidding? Wong doesn't play nice, and from what I hear, his terms suck. Everyone knows that. You're going to get yourself killed, you know that?"

"I needed a lot of money fast," I say. "Everything will work out. It has to. Four more weeks is all it will take. But Sophie, I need you on board. If you go, Halo is going to get skittish."

Sophie shakes her head and rolls her eyes.

"Another three hundred thousand," she says, "or I walk."

I let out a loud breath. "Ok."

"So, just how are you going to close this deal?" she says.

"Apparently, I haven't been firm enough with Abbie Sterling. I'll talk to her tomorrow and get this train back on the track."

"You've got two weeks, Christian," says Sophie, as she steps back from the car. "Then, I'm outta here. Sorry. It's just business."

# CHAPTER 37

After Sophie's poorly timed ultimatum, I now have to make things happen much faster. But I'm prepared, and know exactly what levers to pull to speed things up. Sophie isn't wrong. We've been getting mixed signals from Jason Sterling for a few weeks. The Halo Group's investment in my business isn't a forgone conclusion.

Time to turn up the heat on Abbie and get her to push the deal through. I see the way her husband looks at her. He's all in on her. He'd do anything she asked him to do . . . as I'd hoped.

That night when I met them in the restaurant, Abbie mentioned she volunteers at St. Vincent's on Wednesday mornings. I just made an appointment with the director of admissions there to take a tour this Wednesday at 11:00 a.m. I told the woman that I was looking for a place for my elderly and infirm mother.

"I've heard good things about St. Vincent's," I told her. "I want see if it would be a good fit for my beautiful mother." Of course, my real mother was a drunken bitch, and thankfully, is dead. But nobody has to know that.

On Wednesday morning, I pull into the entrance of St. Vincent's ready to go. Driving through the visitor's parking

186

lot, I spot Abbie's blue BMW SUV. I get out of my car, walk past hers and place my hand on her hood. It's still warm. She's just arrived. Perfect timing.

I enter the lobby and wait for the admissions director to collect me for my tour. A few minutes later a short stocky woman with wavy gray hair walks towards me. She's dressed in a no-nonsense navy pantsuit and her hand is extended. I shake it.

"Mr. Wendt?" she says with a smile. "I'm Robin. I'll be showing you around today."

I make small talk with the older woman telling her all about my fictitiously wonderful and sweet-natured mother and how difficult it's been watching her struggle with everyday things. The truth is my mother expired by choking on a chicken and waffle sandwich inside some trailer park. If only I could have seen that. A fitting end, in my opinion.

"We hear that from families all the time," says the director with a comforting smile. "Is Mom still ambulatory?"

I nod. "She has some difficulty walking, but she can still move on her own, God bless her," I say, dabbing my right eye for effect. "She's such a dear person. Wait until you meet her. You'll love her. Everyone does. That's why this is all so painful."

We talk about managing my mother's extensive medication regimen. Robin assures me the staff at St. Vincent's can handle it. With my bogus concerns resolved, I share some stories about my poor mother's recent cognitive decline to leave a lasting impression.

We finish the walk-thru tour of the building and end up in the lobby where we started.

"Mr. Wendt," she says, "I want to assure you that we're fully equipped to handle residents at any stage. I'm sure we could make your wonderful mother comfortable here. I for one can't wait to meet her. She sounds delightful. Would you like to see our outdoor space? We have beautiful gardens."

After looking at the gardens, the tour concludes. I tell the director that I'm going to give very serious consideration to St.

Vincent's. I see dollar signs flash in her eyes when I ask her if I might sit in the garden for a few moments before heading back to the city.

She nods enthusiastically, already counting her commission. Everyone has an angle, including nursing homes.

"Feel free to take another look at the dining and recreation rooms as well," she says, as she walks off.

As soon as she gets on the elevator, I slip away and head directly into the resident wings to look for Abbie Sterling. Starting on the Maple Wing, I spot a metal cart in the hallway loaded with what looks like craft supplies. I approach the door next to the cart and peek into the room.

Through the crack, I see an old man in a wheelchair staring off into space. Seated in a chair next to him is Bianca, the dark-haired woman with the great legs I met at the Sterling's Memorial Day party.

My first instinct is to leave before she sees me and continue searching for Abbie. I'm about to turn and walk away when I hear a voice calling my name.

"Christian?" Bianca says, looking up and spotting me through the open door.

I feign confusion as she gets up and comes out into the hall.

"It's me, Bianca," she says. "We met at Abbie and Jason's barbecue a few weeks ago. You saved the day, remember?"

I squint, tilt my head for added emphasis and make a face like I'm scrolling through a trove of memories to recall her.

"You saved me from dropping the cake on the lawn," she adds, coaching me.

I open my eyes wide and smile. "Of course, you're the cake lady."

She smiles, and I quickly explain why I'm there before she has time to ask.

". . . so after hearing Abbie Sterling talk so highly of this place, I wanted to check it out myself . . . for my mom."

"Abbie's here today," says Bianca, getting excited. "At least I think she is. We took separate cars and I was just about to go look for her. I'm sure she'd love to say hello. She'll be so surprised to see you."

*Yes, she certainly will.*

Together, we head down to the Birch Wing. Soon, I spot a similar cart to the one Bianca had sitting at the far end of a long hallway.

"She must still be in Father Cleary's room," says Bianca, holding several large bags. "She always ends her visits with him. I think he's her favorite."

I offer to carry one of Bianca's bags as she chatters non-stop, which gives me time to go over my canned lines. As we get closer to the cart, I hear a man shouting in Latin.

"*Ego te absolvo!*" a loud male voice echoes as we get near the last doorway. "*Ego te absolvo.*"

Loud riffs in Latin are followed by a stern female voice speaking in English.

"That's enough for today, Father. I think you should go now. Father needs to rest."

A moment later, Abbie Sterling emerges from the room. I'm standing off to the side and Abbie only sees Bianca at first.

"What's all the commotion?" says Bianca. "Father Cleary going off the rails again?"

Abbie nods, but still hasn't noticed me.

"Everything was fine when I first got in there," whispers Abbie to her friend. "Then, that damn nurse shows up. That's when Father became really agitated. I swear, I think it's her. I was just about to call for . . ."

Abbie turns her head and her eyes land on me. A look of surprise splashes across her face. I respond with my warmest smile.

"Surprise," I say, lifting my arms up in the air to make the moment festive.

Her eyes grow round and her brows go up as she takes two steps backwards.

"What are you doing here?" she says, barely above a whisper.

"Isn't it crazy?" says a smiling Bianca. "Christian remembered you talking about St. Vincent's. He came to look at this place for his mom. She's not doing well. What did you think, Christian? It's beautiful here, isn't it?"

Abbie's staring at me now with a mix of anger, disbelief and fear in her eyes. Perfect. That's exactly the effect I had hoped my appearance would have today.

"It does seem like a wonderful place," I say, still smiling. "Except for all the shouting in Latin. What was that all about?"

Abbie forces a smile. It's a strain for her. Good.

"Just one of our patients," she replies curtly. "He's an elderly priest and sometimes gets confused. He thinks he's saying a mass."

I give Abbie a lot of credit right now. Out of nowhere, I spring myself on her and she's holding it together. She's not as weak and pliable as I thought she'd be, but I can handle it. I like a bit of a challenge.

I accompany the two women out of the building and into the visitor's parking lot. When we get to Abbie's car, Bianca realizes one of her bags is missing.

"Oh, I'm sorry," I say. "That was the one I was carrying. When the priest started shouting in Latin, I put it down on the floor. I can go back and look for it."

"I'll go," says Bianca. "I know my way around. I'll be back in five minutes."

As I'd hoped when I deliberately left the bag behind, it gives me the alone time with Abbie that I need.

"I didn't know you were looking for an assisted living facility," Abbie says, keeping her physical distance from me. "What a coincidence you're here at the same time as I am."

I smile again and inch closer.

"It's crazy, isn't it?" I say. "May I be honest with you?"

She lets out a disingenuous laugh. "Please, do be honest with me. I'd really appreciate it."

I sigh deliberately for dramatic effect. "It wasn't an accident that I ran into you here," I say. "At dinner that first night, you mentioned you often come here on Wednesdays in the late morning. I scheduled my tour for today with the hopes that I might bump into you."

"Why? What do you want?"

I make a tsk-ing noise and put on a sad face. "If I were a more sensitive man, I'd think that you're not happy to see me. And we used to be such good friends, too."

Abbie's face goes white. I've finally acknowledged what she's been thinking since the first night we met in the restaurant. *You're welcome.*

"But you're dead!" she gasps and starts to back away. "You died in a car accident."

"You just can't keep a good man down. Here I am in the flesh," I say my arms outstretched. "Miss me?"

Her eyes dart around as panic sets in. Truthfully, I'm kind of enjoying this.

"What do you want, Travis?" she says, in a hoarse whisper. She's shaking. That means she'll do what I want her to do, just like she used to.

"The name is Christian now," I say.

"I knew it," she says, under her breath. "I don't care what you call yourself. Go away and leave me and my husband alone."

At that exact moment, Bianca steps out of the lobby door and begins walking towards us. I inch closer to Abbie.

"Meet me tomorrow morning in Westport," I whisper. "I'll take the train up from the city. There's a little coffee shop across the street from the train station. There's something urgent I need to discuss with you before my meeting with your husband tomorrow afternoon. Be there by 10:00 a.m. Don't be late. You know I don't like to be kept waiting."

# CHAPTER 38

*Abbie*

After Travis showed up at St. Vincent's yesterday, I was a total wreck. I didn't hear a word Bianca said on the drive home. I was prepared for an awful night of terrifying dreams last night. But that didn't happen, because I didn't sleep the entire night. I tossed and turned for hours, obsessing over my meeting with *him* today. I was so restless, and moved around so much that I woke up Jason twice. He's so worried about me and I can't explain anything.

This morning Jason left for the city and I got the kids off to school. Now, I'm in my room trying to find the least attractive outfit I own. I want something drab and eventually settle on a pair of jeans, flat brown sandals and a loose over-sized high-necked white top. Nothing remotely sexy or too attractive. This meeting needs to be all business.

I pull my hair up into a ponytail, and put on only tinted moisturizer before heading out the door. I'm on edge as I start my car, wondering how this day is going to end. It takes me twenty minutes to get to the Westport train station. The closer I get, the larger the pit in my stomach grows. I keep imagining what Christian is going to reveal and stressing out over what exactly he wants from me. Whatever it is, it's not good.

I can't deny that Travis helped me when I had no one else to turn to. He fixed everything with the cops for me, but he was also the one loose end left. Years ago, when I found out he died in a car accident, everything changed . . . my loose end was gone. I could finally live my life without fear. By the time I met Jason, I wasn't worried about my past catching up with me because the only real witness was dead. I stopped looking over my shoulder.

Then, when I ran into Father Cleary at St. Vincent's, all those fears came flooding back. I must have blocked out the priest and my confession until the day I saw the old man. What I told Father is more than enough to put me in jail. But as far as I know, he's said nothing specific that could cause me any harm. As long as Father Cleary sounds befuddled and confused, no one, including the police, will take his words too seriously.

Driving through downtown Westport, I spot the road to the train station and turn on to it. I look around for a coffee shop and see one tucked among a few other stores. I check the time as I hunt for a parking space. The Travis I knew twenty years ago had a very short temper and didn't like to be kept waiting.

I find a spot several blocks away and can easily make it to the coffee shop on foot by 10:00. Walking up the front steps of the storefront, I see Travis sitting outside at a little metal bistro table sipping a cappuccino while reading something on his phone. To anyone else, he looks so normal. But normal he's not.

He looks up. "I appreciate you being on time. Punctuality is so important," he says, smiling. "Do you want a coffee before we begin our chat?"

I stare at him with a mix of fear and loathing, feeling like a hostage. Instead of drinking a hot coffee, I'd rather throw one in his face. I want to tell him that I wish he *had* died in that car accident, so I didn't have to be here with him today. But I keep my mouth shut. I have to remember my family.

Looking into the dark eyes that I once found so alluring, I'm suddenly afraid. Now, those eyes scare the hell out of me.

"No coffee," I say, feeling myself tremble but trying to look tough. "Tell me what you want and let's wrap this up. I have a million things to do today."

"I so appreciate you taking the time out of your busy schedule to meet. It's a shame, though. I thought this was going to be a happy little Warwick reunion. You seem to want it over before it starts. I'll admit, that stings."

Now, I feel myself sweating. My armpits are dripping and it has nothing to do with the high summer temperatures today. The beginnings of an anxiety attack are surfacing. I'm not sure how long I can sit here before I lose it.

*Hold it together. Protect your family.*

I take a deep breath, pull out a chair and take a seat. Now, we're only inches from each other.

"What do you want, Travis?"

"I hate to correct you again, but it's Christian. I'd prefer you call me that."

I take another deep breath. "What do you want, Christian?"

He smiles condescendingly, as if I'm a child unable to comprehend a grown-up conversation.

"It's not what I want, Abbie. It's what *you* want."

"I don't know what the hell you're talking about. The only thing I want is for you to go away."

He smiles again and folds his hands in front of him on the tabletop. "But you *do* want something from me. You want my silence, isn't that correct?"

I start to get up, because my anxiety is taking over.

"Sit down, Abbie," he commands, all niceness gone from his voice.

I freeze. His stark, ominous tone takes me back twenty years to Warwick. He used to speak to me that way all the time.

"Sit down," he says again. "We've got important things to discuss and I don't have much time."

# CHAPTER 39

As I sink into the chair, my legs go weak and I feel like I'm going to puke. There's a lump in my throat and my hands have visibly started to shake. Of course, he notices; I see the faint glimmer of a smile on his face.

*Don't let him see you're scared.*

Staying in my chair like an obedient child, I wait for him to start.

"Since you're obviously not interested in skipping down memory lane with me," he says, "I'll get right to the point. I need your help with something."

"Why did you pretend you didn't know me when we first met?" I blurt out.

He lets out a little mocking laugh which irks me.

"I might ask you the same question," he says. "I presumed your husband knew nothing about your past or your relationship with me. Given that, since I'm trying to broker a deal with him and his group, I thought it best to keep silent."

I stare at him trying to read his face.

"Bullshit," I spit out. "You pretended not to know me at our barbecue, too. Why do you keep showing up around my family? I want it to stop, now."

Christian leans back and puts his hands behind his head intertwining his fingers. He smiles at me in the smarmiest way possible.

"I don't think you're in a position to make any demands," he says.

Now, my heart's pounding and everything in my stomach starts to gurgle. I need to get out of here. As I start to get up, he reaches out and grabs my wrist before I can move.

"Sit down, Abigail," he hisses through clenched teeth. "I'm not finished yet."

Like a naughty child, I do what he says.

"You and I both know what really happened all those years ago in your mother's house," he says, looking directly into my eyes. "You did something unspeakable, horrible — and, I might add, extremely illegal — that day. After you went on your murderous rampage, you called me to clean up your mess."

My breath catches in my throat. I reach into my bag, dig out a bottle of water, and take a much-needed swig.

"Remember?" he continues. "I was the one who got rid of the murder weapon for you. I helped make it look like there was a home invasion, to get you off the hook. You owe me for that."

"What do you want?" I say, barely whispering.

"In case you're wondering, I've taken very good care of that gun all these years. You know the one I mean. You used it to put three bullet holes into your poor mother's chest."

"Shut up."

"Wait," he says, holding up one palm in front of my face. "Don't give it another thought. Your gun is safe and sound. I put it in an airtight plastic container and left it in a place where no one will ever find it."

"You . . . you still have that gun?"

"The one with the little Irish shamrock on it. I didn't want it to slip into the wrong hands. After all, you were my first love."

I want to scream, cry, kick my feet and throw up all at the same time. But I don't and try to maintain a cool exterior composure. I can't let him rattle me or I'll lose everything.

"Are you threatening me?" I say.

He smiles again in a way that sends another shiver down my spine.

"Threatening you?" he says grinning. "I haven't yet. But I'm about to."

Suddenly his whole face changes and grows dark.

"You need to make sure your husband invests in my company. We're looking for a ten-million-dollar cash infusion. That's a drop in the bucket for Jason Sterling and the Halo Group. I want you to make that happen."

"Jason would know something was wrong. I never get involved in his business."

"Then, it's high time you did. This money needs to be in my account within the next couple of weeks. I'll leave it up to you how you do it. Just make sure he pulls the trigger. Oops. Sorry for the pun. I couldn't help myself."

"Or what?"

Christian starts to laugh.

"You're funny," he says chuckling. "I thought it was pretty obvious. But if you want me to spell it out, I can do that. Here goes. You get your husband to do this deal with me or that gun is going to find its way to the police. For clarity, I'll send it with a little note explaining what really happened that day with your mommy."

"Why are you doing this to me? I have kids. You've met my girls. This could ruin their lives."

"Not if you do what I ask. Don't make such a big deal out of it. It's just business," he says, all humor gone as he gets up from the table. "Do yourself and your kids a favor and make it happen. I'd hate to think of a pretty girl like you spending the rest of your life in prison. How would your daughters live with the stigma of having a mother who's a murderer? A mother who murdered their grandmother."

"You won't do that."

"I can and I will," he says, with no emotion, his eyes full of anger.

"But how am I going to get Jason . . ."

He puts his fingers to his lips. "Shhh. No excuses, Abbie. Just get it done. Then, you, Jason and little Grace and Luna can go back to living your perfect privileged life in your ten-thousand-square-foot home in Connecticut."

"But I—"

"I'll be in touch."

"But Jason will know something's up. I never interfere in his—"

"I don't care how. Just fucking do it."

He takes two steps before he stops and turns back to me.

"And what was the deal with that priest at the nursing home yesterday?" he says. "I saw his name on the door, Father Michael Cleary. Wasn't that the same name of the priest in the church in Warwick?"

I let out a snort. "Like you ever went to church."

"Don't be rude, Abigail. My grandmother used to take me to that church from time to time, after my mother took off for parts unknown. It doesn't matter anyway. Don't forget you have a job to do. Two weeks and the money needs to be in my account."

As I watch him walk away towards the train station, I can't feel my limbs. They're numb. All these years, I thought I was in the clear. I've tried to put all those horrible memories behind me and lead a good and normal life. Other than the occasional update from the Warwick Police whenever a random lead popped up, everything's been quiet.

Now, in the span of a few months, two entirely different entities have surfaced. One is deliberate and lethal, and the other loud and confused. Regardless of their respective motivations, they're both a danger to me and my family. Either one of them could be my undoing.

The one person I would normally turn to for help is Jason, but that's not an option.

It never will be. I'm on my own.

# CHAPTER 40

*Christian*

Riding the Metro North train back to New York City, I check the time on my lucky Rolex watch. It's almost 1:15 p.m. My train will be arriving at Grand Central Station in a few minutes. That gives me plenty of time to get downtown for my meeting with the Halo Group.

I plan to dazzle them today. After I show them the new numbers and testimonials that Sophie invented and then mocked up last night, they'll be eating out of my hand. They'll be begging to give me their money. And, if for some reason I don't seal the deal today on my own, I've always got Abbie — my little secret weapon.

I've watched Jason Sterling around his wife; he's crazy about her. He'd do anything to make her happy. Even as a teenager, Abbie was always a smart girl and a good little actress. She used to lie to her mother without even flinching. If she's as smart as I think she is, she'll talk up her commitment to saving the planet from climate change. She has one job — convince her husband that investing in RDV really matters to her. That should sew up the deal.

When the half empty train comes to a halt, the doors open and the passengers within scramble to the exits. I make my way through the iconic terminal and head outside onto 42nd Street. After ordering an Uber, I people-watch until my car pulls up.

"What's the traffic like today?" I say to the driver as I climb into the back seat. "Let's take the FDR Drive. I've got an important meeting to get to."

The driver does what I ask. It turns out that the traffic is fairly light and we sail downtown arriving earlier than I had anticipated. The Halo Group meeting doesn't begin for another forty-five minutes. If I go up to their offices too early, I'll look overly eager. I might even look a little desperate. Can't have that. To kill some time, I text Sophie and tell her to meet me at the Starbucks on the next block.

Once there, I order a coffee and park myself at a table in the corner to wait for my partner in crime to arrive. While sipping my double espresso, I send a text to Mrs. Sterling tightening the screws a little bit more.

*Abbie, I'm meeting with your husband in 30 minutes. Grease the wheels for me before I get there. Wouldn't want to slip up and say something about your past during my presentation. Be smart.*

That should do it. A quick phone call from Abbie to her husband before my meeting would help put a positive spin on me and my company. Her endorsement will go a long way with her husband.

"What are you smiling about?" says Sophie, standing over me holding an iced latte.

"Just adding another piece to the puzzle."

"A critical piece?"

"Absolutely. In fact, I think you'll see the doors swing open for us from now on," I say, pulling out a chair for her to sit on.

"What did you do?" she says, her eyes narrowing. "Sprinkle some of that Christian fairy dust around?"

I look at my partner and smile. As far as I'm concerned, the backstory on Abbie and me is on a strictly need-to-know basis. I won't be sharing that with Sophie. All she needs to know is that I've got Abbie Sterling under control and working for us.

"You've got something on Abbie, don't you?" Sophie says, her left eyebrow arched. "What is it?"

"It's better if I keep my own counsel on this one. Trust me."

"Fine. Whatever," she says, shrugging, as she takes a sip of her drink. "I don't care as long as we get our goddamn cash. Remember, my clock is still ticking. My guy in Boston wants an answer from me . . . yesterday."

*How many times is she going to remind me she has another job? She needs to finish this goddamn job first.*

"Did you confirm all the references at the five new dairies we put into the prospectus?" I say, trying to switch gears and remain businesslike.

"Can you get off my back?" she says bristling. "I know how to do my job. Yes. Everything's set."

"We've got a lot riding on this."

"You think I don't know that?" says Sophie, her voice getting louder.

Right away, I realize this was the wrong time to antagonize her. I need her cool and calm in this meeting.

I lift up my open palms.

"*Mea culpa*," I say. "Of course you know what you're doing. I didn't mean to insinuate anything else. Why do you think I brought you in on this job in the first place?"

"I'd love to know."

"Because you're the best, that's why."

"Damn straight," she says, sitting back in her chair.

"Soph, we're almost at the finish line. Our big payday is right around the corner. Can't you feel it? We can't screw this up now. You gotta trust me. Let's go over the new set of numbers one last time before the presentation."

Twenty minutes later, we get out of the elevator and walk into the Halo Group's reception area. This is my fourth time here, and the receptionist greets me by name. I like that.

"Mr. Wendt," she says, smiling. "Nice to see you again. I'll let Jason and the others know you've arrived."

"Thanks, much appreciated," I say. "If you don't mind me saying, that's a beautiful teal pattern on your dress. It brings out the aqua blue in your eyes." She giggles and blushes before she walks away to find the team.

"Always workin' it, aren't you?" whispers Sophie, while we sit down next to each other on the gray reception couch.

"I prefer to call it *closing*," I whisper. "If you don't close the door, you leave it open for someone else to steal the prize."

# CHAPTER 41

*Abbie*

Since I got home from my gut-wrenching meeting this morning with Christian, I've been pacing non-stop around my kitchen for hours. I check the clock on the oven door. The girls will be home from a playdate in fifteen minutes. If I'm going to do something to stop my free fall, I've got to do it now.

That meeting at the coffee shop in Westport was surreal. Being there with him took me back to when I was a kid and totally freaked me out. He hasn't changed. He's still a liar and a cheat. How can I trust him to keep his promise, even if I do what he says? On the other hand, do I have any choice? If I convince my husband to pour money into Christian's energy company, at least it will help save the planet. But what's to stop Christian from asking me for more money or for something else? As long as he has that gun, he could come back in a month demanding another favor or more cash.

I've looked at it from every angle and come back to the same thing. I'm screwed.

With no other choice, I call my husband. He answers on the third ring.

"Hey babe," he says, "this is a pleasant surprise."

"I was wondering about dinner tonight," I say. "Luna's got piano and Grace is going to a friend's house. After I drop them off, I was going to run into the town to pick up something for dinner. I'm making something special and thought we could open a good bottle of wine."

"What are you making?"

"It's a surprise," I say, trying to sound cheerful, when I really feel like jumping off a bridge. "What time will you be home?"

As the words fly off my lips, I hear a message ding on my phone. It's from a number I don't know. While still chatting with my husband, I click on it. A picture of an old gun nestled on a piece of cloth fills my screen. There's a small shamrock on the grip.

*Oh, my God. This can't be happening.*

"Not sure what time I'll be home yet," says Jason. "I'm about to go into a meeting with Christian and Sophie. Our group is taking one last look at their proposal."

"Are you going to invest?" I say.

"Not sure. I do like what they're doing but . . ."

"You should do it. I think he's got . . . an amazing concept," I say, going into full sales mode.

"How do you know so much about it?"

"Because . . . Christian and Sophie explained their whole operation to me at the soccer jamboree."

"I don't remember that."

"You went to get a hot dog, remember? You were gone a while. They shared their whole vision. I think investment groups like yours have an obligation to help companies like RDV. It's the only way we're going to stop climate change. We're reaching a critical point as a planet."

My husband doesn't respond.

"Jason, are you there?"

"Yeah."

"Why aren't you saying anything?" I ask.

"You've never commented on my business before."

I respond maybe a little too quickly, but I can't help myself.

"Normally, your deals are so complex. Also, I never meet any of the people who pitch you. Unlike your other deals, I've met Sophie and Christian a few times," I say. "After getting to know them and seeing their passion firsthand, I'm sold."

My husband doesn't say anything.

"Jason?"

"I thought you didn't like Christian," he says.

*How do I wiggle out of this? I've been throwing Christian under the bus from the first time we met at the restaurant.*

"You misread me. I think Christian's great. In the beginning, I didn't fully understand the scope of his project. And, maybe I was being overly protective of you. I was afraid he was trying to sell you a bunch of bull."

"And now?"

"After they explained their business and environmental goals to me, I changed my mind. Every time I talked to them, their commitment and passion for their project was so contagious. I'll admit it, I've had a complete change of heart."

There's another long silence and I wait.

"Fair enough," my husband finally says. I let out a breath and feel my entire body relax. I hadn't realized how wound up I'd been.

"As it turns out, I agree with you," says my husband. "We do have an obligation to stop climate change. I started Halo to invest in companies that will do good things. Our return on investment might not be as great as other firms, but at least we'll do some good."

I take a deep breath and let it out slowly, filled with relief. He's still considering Christian's proposal.

"Then, you're going to do it?" I say, smiling. "You'll invest in RDV? That makes me so happy."

"We're not there yet. But since you feel so strongly about it, if everything checks out, then . . . yes."

I smile. "That's great. So when will you—"

"Babe, I gotta go. They're here."

I tell Jason I love him before he hangs up, and he says the same to me. I hate lying, and despise myself for what I just did. But it's the only way to keep my family safe. That's all that matters to me now.

I look out the window at the woods on the far end of our property and wonder what good would it be for anyone if I were arrested? Being thrown in jail won't bring my mother back. And it would ruin the lives of the three people I love most in the world. I can't let that happen.

I text Christian.

*Jason's on board. It's yours to lose. I did my job and I never want to hear from you again. I want that gun or I'll blow this whole thing up.*

# CHAPTER 42

After my phone call with Jason, I feel sick to my stomach. Lying to my husband feels so wrong. As anxiety bubbles up inside me, I feel myself heading into a panic. With so much coming at me, I can hardly breathe. For weeks, I've juggled all kinds of poison darts coming at me in the form of Christian and Father Cleary, and I'm exhausted.

Leaning on the kitchen counter, I count to ten. As I catch my breath, I remember that the kids are leaving for summer camp this weekend. I've got a lot to do to get them ready for their two weeks at Camp Louise. While I'll miss them, with all the crap that's been going on with Christian, it's better that my kids aren't around.

Lately, the pressure's been overwhelming. This morning, I made breakfast for the girls and accidentally gave Grace a cup of coffee instead of her milk. My mind has been jumping from Christian to the old priest and catastrophizing everything. There's been little room for anything else.

The truth is, I've been on edge since that first time I ran into Father Cleary. Although my nerves have become much worse since Christian showed up. I've been so worried about being found out that I can't think straight anymore. All I know is that one way or another, I have to get Christian out of my life for good.

Around 4:00, a neighbor drops the girls off from a play-date. I send them both directly up to their rooms with their camp packing list.

"It's your last chance, girls. Make sure you've got everything and check it twice," I shout, as they go up the stairs. "I'll be up in a few minutes to have a look."

Later, I go up to their rooms and we go through each bag checking off every item on the list.

"I think we're good," I say, letting out an exhausted sigh before plopping onto Luna's bed.

Suddenly, there's a noise downstairs and all my senses go on high alert. I look at the time on my phone. It's only 5:00. Jason promised he'd be home early so we could eat together on the girls' last night. But this is *too* early.

"Girls," I say, "stay here. I'll be right back."

"Where are you going, Mom?" says Luna.

"Just do what I say."

I leave Luna's room, closing the door behind me. Tiptoeing silently down the hallway, I reach the top of the stairs and listen carefully for any kind of sound. At first I hear nothing, but then I hear the faint distant squeak of the basement door hinge opening. I'd been meaning to spray it with some silicon for months, but never got around to it. I hear it a second time. *Shit.* Someone's in my house. My anxiety shoots up to warp ten.

I look around for something to use as a weapon. Passing the doorway to Grace's room, I see her lacrosse stick on the floor next to her bed and grab it. Now at least, I'm armed. Sort of.

Slowly, I descend the stairs, listening for sounds. I don't know if it's my nerves, but I could swear I hear something on the other side of the house. I slink down to the bottom step, the lacrosse stick up high over my shoulder, poised to attack.

Should I call out? After a three-second debate with myself, I decide a surprise is better to maintain my advantage. I creep along the hall towards the noise, the stick gripped in my hand.

My heart is pounding as I chant, "Protect the family" over and over in my head.

I turn a corner, and from that vantage point can see into both the living and dining rooms. Both are empty, so I turn and walk down the hall towards the kitchen passing the powder room. I'm about to walk through the archway of our kitchen when I hear a door shut from behind me. My heart jumps into my throat as I spin around with my stick ready to strike.

*Protect the family.*

Before I can identify who or what is making that noise, I start swinging the stick with all my might.

"Abbie! What are you doing?" cries Jason, as he jumps back and puts up his hands to protect himself.

I drop the stick and lean back against the wall. My legs are about to buckle underneath me as I try to catch my breath.

"Oh, my God. Jason, it's you," I say, hyperventilating.

"Who else would it be? I told you I'd be home early. What's going on with you lately? You're so jumpy."

"I was upstairs packing with the girls and heard a strange noise. I thought someone had broken in to our house."

"Daddy!" scream both girls as they race down the stairs. So much for them staying in their rooms. While I remain in the hallway for a few seconds trying to compose myself, Jason and the girls go off to the family room. By the time I get there, Luna and Grace are sitting on either side of their father talking non-stop.

Despite the crazy beginning to our night, we end up having a wonderful family dinner and get the girls in bed by nine. Once they're quiet, Jason and I sit on the couch in the family room with a glass of wine trying to decide what to watch on Netflix. While he's flipping through our options, I take the opportunity to bring up Christian's energy company again. This investment *must* happen. I need to get that creep out of my life for good.

"How did your meeting with Christian go this after-noon?" I say, as I pick up a travel magazine on the coffee table and flip through the pages. "Did you finalize everything?"

"You're really interested in this one," Jason says, adding a little more wine to his glass.

"Harnessing energy from cows could be so important for the planet," I say, hating myself for lying again.

"I've never seen you so curious about my work before."

"You know I'm passionate about this topic. Christian's company struck a chord with me. They're doing something important. It could be amazing."

Jason picks up my empty glass and walks over to the wine fridge. He takes out a new bottle and refills his glass, then mine.

"I like what RDV is doing, but I'm not ready to commit yet," he says, as he hands me my glass. "They look good on paper. Some of our guys also spoke to their references."

"And?"

"Reviews so far are great. I don't know . . . something's keeping me from pulling the trigger."

*Oh God, help me. Jason's usually so decisive. Why is he flip-flop-ping on this?*

"What's holding you back, then?" I say. "You like Sophie and Christian. They've even been guests in our home. They're thinking of moving here to Eastport. It seems perfect to me."

Jason tilts his head and peers at me. "I always go with my gut. So far, it's never let me down. Something about RDV is nagging at me. I'm not sure it's right for our group."

My internal alarm bells go off. I'm losing him.

"Did you already tell Christian no?" I say, choking on the words.

"Not yet. A couple of our junior partners are still check-ing out some of the dairies. To be fair to Christian, I'll let my guys finish their due diligence before we make a final decision. One way or another, we should have it wrapped up by the end of next week."

Later that night, I'm awakened by my own screams.

"Wake up, Abbie," Jason says, his arms around me. "It's okay. I'm here. I'll always be here."

## CHAPTER 43

The next morning is camp day, and we're all up early. The girls are supposed to check in at Camp Louise by 10:00 a.m. According to the schedule, there will be one orientation for parents and a separate meet-and-greet for the campers. Afterwards, everyone will gather in the cafeteria for lunch, followed by family relay races. By mid-afternoon, the parents say goodbye and head home.

We're on the road by 7:30 a.m. Luna talks non-stop in the back seat for fifteen minutes straight, rattling off every single thing she plans to do during her two-week stay. It's her second year at Camp Louise; she knows the ropes and is proud of it.

Grace, on the other hand, is unusually quiet during our drive. This is her first time away from home, away from us. I have a feeling she's getting a little homesick.

"You okay, Gracie?" I say gently, interrupting her sister. I turn around in my seat to look at her.

Grace nods ever so slightly, but without a smile. She's usually a big talker, so when she's quiet like this, I know something's wrong.

"Are you a little nervous about being away from home, sweetie?" I say.

She nods again.

"You'll be okay. Remember, your sister will be there with you."

Tears fill my younger daughter's eyes. I reach my hand out and take hers. "Honey, you're going to love camp. Your sister had a great time last year, didn't you, Luna?"

"You're going to have so much fun, Gracie," Luna says, taking her little sister's other hand. "You get to go swimming and kayaking and horseback riding. And there's campfires where we roast marshmallows and make s'mores. You love s'mores, Gracie."

Grace sniffles a little, and she fights a smile after hearing about the marshmallows and chocolate.

"C'mon, Grace," says Jason, as he drives through the front gates of Camp Louise, "you're going to have a blast. I'll bet you won't want to come home when it's over."

"I will," says my younger daughter emphatically.

"Remember," says Jason, "we're only an hour away. Anytime you need us, we can be here right away, okay?"

We picked Camp Louise partly because it *is* only an hour away. But also, the property is amazing. Camp Louise accepts about six hundred and fifty female campers, ranging in age from seven to fifteen, every summer. It's nestled on a couple hundred acres of pristine wooded land in northern Connecticut.

They have beautiful new cabins, a professional theater, dance studio, lake, hiking trails, stables and a petting zoo. Just about anything you can dream up is there. The camp food service is even supervised by a licensed nutritionist and has gluten-free and vegan options. There's also a doctor and a nurse on premises at all times. I'm confident my girls are in very good hands.

The four of us walk up to the check-in desk lugging the girls' bags. Luna and Grace go one way to the campers' ori-entation, and Jason and I are sent off with hundreds of other parents to our own session. After the meetings are over, we have a little free time to explore the grounds before the lunch begins in the enormous state-of-the-art cafeteria.

It's a spectacular day, sunny and warm. I'm trying to enjoy myself, but I can't get Christian and the threat he holds over me out of my head. I make small talk with my husband, but my mind is elsewhere.

*Would he really turn me in to the police? He's not innocent in all this. Outing me would ruin everything for him and his energy company. Maybe he's bluffing. Can I take that chance?*

I talk myself off of the proverbial ledge as Jason and I head to the cafeteria to meet up with the girls. The large cathedral-domed room is filled with hundreds of parents and campers all talking at once. The noise is deafening.

"What do you think of Camp Louise so far, Gracie?" I shout to my tentative seven-year-old. "It's nice here, isn't it? Did they take you down to the petting zoo yet?"

Grace smiles and nods. "I made a new friend, Mom. Her name is Kayla. We're in the same cabin. She's seven, too."

Relieved my daughter is starting to get into the swing of things, we sit down at a table for lunch. After everyone's finished eating, a couple dozen enthusiastic teenage camp counselors take us outside. They lead us in camp songs, and we join in on a sack race with our kids. By 2:45 p.m., a whistle blows informing us that it's time for the parents to leave.

We walk with the girls to the departure point and give them each a hug and a kiss. Jason takes Luna back to her group, while I say a final goodbye to Gracie.

"You're going to have a great time, honey," I say. "You'll make all sorts of new friends here. There might even be some kids here from Eastport."

She nods. "I saw someone from Eastport today."

"You did?" I say, smiling. "Who?"

"He was at our barbecue."

"On Memorial Day? Who?"

"I don't know his name," she says, as Jason walks up.

"Ready to roll?" he says to me.

"Grace thinks she saw someone here from Eastport," I say, "She said it was someone who was at our barbecue. Did you see anyone that we know?"

Jason shakes his head.

"Who could it be?" I say, to no one in particular.

"It was a man who was at our house."

"A man?" I say, alarm bells ringing. "What did he look like? Did he say anything to you?"

Grace shakes her head. "No, he was at our party with a woman with dark-brown hair. I think her name was Sophie. She was nice. She got me an ice cream pop."

Acid washes up into my throat as I look over at my husband.

"Christian?" I say, looking around at the faces of all the adults heading to the parking lot.

"Why would Christian be here?" says Jason, also looking around. "He doesn't have kids. Grace, are you sure it was him?"

"I saw him, Daddy," says my daughter, nodding. "He waved to me."

With a perplexed look, Jason crouches down in front of our daughter.

"Gracie, did you ever hear the word doppelganger?" says my husband, now eye-to-eye with Grace.

She shakes her head.

"It's a funny-sounding word, isn't it?"

Grace nods.

"Sometimes," he says, "there are people in the world who look a lot like other people, and they're not even related. Isn't that crazy? Some people even believe that each one of us has an identical twin somewhere in the world. They call them doppelgangers."

Grace's eyes open wide. "I have a twin?"

Jason laughs. "I said 'some people' believe that. I'm not one of them. My guess is whoever you saw was probably someone who just *looked* a lot like someone who was at our party."

Grace seems satisfied with my husband's explanation and takes his hand. I kiss her goodbye and they go off to find her

214

counselor. As soon as they leave, I frantically scan the crowd, gripped with fear. Jason may think our daughter saw a doppelganger, but I know Grace isn't wrong. He's here and he's sending me a message.

The sick feeling in my stomach grows as I examine each face in the crowd. Somehow, I've got to get Jason to make that investment in Christian's energy company. If I don't, something really bad is going to happen.

# CHAPTER 44

*Christian*

When I called Sophie a few days ago and told her about my
plans to visit the Sterling kids at camp, she pushed back on
me hard. I hadn't expected that. I thought she was made of
tougher stuff.

"We've got to close this deal," I said. "The Sterling kids
are leaving for camp on Saturday. A little surprise visit from
me should be just the thing to compel Abbie to make our deal
happen."

Sophie remained silent on the phone for a long five seconds. I waited for her reply.

"I only agreed to keep working this scam because you told
me you had some ace in the hole with the wife," she said. "Now,
you're stalking their kids at camp to get this thing done?"

"It's not like that," I told her.

"I don't do jobs involving kids or animals," said Sophie,
with a defiant tone in her voice. "That's not my brand. Kids
don't have a say in what grown-ups do. I'm totally cool taking
stupid, greedy adults for everything they've got, but leave their
kids out of it. Are we clear?"

I need Sophie and didn't want to push my luck. I agreed to skip the camp visit in order to keep her onboard and focused. What can I say? I lied. I drove up to northern Connecticut alone from New York City and did what needed to be done.

When I pulled onto the grounds of Camp Louise, the visitor parking area was filled with only new high-end cars — BMWs, Porsches, Mercedes and even a Bentley or two. My five-year-old Kia with a dent on the side sticks out like a sore thumb. I park it in the back of the lot.

From what I read online, Camp Louise is one of the most expensive girls' camps in the country. A week at this place runs many thousands, not to mention all the additional fees. Must be nice to have that kind of disposable income. That's what I want: enough money so that I never have to ask the price of anything. The steep cost of this country club camp would make most people's heads spin. It's pocket change to Jason Sterling.

When I do get that kind of money, I won't be spending it on summer camps and violin lessons. I'll be in my private jet on the way to my private island drinking Cristal champagne to wash down my king crab legs.

After I park my car, I slip into the crowd of families dropping off their kids. My objective is simple — remind Abbie that I'm deadly serious. She needs to lock in my money, or her life will become very unpleasant.

I didn't know it at the time, but it turns out that holding on to that gun was one of the smartest things I ever did. Something told me it would come in handy one day. Just my dumb luck that little insecure Abigail Lester ended up marrying a multi-millionaire. If she'd married a carpenter or a school teacher, I'd be out of luck.

For years I worked scams, picking up a few grand here and there. It was never enough to live the way I really want, the way I deserve. When I read that article two years ago in a financial magazine about Jason Sterling's Halo Group, and saw who he was married to, I knew my payday had arrived.

I didn't rush it. I took my time. To pull off something as big as this, everything had to be perfect. Jason Sterling didn't make all those millions by jumping at every opportunity that crossed his path. I had to come up with something clever and in line with his philosophical and business goals.

Doing research, and learning the Halo Group made only environmentally conscious investments, gave me an idea. I'd create an energy company on paper and peddle it to him and his group. If I was going to present a phony energy company and get him to invest millions, my execution had to be flawless.

For the next six months, I did my homework and found a niche in the market that wasn't being addressed. I worked all the angles and did a deep dive into the renewable energy market. I now know more about that business than most of the people working in it. I had an amazing idea that would allow me to take a lot of money from a lot of people, but didn't have the financing to execute it. Pulling off something this big requires a lot of cash.

I made some inquiries through back channels that eventually led me to Kenny Wong. I had heard about him over the years. Wong's the man to see when you need a loan and have no collateral. The terms of his deals are skewed strongly in his favor, and you don't want to be late returning the money. That makes him angry.

Using the five hundred thousand borrowed from Wong, I set up a network of fake dairies and references all over the country through both an online and offline presence. I paid off a slew of people until the whole venture looked legit on paper. Then, I started raising my profile at energy events and cozied up to big shots in the industry. I took out some promotional ads in industry newsletters and test drove the pitch with some small investors to find out where the holes were. Once I got a couple of people to invest a few thousand, I was ready to go for the big enchilada. But to do that, I needed some help. That's when I brought in Sophie Boyd. She's a pro.

Sophie and I worked together on a successful credit card scam about five or six years ago. She's smart, buttoned-up and thinks on her feet. Plus, she's a goddamn chameleon if ever I saw one. People take to her instantly. She was perfect for this job. Her one flaw is her big heart. You can't get emotional in this business. It's kill or be killed. I have to remind her of that all the time. Once you start second-guessing yourself, or feeling sorry for your marks, you're done. Game over.

Sophie's not looking at the big picture. We're almost at the finish line. If Abbie does what I've told her, Sophie and I will be counting our money in a few weeks. After this is all over, I'll lay low for a few years. Eventually, I'll be back for a second dip into the well. As long as I have that gun, Abbie Sterling is like an annuity for me.

I arrive at Camp Louise early and walk the grounds making sure I'm not seen by Jason Sterling. Obviously, my presence would be hard to explain. Regardless, I'm prepared. If he spots me, I'll tell him I had business in Boston and my sister asked me to check out the camp for her son on my drive back to New York. I even pulled pictures of a ten-year-old boy off the internet and loaded them onto my phone so I can play the proud uncle if need be. Never leave anything to chance.

I pick up the camp schedule for opening day from the check-in area. It says the kids will split up from their families in the morning and get back together for lunch. I plan to make my presence known to the younger daughter while they're separated. Sophie spent some time talking to the kid at the Sterlings' barbecue. I was standing next to Sophie the whole time. The kid should remember me; she looks smart enough.

I walk around to the far side of the Olympic-sized swimming pool watching the crowds from a distance. Suddenly, the children move to the left and the parents to the right, so it's time for me go into action. I follow the kids being led by their group leaders through the woods. It looks like a lot of parents skipped the adult orientation and are just walking around by themselves, so I don't stand out.

In the distance, I see several groups of girls sitting in large circles in a big open field. I locate Grace's group and lean on a nearby tree pretending to be on the phone. I make sure to position myself directly in her sight line and talk animatedly to attract her attention. Eventually, she sees me and our eyes lock for a split second. When I see that flicker of recognition on her face, I subtly smile and nod to her.

Mission accomplished.

After a few minutes, I end my fake call and head back towards the parking lot. I've done what I came to do. If Abbie is having any second thoughts or thinking she could outmaneuver me, my camp visit should make her think twice.

If the fear of going to jail for murdering her own mother isn't enough of an incentive to get me my money, her kids' health and well-being should tip the scales in my favor.

I can already taste the crab legs and champagne.

# CHAPTER 45

"You did what?" says Sophie, sitting on the beat-up couch in my apartment. I just told her where I've been all day and about my visit to Camp Louise. I hadn't planned to. I guess I was boasting about my handiwork.

"Why the hell would you go to their kids' camp?" she says, anger in her voice. "This is between us and the parents. I thought I was clear about that. Kids stay out of it."

"Relax," I say, sitting down next to her. "Nobody got hurt. Besides, I didn't have a choice. Kenny Wong's breathing down my neck about his money, and I was getting the sense Abbie was running cold. She tells me she's taking care of things, but her husband's still not on board. I'm not getting positive vibes from him."

Sophie gets up, crosses the room and stares through the window into the night sky.

"What are you looking at?" I say.

She doesn't answer. Instead she turns around, her face red and angry.

"I can't believe you went to their kids' camp today. That kind of shit is not what I signed up for."

I roll my eyes. "Things don't always go as planned in this business. You've got to improvise."

Sophie turns and looks out the window again.

"I don't like the direction this is going in," she says, shaking her head. "You begged me to come on board to do a simple con. You said it was 'a piece of cake'. You didn't mention getting financing from Kenny Wong or anything about threatening little kids. I would have given you a hard 'no' if I knew that was your plan."

"I didn't say a word to those kids."

She spins around. "But they saw you, didn't they?"

I shrug my shoulders.

"Well, that's fucking creepy," she says, disgust in in her voice. "Why did you involve those two little girls? They have nothing to do with this. They're innocent."

"I told you. Abbie Sterling needed more incentive. Her children are her Achilles' heel. Do you want your money or don't you? Our deal is about to fall apart. I had to do something."

Sophie reaches for her glass and pours herself another glass of wine. Walking back to the window, she stands with her back to me again.

"You know I have a daughter around the same age as those two kids," she says.

"I know."

"She lives with my mom outside of Chicago. Almost all the money I make on jobs like this pays for her private school and all the other things I never had."

"You're a good mother."

Sophie turns around, her face now in a snarl. "Fuck off, Christian. I'm just doing this job to get enough saved up to be a *real* mother to my daughter. If it's not coming together like you promised, I need to cut my losses and move on now."

I walk over to her. Though we're not technically romantically involved, we've had a few drunken encounters where business lines blurred. I put my hand on her shoulder and give it a rub, hoping to appeal to that part of her. She quickly brushes it off and moves away from me.

"That wasn't very friendly," I say, taking a step back to give her some space.

She faces me and downs half of her wine before speaking.

"Let's keep this professional, okay?" she says. "You brought me on board to help you convince entitled rich guys to invest in renewable energy farts from cows. That, in itself, sounds ridiculous when I say it out loud. But hear me on this point. I didn't sign up to be your girlfriend. Are we clear about that? I think it might be time to end this partnership."

*Shit. I need her or it's all going to fall apart.*

I take another step backwards, raise both my hands in submission and speak softly.

"Message received. I'm not trying to be your boyfriend. I'm your business partner, nothing more. I'll admit, we've hit a few snags lately. Rest assured, I've been doing everything possible to close this deal."

She finishes the rest of her wine and places the glass on a table.

"This whole thing is taking too long," she says. "The offer I've got up in Boston is a short-term sure thing."

"Come on, Soph. You can't leave me now. We're almost there."

She walks over to the door and picks up her bag.

"If you have to threaten little girls at a sleep away camp," she says, "we're not almost there."

She swings her bag over her shoulder and opens the door.

"Like I said, I'm a mom. This job isn't for me anymore."

"Sophie, c'mon, can't we talk about this?"

She wrinkles her nose as if she smells something awful. "I don't want to talk about it. It's over," she says, with one foot out in the hallway. "I warned you, no kids. Also, I kind of like Abbie. She's a good person. She's the kind of mother I hope to be one day. Honestly, this whole deal stinks."

I run over to the door and grab her arm. "You can't bail on me now. We're almost there. Think of all the money you're leaving on the table."

Sophie laughs, pulls her arm away and moves out into the hallway.

"In case you forgot," she says. "Jason Sterling isn't stupid or a pussy. When he finds out you went near his kids, things are going to get real very fast. Lose my number."

The click of Sophie's heels reverberates on the bare stairway walls as she walks down three flights of steps. The entire time, I'm hoping she'll stop and change her mind. When I hear the downstairs door open and close with a thud, I know she's gone for good.

Now, I'm working this job solo, which complicates things. But I'll make it work one way or another.

# CHAPTER 46

*Abbie*

After leaving the kids at camp, Jason and I don't say much during our drive home. He's quiet because he's got several big deals coming to fruition and they're occupying all of his brain space. He always gets like that when things are about to close.

I'm silent because I'm quietly terrified after what just happened at the camp. Jason blew it off so easily when Gracie essentially told us she saw someone who looked like Christian. My husband chalked it up to a confused seven-year-old, something I would never do.

I knew my daughter wasn't confused. She saw Travis or Christian or whatever the hell he calls himself this week. He was there. I feel him in my core.

As our car glides south on the parkway, I wrestle with what to do. I'm a little surprised Jason wasn't alarmed after what Grace told us. For a guy who does so many big deals, my husband can sometimes be too trusting.

Case in point . . . he married me.

When we're ten minutes from home, I get a text. Before I even look at it, I know who it's from.

*My deal is hanging by a thread. You've got seventy-two hours to make it happen before I spill the tea all over the table. Be smart.*

"I meant to ask you," I say, trying to sound casual as Jason pulls off the highway. "What's the upshot with Christian and Sophie's dairy deal? Is Halo going to make the investment?"

With his eyes still on the road, Jason presses his lips together.

"I don't know. Something's keeping me from moving forward. That has to mean something, right?"

*Oh, my God. Jason does huge deals every single day, but on this one, he's skittish? I've been promoting this stupid dairy concept and talking non-stop about climate change. I've got to get him to do this.*

I turn in my seat to face him. "Jason, I've never asked you for anything when it comes to your business," I say, laying it on thick.

He turns his head and grins at me. "And I so appreciate that."

"I always stay out of your business," I say.

"That's true."

"But there are some global issues that really matter to me. Things that I'd like to be a part of — or should I say, be part of the solution."

"Ok."

"You know how I feel about climate change and all the other terrible environmental things we're doing to our planet."

"I know how you feel, and I agree with you."

"Good, because Renewable Dairy Ventures really speaks to me," I say. "I think it's an amazing opportunity to do something great for the world. What Christian and Sophie are doing could have far-reaching implications. Not only is it potentially a lucrative investment, but you'd be doing something incredible for the environment."

"I had no idea you were so passionate about cows," he says, clearly making fun of me.

"Well, I am passionate. Did you know that about forty percent of the world's climate problem is caused by gases from livestock?" I say, my voice growing stronger and more confident with each word. "We'd be at the forefront of this whole planet-saving movement. We might make a real difference. You could help take RDV global. Think of what that would mean."

Jason turns left onto our street. "I thought you didn't like Christian when you met him. What changed since then?"

*Oh God. I hate lying to Jason, but I don't have a choice.*

"I didn't *dislike* Christian. I was really sick that night, remember?"

"I guess," says my husband, as he pulls our car into the garage. "We haven't made a final decision on RDV yet. A few other investors in the group really like them. To be honest, I'm one of the last holdouts. But if it matters that much to you, I'll give it another hard look."

I smile. "It would mean a lot to me. It's such a small investment in the scheme of things. Most of your deals are so much bigger, aren't they?"

"They are," he says, as we get out of the car. "Regardless, I don't make bad investments. But you're right. It's a small one and if it makes you that happy, I'll try to make it happen. Okay?"

When we get inside the house, I make myself a cup of tea while Jason goes upstairs to change. As soon as I hear him up on the second floor, I go into the powder room and text Christian.

*Call Jason on Thursday and close this damn deal. I want it over. Stay away from my kids. If you go near them again, I'll kill you.*

# CHAPTER 47

That night, Jason and I crack open a good bottle of red and argue over which movie to watch. He's in the mood for a thriller. But since my life has become one, I convince him to watch a lighthearted romantic comedy, to distract myself from the doom and gloom that currently surrounds me. We finally agree on a rom com called *About Time*. It's about a young man who can time travel to earlier points in his life and change the outcome, usually for the better.

As we watch the movie unfold, I fantasize about how my life would be so different if I could travel back in time, too. What if I could step in a time machine and change what happened in Warwick twenty years ago? I'd still have my mom in my life. My children would know their grandmother and Christian/Travis wouldn't be threatening my family's existence.

After a long day at Camp Louise, we go up to bed right after the movie. I notice Jason yawning as we climb the stairs. It's weird having both of the girls gone. The house is so quiet without them here. I miss them.

By the time I've brushed my teeth, Jason is asleep and softly snoring. Still agitated, I climb into bed and turn my back to him. Curling up into my normal side position, I hope that sleep will soon overtake me. My mind needs rest, but instead it races along, summoning every possible catastrophe that could ever happen. Dozens of what-ifs flip-flop through my brain.

The next thing I know I have the sense of being trapped. It's dark. I can't see anything and start to sputter and choke. Someone or something is holding my body down. I try to move, but their grip is tight and won't let me go. I struggle with all my might and start to scream as if my life depends on it, because somehow I know it does.

As I gasp for air, the lights in the room flicker on.

"Abbie, wake up," says a familiar voice. "You're okay, you're safe. Wake up. I've got you, honey."

My eyes spring open and Jason's face hovers inches from mine. I cling to him and begin to sob.

"Oh, my God. I thought I was dying," I say, trying to catch my breath. "He was coming after me. He was going to kill me."

"Who? Who was trying to kill you?"

I shake my head as tears spill from my eyes. "He didn't have a face. He was just a dark figure and he had his hands around my throat."

Jason holds me for half an hour until my heart rate and breathing slowly get back to normal.

"You're soaking wet," he says to me, when I start to shiver. He's right; I was in such a cold sweat that my nightgown and the sheets on my side of the bed are drenched. While I change my clothes, he makes me promise to go see Dr. Goldberg on Monday. I agree, even though my therapist won't be able to help me. No amount of therapy is going to bring my mother back or get Christian Wendt out of my life.

When I wake up in the morning, Jason's gone out for a run. Being left alone triggers my anxiety. I consider having a glass of wine to calm myself down until I look at the clock. It's only 9 a.m. That's even too early for me.

Getting out of bed, I send a panicky text to Dr. Goldberg. Fifteen minutes later he responds, offering me an appointment on Wednesday morning. Even though I routinely tell him a pack of lies, I do feel better after I see him. I often wonder how much bullshit I can throw at my therapist before he finally figures out I'm a liar. Goldberg's not a stupid man. I wouldn't be surprised if he's already figured out I'm a fraud.

Or maybe he just thinks I'm nuts?

## CHAPTER 48

Wednesday at 8:00 a.m., I meet with Goldberg. As always, I dance around the real issues that haunt me and give him my usual line of bullshit. He asks me a lot of questions, and I respond with plenty of detailed answers. Unfortunately, most of them are made up.

With my hour almost over, he shows me a few deep breathing exercises. Then, for the first time, he broaches the idea of medication.

"You think a pill could help me?" I say.

"Some of my patients have had a great response. I'd say it's worth investigating."

He gives me the phone number of a psychiatrist and I promise to make an appointment. Oddly, despite having shared nothing significant today, I walk out of his office feeling lighter. I guess talking works. Maybe medication will help me as well. At least a pill won't ask me questions I don't want to answer.

My post-therapy calm doesn't last long. By the time I get home at 9:30, I'm like a caged lion pacing around my house. Bianca calls. She's going out to St. Vincent's in thirty minutes, and wants to know if I can still go with her. We're supposed to drop off costumes and props for a vaudeville show being performed later in the week that is sponsored by our committee. I'm not ready to go, so I tell her I'll meet her there.

An hour later, I pull into St. Vincent's, carry a large box of costumes from my car into the building and stow them in a storage room. I text Bianca to let her know I've arrived and what time I'll meet her later. Then, I head off to the Birch Wing.

Cruising down the hallway, I stop in to see Mr. Sala, Ms. Gill and Sister Joan. Mr. Sala and Sister Joan are asleep. But Ms. Gill, as always, is dressed for a fancy dinner and a show. Even her purse is packed and sitting on the tray of her wheelchair.

She and I chat for few minutes before I drop in on Father Cleary. When I enter the room, the priest is in bed. The good news, Nurse Peggy isn't there. Quietly, I tiptoe over to see if Father's sleeping. His eyes are closed.

"Father?" I whisper. "Are you awake?"

His eyes flutter, and after a moment they open. Despite his advanced age, his eyes are a bright sparkly blue. My mom's were the same color, and I feel myself getting weepy.

"I hope I didn't wake you," I say, wiping away a tear.

"You did," he says, with a smile as he stretches his arms, "but it was well worth opening my eyes to see the face of an angel standing over me."

A pit forms in my stomach when he says that. 'Face of an angel' couldn't be further from the truth. I've done dreadful things and have spent my life covering them up. I've perverted the truth to save my own skin. My worst offense: I lie to my husband, the person I love most in the world, after my kids.

"An angel?" I say, with a rueful smile. "I don't qualify for that title. I was in the building dropping something off for Friday and thought I'd stop in to say hello."

"You know, it's the darnedest thing," says the priest. "Every time I see you, I have this feeling I've seen you before. But not here, somewhere else."

I feel my eyes involuntarily open wider as I search for an appropriate response.

"I . . . don't know where we could have met . . ."

"Sorry to interrupt your visit," says a young male nurse, entering the room with a wheelchair. "I'm supposed to take Father up to physical therapy now. Let's get you into this wheelchair, Father. Got to keep those limbs moving. You don't use it, you lose it."

As Bianca and I leave the facility, we make plans for returning to see the vaudeville show before heading to our separate cars. I wave to her as she pulls out before I notice a piece of white paper stuck on my windshield. My stomach twists as I pick it up and read it.

*Look to your right.*

I jerk my head to the right. It takes me a few seconds, but then I see him. Christian's sitting in a chair next to the building waving at me. I'm instantly nauseous, get in my car and race out of the parking lot as fast as possible.

Honestly, I don't know how I got home. I don't remember the drive at all. All I know is I must have been speeding, because it normally takes me twenty-five minutes and I was home in fifteen. I grab a bottle of water from the fridge and go outside to sit on the deck, enjoy the sunshine and try to decompress. I can't stop thinking about my situation. To distract myself before I implode, I reach for my phone to check my messages. As soon as I pick it up, it rings. I don't recognize the number but answer it anyway.

"Hey, miss me?" says a man's voice.

It's him.

"What do you want?" I say, standing up, my nerves firing in every direction.

"That sounds like a hostile tone in your voice, Abbie," he says. "It seems rather misplaced, given that we used to be lovers?"

His comment makes me want to vomit, but somehow I hold it together.

"What do you want from me, Travis?"

"It's Christian."

If I could reach through the phone and strangle him right now, I'd do it in a heartbeat.

"I've done everything I can," I say. "I can't force Jason to give you the money. The last time he and I talked about it, it sounded like he was ready to invest in your stupid cows."

"Sounded like? That's the difference between you and me. I don't leave things to chance. I talked to your husband this morning. He's still not sold. He wouldn't give me an answer. Clearly, you haven't convinced him. That was our deal."

*This can't be happening.*

I clear my throat in an attempt to sound official and in control, which I'm not.

"I told you to call him tomorrow, not today," I say. "If my husband hasn't said no to you, it means he's still considering it. You're reading more into it."

"I'm not an idiot," says Christian, icily. "Jason obviously still has reservations. That means you haven't done your job properly. This is your last chance, Abbie. Get him to invest the ten million in my company, and I'll vanish."

"I've tried everything I can think of and—"

"Then I'm afraid I'll have no choice. I'll have to let the authorities know it was you who killed your mother. I still have that gun with your fingerprints all over it hidden in a very safe place. In fact, I'm looking at it right now."

At the most inopportune time imaginable, I begin to hiccup. My world is literally crashing around me and I've got the freakin' hiccups.

"Why are you doing this to me? I have kids."

"That's what's so sad about this whole thing. Those poor little kids," he says, faking sympathy. "Imagine what it will do to them when they find out that their mother's a murderer. It will probably scar them for life. None of the kids in Eastport will be allowed to play with yours when their parents learn you killed your own mother in cold blood."

Standing alone in my yard, I shout into the phone. "You're being unreasonable! I can't *make* Jason give you the money!"

"But I think you can," says Christian.

"Please, I need more time."

"Unfortunately, that's the one thing we don't have. I'll need that money in my account by Friday. It would be such a shame for your two girls to grow up without a mother, the way you did."

*Click.*

# CHAPTER 49

*Christian*

When Sophie unexpectedly walked out on me, I had to recalibrate everything. The days of me playing the earnest entrepreneurial businessman were clearly over. Sophie's presence softened me and made us look legit. I've always made people a little uneasy, but they feel comfortable with her. She was the perfect yin to my yang. Everything was humming along like clockwork, until she went all soft on me over those kids at camp.

When I think about all the planning we did and the documentation we provided to these prospective investors, I'm pretty damn proud. If I say so myself, we executed an amazing con. We created professional charts illustrating our proprietary mechanical systems, along with reams of statistics showcasing our massive projected revenue. For a little cherry on top, we even provided glowing, albeit fake, references from dairies all over the country, singing RDV's praises. Between the two of us, Sophie and I were able to show solid reasons for investors to give their money to us. It was a flawless scam, one for the history books.

Granted, I specifically approached Halo because I had an ace already up my sleeve. If I couldn't make this deal happen the old-fashioned way, through a good, old, well-thought-out swindle, blackmailing Abbie was always my backup.

Unfortunately, playing it quasi-straight didn't work out, and here we are. Now, I'm forced to play my ace — Midge Lester's murder weapon. Twenty years ago, something told me to hang on to that gun. Every time I thought about ditching it, tossing it into the ocean or a landfill, a little voice in my head told me to stop.

Without that weapon now, I'd have nothing, no leverage whatsoever. This deal would have been dead a long time ago. But I knew when all else failed, that gun with the shamrock would be my safety net.

So I visited those snotty, entitled kids at camp last weekend. Big deal. Sophie blew it out of proportion and took it way too personally. She was always a little soft. In this game, being weak or empathetic is a liability. With her gone, I'll have to change gears.

Plan B, here we come. Now, I can operate in a way that's more natural for me. I'm more of a 'give me your fucking money or lose a finger' kind of guy than a gentle breeze. I tried to do it the nice way. It didn't work out.

My gut tells me Abbie's stalling, which surprises me. I thought my visit to Camp Louise would have been enough of an incentive, but clearly it wasn't. If Abbie wants to keep her family intact, she needs to try harder. I'm not a good loser. If I don't get Jason's money after all the time I've put in and the work I've done, I'm going to blow up Abbie's life just for the hell of it.

Also, I've got big plans for that money. I'm planning to move to South America for a while until things quiet down here. I hear the American dollar goes a long way in Argentina. I could learn how to do the tango in Buenos Aires. With all that money, I'd find myself a pretty little senorita and maybe have a couple of little Argentinian kids. I'd be a great dad.

I turn my car onto the Sterling's street keeping my eyes peeled for the mailbox with their address. I've still got one more hand to play before I pull the plug on the whole operation. I see number 151 Foxcroft, and drive past it continuing around the bend in the road. When I can't see the entrance to the Sterling property in my rearview, I pull over onto the shoulder and turn off the engine.

A thousand feet past their driveway, I put on a baseball cap and dark aviator sunglasses, lock my car and casually walk back up the road towards their house. It's rural in this part of Connecticut, and few people live in this end of town. I whistle as I stroll along to 151, grateful that not a single car passes me.

Once I get to their driveway, I look around in all directions. With not a soul in sight, I walk up the long driveway through their deep wooded lot. Their home sits on five or six acres and it takes me a few minutes to get up to the house.

All I hear is the sound of birds chirping and one lone woodpecker hammering away on the side of a tree trunk. I creep over to the garage door and peek through the window.

Abbie's blue SUV is parked inside. Jason's car is missing, as I knew it would be.

She's alone.

# CHAPTER 50

*Abbie*

After that horrific phone call with Christian yesterday, I was a basket case. I tried to act cool, but last night when Jason got home, he noticed I wasn't myself.

"You're going to wear out the floor," he said to me, as I flitted to different spots around our kitchen for no particular reason.

"I guess I miss the girls," I said, blurting out the first excuse that popped into my mind.

"They'll only be gone for two weeks," he said. "Try to relax. Remember, they're having a great time. You need to remember that."

Last night, I lay awake in bed running dozens of possible escape scenarios through my mind. I kept searching for the one reason that would convince my husband to give Christian his goddamn money. I came up with a half dozen: some crafty and complicated, and some just plain stupid.

This morning, the answer came to me. My safe harbor is, and always has been, Jason. He loves me and would move heaven and earth if I asked. Tonight, I'll simply ask him straight out to invest in Renewable Dairy Ventures because it's important to me. Period. I'll ask him to do it simply because it will make me happy.

With my new plan of attack, I relax a little this afternoon while I wait for Jason to come home. Christian gave me until tomorrow to make the money transfer happen. The minute Jason gets home tonight, I'll speak to him. If all goes the way I hope, Christian will get his money tomorrow and I can put this whole nightmare behind me.

I make myself some lunch, and settle in at the desk in the family room off the kitchen to do some work. I've got a mountain of household bills to pay; and it's a good distraction. I'm about to sit down and dig in, when I notice how hot the house is. We usually keep our windows open to let in the fresh country air. But today, it's very warm, so I close the windows and turn on the air conditioner.

At around 1:00 p.m., I get to work. I lose myself for a couple of hours paying the bills and making some phone calls. When I finally wrap up and look at the clock on the wall, it's nearly 4:00.

Jason told me he has a late meeting in the city today and won't be home until eight at the earliest. That gives me a few more hours of alone time before I have to start dinner. I make a cup of tea and hunt online for any information about Christian Wendt and his company. There are a few new postings about RDV, but not much.

I'm scrolling through an energy convention brochure when I hear a strange sound coming from somewhere in the house. I look at the clock. It's 5:30. Staying absolutely still, I listen for the noise again.

Motionless for at least thirty seconds, which feels like an eternity, I strain to hear the sound. There's nothing.

*It's just the house settling, or the wind blowing through the trees.*

I wait a few more seconds, hear nothing more and admonish myself for being such a baby. I go back to my online searches. After clicking on another energy symposium article, I hear a scraping sound.

240

*It sounds like the noise is coming from inside the house.*

I'm about to turn around when I feel two hands slip around my neck and instantly tighten. I reach up to pull them away, but the grip on my neck only gets stronger.

Unable to see my attacker, I gyrate and flail my arms, trying to get loose. I can't even scream, because no air is getting in. Now, I'm fighting with my entire being, certain I'm going to die.

# CHAPTER 51

*Christian*

I enter the Sterlings' house knowing this is the day that will make or break everything. Given Jason's vast wealth, he has a state-of-the-art home security system that's tied into the police station. I expected nothing less and came prepared.

I'd like to take all the credit for cleverly gaining access to this house, but it was a case of dumb luck. When Abbie's friend Bianca showed up late for their Memorial Day barbecue, an opportunity presented itself. I took advantage of it.

That day at the barbecue, I was walking around the property enjoying the manicured grounds — or, as they say in the business, 'casing the joint'. From a distance, I saw this hot woman nearly drop a large white cake box on the front lawn. A veritable knight in shining armor, I sprung into action.

At first, I thought I was just cozying up to one of Abbie's friends, thinking she might prove useful at a later date. To my surprise, Bianca led me right through the front door of the house. Turns out, she had the code to the Sterlings' security system. Once she punched it in, I had it, too.

It was so easy. This afternoon, knowing Jason wouldn't be there, I let myself into the house through a door on the lower level. Once inside, I found myself in their finished basement, which had been converted into a professional gym — rowing machine, elliptical, treadmill, recumbent bike and a separate full-sized sauna room. Impressive. Must be nice to have that much money. I hadn't thought about it before, but now I want a top-of-the-line home gym, too. Maybe I'll build one in my hacienda in Argentina with my ten million.

I walk over to the steps that lead upstairs and listen for any sound. The house is relatively new and the stairs are carpeted. I move slowly up to the first floor. Once at the top, I reach for the brass doorknob and turn it until it can go no further. Gently, I push the door open an inch and peer through the narrow gap. I try to get my bearings. I think I'm in a hallway, because I see nothing else around me except walls.

All is quiet as I push the door open another six inches and poke my head out to see where the hell I am. I took mental notes of the layout the day I came for the party. To my right is the living room and dining room. To my left is the kitchen, and beyond that, the family room. As I step out into the hallway, Abbie's voice rings out in the distance. I freeze.

"Hey Jen, it's Abbie. I'm almost finished with the seating charts for the breast cancer fundraiser dinner. We're going to blow out our donations for the hospital. I should have it finished for you by tomorrow."

As Abbie leaves her message, I creep slowly down the hallway following the sound of her voice. Nearing the entrance to the family room, I wait a moment, contemplating my next move.

I don't want to hurt her, at least not right now. I need her. Hopefully my unexpected visit today will provide the additional motivation. *Get me my money.* What's so freakin' hard about that?

Standing hidden in the hallway corner, I can see the back of Abbie's pretty little head. She has no idea I'm here. Perhaps my presence will further persuade her to make the deal happen. After all, I'm only asking for ten million. Last time I checked, Jason Sterling was worth over two hundred and fifty million. Ten million is nothing to him . . . but it's everything to me.

I slowly cross the room towards my target. I'm twenty feet away. Now ten, now five. I'm surprised she doesn't sense my presence because she doesn't turn around. When I'm within three feet of her, I lift my gloved hands over my head and bring them down on either side of her neck. Then, I squeeze. Stunned and scared, she instinctually grabs for my hands and begins kicking and trying to loosen my grip. I tighten my fingers around her throat a little more. She struggles to get free. That's never going to happen, not unless I want it to.

When I feel her start to lose steam, I lean over from behind and whisper into her ear.

"Are you playing hard to get? How about a little romance for old times' sake? It's been so long. We used to be so good together. Remember?"

Hearing my voice and amorous suggestion sends her into a frenzy. I almost lose my hold on her. For a second, I'm a little insulted by her violent reaction to the idea of a quickie.

From the way she starts fighting me, it's pretty clear my idea didn't turn her on. *Relax, Ms. Sterling, I didn't come here to rape you. I just want my fucking money.*

When I finally twist her around, and let her see my face, she doesn't appear surprised. She looks scared. My guess is she knew it was me the minute she felt hands around her throat. Realistically, who else would it be? It's not like she's an international spy being followed by assassins.

"Let me go or I'll scream," she says loudly, mustering up some defiance.

I tilt my head back and squint at her. Abbie just said the dumbest thing imaginable. The Sterlings' property is a multi-acre lot in the middle of woods; the nearest homes are on as many or more acres. The closest neighbor is so far away that Abbie and I could both scream for an hour and no one would hear us.

"Go for it, Abbie. Scream your head off," I say, still maintaining my hold on her. "No one's going to hear you and you know it. There's really no need to exert so much pointless energy. I just stopped by to have a friendly little chat with you."

She catches her breath, but I maintain my hold.

"I've done everything you asked," she says, coughing between words.

I release her, take a step backwards and pull out a folded piece of paper from my pocket.

"Dear sweet Abbie," I say, shaking my head with disappointment. "It appears you're still not clear on what our mutual business objectives are. I've always considered myself an excellent communicator. Have I not been specific about my needs?"

"Jason will be home any minute," she says, her eyes darting all around the room, presumably looking for an escape hatch.

I circle her as I speak. "Oh, you think Jason is going to save the day? Let me review things, so we're both on the same page."

Abbie rubs her neck as I continue.

"I require at minimum ten million dollars, and I need it now," I say, as I hand her the piece of paper. "I tried to do it the old-fashioned way, by pitching a bogus company to investors, including your husband. For whatever reason, that didn't work out."

"I tried to get you the money!" she shouts. "Really, I did. I told him how much I liked what you and Sophie were doing and how—"

"I appreciate your support. But if your husband isn't going to invest in my cow farts energy endeavor, you'll just have to withdraw the money from your joint personal account. I know you've got it. You can wire transfer the money to the number on the piece of paper I just handed to you."

Abbie's brown eyes get very large. She's frightened. That was my intention, and frankly, I'm kind of enjoying it.

"I can't just withdraw millions of dollars from our account," she says. "Jason will know it's missing. What will I tell him?"

"Not my problem," I say.

I can see in her eyes, she's getting a second wind.

*Ok. I'll play.*

"If you don't leave right now," she says, getting up and reaching for her phone, "I'm going to call the police."

I get to her phone first and smash it on the floor with my foot. She turns to run, but I'm faster. Grabbing her by the hair, I push her up against a wall.

"You'll do whatever I tell you to do, because I've still got *the* gun. You know the one: your grubby little prints are all over it. As long as I have that, I'm running this show, not you. Are we clear?"

# CHAPTER 52

*Abbie*

Christian slams me into a wall and presses his body against mine. I can smell him — a mix of garlic, perspiration and some overpowering men's cologne. It's revolting. I don't know whether he's just trying to scare me, or if he's on the brink of becoming violent. He's capable of violence, so I can't underestimate what he'll do. Looking into his eyes, they're as black as coal and I can't read them.

"Please . . . let go of me," I say, pushing him back while trying to wriggle away. "It's not too late. You can still walk out of here and we'll forget this ever happened."

He starts to cackle like an old witch.

"Shut the fuck up," he says, in a gruff, almost inhuman-sounding voice. "You think I'm going to walk away now? I've come too far and sacrificed too much to change course now. When I think of all the times I sucked up to your husband and his crew of entitled assholes, it makes me sick. I twisted myself into a pretzel trying to prove the worth of my company to them. The whole time, they were just playing with me because they could."

From the sudden looseness of his talk, I can tell he's starting to lose some of his self-control. I remember Travis being like that when things didn't go his way. He'd go into a rage.

Up until now, I'd only been afraid of him outing me to my husband and the cops. But today, I sense another level of desperation in him, much more than before. He's given up trying to present an image of refinement and legitimacy. I know him. His basic instincts are essentially for self-interest. That's what drives him. Right now, I'm standing in the way of him achieving his goals. He's going to hurt me. My only way out is to talk him down.

I swallow. "No one was laughing at you," I say. "Jason told me many times that he was impressed by your presentations and respected what RDV was trying to accomplish. As far as I know, they're still considering your proposal."

He lets go of my neck, takes a step backwards and stares at me. I must have given him food for thought, because he's got a strange look on his face. I take this momentary break to plan my escape. If I can get to the basement door, it's got a lock on the other side. I can lock him out, run down the stairs, jump in my car and get out of here.

I start to make my move when he catches my arm and throws me up against the wall again. My head slams into the crown molding around a closet door. I start to see stars.

"Wait. Stop," I say, pushing him away with all my strength. "We can figure this out. I thought your dairy ventures company was a really good idea. I did everything I could to get Jason to pull the trigger, but I'll try again. I'll make it happen."

Christian releases me, right before he pulls a gun out of the waistband of his pants and points it directly at me.

"Is that the gun from when—" I start to say.

"Are you kidding?" he says, his nostrils flaring. "You think I'm that stupid? Sorry. The gun you used to blow your mother away is in a very special and secure place . . . like I told you."

Circling me, he waves the gun and touches the barrel to my face. Things have now gone from bad to terrible. Before he was just crazy. Now he's crazy and angry. I look around the room for another way out. From where I'm standing, the nearest door to the outside is in the back of the kitchen and leads out to the deck. Christian's between me and it. I calculate my odds, and I won't make it. He's bigger and stronger, and clearly wouldn't hesitate to shoot me.

"Stop trying to find an escape hatch, Abbie," he says, still circling me. "Remember, I'm calling the shots here."

That's when it hits me. I'm all alone on this. No one's going to come and save me. My eyes lock on him as he paces in front of me. Running or fighting won't work as long as he has a gun. I can tell by the tone in his voice that he's desperate and might do anything. I've got to convince him that I'm on his side.

He points the barrel of the gun at my temple and then pushes it up into my scalp.

"I'm getting weary, Abbie. Are you going to transfer the money or not?"

"It will take a little time."

"I don't have time. Everything's all screwed up!" He screams this so loud I feel it vibrate in my chest. Now, he's waving the gun around. I'm afraid it will go off accidentally. "Sophie's gone. The whole deal's falling apart."

"We don't need Sophie," I say, as calmly as I can. "Jason hasn't made any decisions yet. I'm sure once he has another chance to review the—"

"It's goddamn dead and you know it," he yells, his voice getting louder.

For a second, we both stare at each other without speaking.

"Listen to me, Trav . . . Christian," I say, trying to stay composed so he'll calm down. "I told Jason how important RDV was to me. I know my husband. He wants to make me happy. Just give it a little more time."

"I don't have any more time!" he shouts. He walks in a small circle in front of me, recklessly playing with the gun. "You think I'm stupid because I didn't go to some fancy college? I'm smarter than all of you put together. I don't need a degree from Stanford, I've got street smarts, and that's worth more than any college degree. *Comprende?*"

I nod. I've got to talk him down, or he's going to hurt me.

"I always thought you were smart, even back in Warwick," I say. "All the kids looked up to you, remember? You were the mayor. And, my husband thinks so, too. He told me so. Jason said what you were doing with the dairies was nothing short of amazing."

Christian starts to laugh and points the gun directly at the center of my face.

"Funny thing is," he says, sliding the barrel up against my cheek, "there is no RDV. We're not harnessing energy. I have no relationships with dairies. There's no national network or sales figures. It's all a scam, a grift. In your language, it's total bullshit."

My mouth drops open. I knew something was wrong when Christian started pressuring me, but I had no idea the entire company was a hoax.

"You lied about everything?" I say, my heart pounding. "None of it is real?"

"You've finally got it," he says, with big smile as he moves the barrel of the gun up to my forehead. Terrified, I can't move my arms or legs. I'm literally frozen in place and pretty sure I'm about to die.

He continues rambling about life and the unfairness of it. Then, it hits me. He didn't come here to kill me. If he had, I'd already be dead.

"We can work this out," I say, as calmly as I can. "Can you please move the gun away from my head? It might go off."

He grins. He's fucking enjoying this cat-and-mouse game.

"You always were a stupid bitch," he says, as he moves the gun away, but continues waving it in my face. "Let's see you talk your way out of this one."

I take a deep breath.

"Hear me out," I say. "I've got an idea. You want the investment money, right? If you kill me, you'll get nothing. But with me alive, I can still pull the strings to get you your money."

"Then we're in agreement. That's why I'm here today. If I don't get my money this week, there could be accidents. They might happen here, or possibly up at Camp Louise. That's a deep lake. You just never know."

When I hear him threaten my kids like that, whatever was in my stomach works its way up into my esophagus. I taste bile in my mouth and grab onto the molding on the wall to keep myself from falling over.

Despite my nausea, the little voice in my head plays on a loop.

*Protect my family. Protect my family.*

## CHAPTER 53

Christian finally lets go of me and sits down in a nearby chair, caressing his gun like he was holding a baby. I'm repulsed and terrified at the same time, but maintain eye contact. If he's the same person he was twenty years ago, fear only turns him on. I won't give him the satisfaction or let him see that I'm afraid. My kids' lives depend on it.

We remain in a deadlocked stare for nearly a minute until he finally breaks by smirking at me.

"You always were a tough little customer," he says, with a creepy laugh. "Even when you were fifteen, you were a real badass. Remember all the fun we used to have partying, boosting cars, getting high? You liked that sweet wine that tasted like shit. Remember? Good times."

"If you say so," I reply, still trying to come up with a way out of the room. "Jason will be home any minute. If you leave now, he doesn't have to know about this."

Christian smirks again, stands and comes towards me.

"Nice try," he says. "But we both know Jason has a late meeting tonight. I may be rough around the edges, but I do my homework. I checked with his admin. We've got hours to get reacquainted before your husband comes walking through the door."

Without warning, he leans forward and presses his body up against mine. His hot breath covers my face and smells disgusting. He tries to kiss me. I turn my face away.

*He's going to rape me.*

"Stop!" I shout as he puts his hands on me. "Let me go. Please, Travis."

It's like he doesn't hear me, or he doesn't care. His hand slides between my legs. That's when I scream. I pull his hand away. In return, he puts the barrel of the gun under my chin.

"You've got this all wrong. You'll do whatever I say," he growls, in a voice I haven't heard before. "Now, drop down on your knees."

I'm so terrified that I'm physically unable to react and just stand there swaying. He starts to push me down onto the floor, and I instinctively lock my knees. It's at that moment that we both hear the front door open and close. Christian moves the gun up to my lips.

"Shhh," he whispers. "Not a sound or your husband gets the first bullet."

"Abbie!" shouts Jason, from somewhere in the front of the house. "I'm home. My last meeting was canceled. Where are you?"

"Answer him. Make it seem normal," whispers Christian, pulling me up straight against the wall and tucking the gun away under his jacket. "Remember what I said about accidents at Camp Louise. I can be up there in an hour."

"I'm in here!" I shout. "In the family room."

Christian takes a seat on the couch and casually crosses his legs as if this was a friendly visit. When Jason walks into the room, Christian picks up my mug filled with now-cold tea and takes a sip. At first, Jason doesn't see him; he walks directly to me and gives me a kiss. When he steps back he looks at my face, and I see confusion spill across his.

"Are my kisses that bad?" he says, with a grin.

"Of course not," I say.

"Did you get the mail? Abs, what's going on? You've got a funny look in your eyes."

I look over my husband's shoulder at Christian lounging on our couch. The bastard nods and smiles at me. I hate him so much right now.

"We have . . . a guest," I say, forcing a smile.

Jason turns and sees Christian.

"Surprise," says our uninvited guest, holding up my mug of tea.

"What are you doing here?" my husband says, obviously confused.

"I was in the area looking at houses again. Sophie had another appointment and caught the train back into the city. Since I was up here, I thought the neighborly thing would be to drop by and say hello," Christian says, as he gets up and extends his hand to Jason. "I was hoping to bump into you, so that we could have another conversation."

Jason ignores Christian's hand and puts his arm protectively around my shoulders.

"I conduct all my business in the office," says Jason, clearly trying to be diplomatic. "I thought I made it pretty clear at our last meeting that we'd be in touch *if* we planned to invest in RDV."

Christian nods. "You know something? I guess I didn't pick up on that. Sometimes I can be a little dense. From now on, I'll contact you in the office. But as long as I'm here, can I answer any outstanding questions or concerns you may have?"

Bewildered, Jason looks at me, and then back at Christian.

"Not at this time," my husband says starting to simmer. "I hate to rush you out, but Abbie and I have something we have to do tonight."

"When can I expect to get the good word?" says Christian, smiling.

I can tell my husband is about to lose his temper. If he does, something bad is going to happen. I've got to defuse this fast.

"We've got to get going to this thing tonight," I say. "Why don't you two talk tomorrow?"

"You have an interesting concept and execution, Christian," says Jason. "But I've got to be honest, I don't think it's for us."

Christian walks towards us in a quasi-menacing way.

"I'm completely stunned," he says. "I thought you were all on board. Sophie and I are really counting on this. What can I say to you to turn this around?"

"There's nothing," says my husband, now obviously annoyed. "Like I told you, we're not moving forward."

Christian lets out a weird laugh while shaking his head. "I see. Unfortunately, I don't like taking no for an answer."

My husband who is six feet two in bare feet, stands up very tall and puffs out his chest like a rooster in a barnyard. He's got at least three inches on Christian, and looks him directly in the eyes.

"I think you should leave," Jason says, loudly. "Now."

Christian shakes his head and presses his lips together.

"I can't do that. I really need that ten million dollars. In fact, I promised myself this morning that I wouldn't leave here today without it."

"What are you talking about?" says my husband, now furious. "I'm not giving you any money. I want you to get the hell out of my house or I'm calling the police."

Christian appears to be enjoying this altercation and takes a long deep breath before slowly exhaling.

"I don't think you want to call the police," he says, pacing around us. "If they come, they'll ask all sorts of questions. Your wife wouldn't want that."

"Leave my wife out of this," Jason says, as he pulls out his phone. "I've had enough. I'm calling the cops."

Suddenly, Christian's gun appears. He knocks the phone out of Jason's hand with the barrel of the gun. The phone slides across the wood floor and under the couch.

"I *said*, I don't think you want to call the police." Christian holds his gun on both of us. "Take it from me, you never know what the cops might ask you. For example, they might have questions about a murder that happened in Warwick twenty years ago. I believe that's around the time that your wife's mother was killed."

"Why do I feel like we're having two different conversations?" says my husband, staring fiercely at Christian. "Put that gun down and get out of my house."

Christian comes closer again, waving and gesturing with the gun.

"You're not really in a position to make demands," he says. "You never met Abbie's mother, did you? No, I suppose not. Midge was long gone by the time you came into the picture. She was a hard ass, that's for sure. Did Abbie ever tell you about the day her mother died? I'm not talking about what the papers reported. I mean the real truth about what happened?"

Jason looks at me and then back at Christian, but remains silent. I know my husband. He has a very long fuse, but he's about to blow.

"Of course, Abbie wouldn't tell you about her mother's death," Christian says, clearly enjoying his moment in the limelight. "Your wife is very good at keeping secrets, did you know that? Most women are always yapping. Yappity-yap-yap. But not her. She can keep a secret for decades . . . even from you."

Jason looks at me. "Abbie, what's he talking about?"

Before I can respond, Christian continues.

"I'm not surprised she never told you about it," he says, glancing at me and grinning. "It was such an ugly business . . . so much blood."

"You're not making any sense," says Jason, simmering.

"It's hard to imagine a fifteen-year-old girl gunning down her own mother in cold blood," says Christian, looking at me. "But then again, old Midge didn't leave you much choice, did she? Sticking her nose in where it didn't belong. Everyone knows when you do that, bad things are bound to happen."

"Shut up!" I shout. "Stop it. Leave us alone."

Christian smiles like a cat about to devour a canary.

"I'm afraid it's too late for that," he says. "Your husband has a right to know who he's married to. Why don't you tell him the truth, Abbie? Don't you owe him that? Go ahead, tell him he's married to a murderer."

# CHAPTER 54

"What the hell is he talking about?" says Jason, looking first at me and then over at Christian.

"I'm afraid your wife hasn't been truthful with you about her past," says Christian, grimacing. "Would you like to tell him what happened, Abbie, or may I have the honor?"

"Abbie, what's he talking about?"

I'm a mix of fear and nausea infused with adrenaline. I open my mouth, but nothing comes out. Even if I could talk, I wouldn't know what to say.

"Cat got your tongue?" Christian says, in a cold, dead voice, still holding the gun on both of us. "No worries. I'm happy to fill your husband in on your past . . . indiscretions. Let's start at the beginning. I'm betting your wife never told you about us."

Jason pulls his head back, cranes his neck around and stares at me.

"That's right. We were a thing twenty years ago," says Christian. "She was a hot little piece of ass back then, pretty hard to resist. She wanted it all the time. Even at fifteen, she was a hard one to satisfy. Remember, Abbie? You could never get enough."

"Shut up!" I shout. "Shut up."

"Too late for that. The cat's half out of the bag. I'll bet your husband's dying to know the full unedited story."

"Leave us alone!" I shout.

"I absolutely will as soon as I get the ten million dollars," says Christian with a wink. He comes closer, brandishing his weapon.

"Fuck you," spits Jason. "I'm not giving you a fucking penny."

Christian clucks with his tongue. "I tried to get it the old-fashioned way by pulling a well-thought-out scam, but you didn't bite. Sophie and I put on a pretty good show. Months of work down the drain. I'm curious. What exactly was it that kept you from pulling the trigger on our proposal?"

My husband steps in front of me and stares into Christian's dark eyes.

"It was you, man. I didn't trust you," he says. "It was that simple."

Christian lets out a menacing laugh. "I hear you, *man*. You gotta trust your gut, right? I live by that, too. The gut never lies. Although yours wasn't working very well when you met your wife. You think I've got skeletons in my closet? Your wife has a whole armoire filled with bones. You want to tell him the truth, Abbie, or should I?"

"We'll get you your money. I promise!" I shout. "Leave now, and I'll get it to you tomorrow."

"Abbie, what the hell is he talking about?" says my husband, frantically looking into my eyes. I see sadness and confusion on his face, and it breaks my heart.

"I didn't mean for it to happen!" I say, bursting into tears.

"At least your wife's consistent," says Christian chuckling. "Those are the exact words she said to me twenty years ago. I believed her, too."

Christian leans back and sits on the edge of an end table.

"Here's how it went down. I'm in the drive-thru lane at Burger King minding my own business, ordering a Whopper, when your wife calls me. She wasn't making any sense. Kept talking about all this blood and how she didn't know what to do. Like a good boyfriend, I got off the line and drove straight over to her mother's house. I didn't even wait for my burger. Now, that's love."

"Please, stop," I say, my face soaked with tears.

"I'll tell you something else. When I walked into that bedroom . . . holy shit. There was blood fucking everywhere — on the walls, the rug and the floor. In the middle of this bloodbath, is her mother lying in a pool of her own blood."

"I don't understand," says Jason, looking at me. "You two know each other?"

"Try to keep up, *man*," says Christian, waving his gun again, enjoying his role as master of ceremonies. "I'm getting there. Abbie's mom didn't like me too much. When she found out I wasn't seventeen like we told her, but closing in on twenty, that woman lost her freakin' mind. Abbie was fifteen, and old Midge said she was going to turn me over to the cops for statutory rape. It was either me or Mom. Your wife was just trying to protect me."

"What are you saying?" says my husband, clearly itching to take a swing at Christian.

"I'm saying," Christian continues, "that twenty years ago on a sunny weekday afternoon, your perfect little bride shot her mother three times in the chest. Then she called me to clean up her mess."

I look up at my husband's face and see an expression of horror, confusion and utter disappointment. He shakes his head.

"I didn't mean to do it," I shout. "Jason, you've got to believe me. It was an accident. I was so messed up. I was taking so many pills. I don't even know how I got the gun."

"How could you keep something like this from me?" my husband says. "Why didn't you tell me?"

"I couldn't," I plead. "I was afraid to tell anyone. You have no idea how this has been eating me up all these years.

That's why I have all those nightmares. I didn't know what to do."

"You could have been honest with me," says Jason, turning to face me, somehow forgetting Christian is still holding a gun on us. "I don't even know you."

"You do know me," I say. "I'm nothing like the person he's describing."

"You can't just brush a murder under the rug, Abbie," my husband says. "You murdered your own mother?"

"I didn't mean to. She threatened us. Everything was all jumbled up in my head."

"You should have trusted me," Jason says.

"If I'd been honest with you when we met, you wouldn't have understood."

"You never gave me the chance," he says, as he looks at a picture of our girls on a nearby table. "Our whole marriage and family is built on a lie."

Christian clears his throat.

"You two can finish this conversation on your own time," he says, walking over to me and leveling his gun at my temple. I feel myself tremble. "Right now, we have some arrangements to discuss."

Jason stands up. "What do I need to do to make this go away?" my husband says calmly, as if he were conducting a board meeting.

Christian smiles. "I see you're a man who understands business. It's simple. All I need is my ten million, and you'll never see me again."

"What's to stop me from going to the police and reporting you?" says Jason.

Christian moves around the room pretending to look for hidden cameras before letting out a laugh.

"Try to keep up," he says, holding out his phone. "You can call the cops, if you're cool having your wife and the mother of your children go to prison for the rest of her life. Here, make the call."

Christian and Jason stare at each other.

"I'm offering you peace of mind. Think of it as a little insurance policy premium. Ten million dollars buys my eternal silence. It's a small price to pay to protect your family. You'll hardly even feel it, Sterling."

Jason looks up at the ceiling for a moment and then back at Christian.

"It's just your word against hers," my husband says. "Abbie's a mother and a respected member of this community. You're a drifter and a grifter. Seems to me that twenty years ago you were a legally adult male who took physical advantage of a fifteen-year-old girl. Who do you think the cops are going to believe, you or me?"

Christian circles us waving the gun.

"I see your point," he says smugly, "if it weren't for one tiny little thing. I'm still in possession of the murder weapon. The one your wife used to shoot her poor mother. Abbie gave it to me that day. At the time, I had full intentions of getting rid of it. But, as I was looking for a place to toss it, this little voice inside my head told me to hang on to it. It said that it would come in handy one day. So, I wrapped up the gun with Abbie's fingerprints all over it and put it away in a safe place."

The room is deadly silent.

"I'll give you the ten million dollars, and you give me that gun," says Jason, all business.

"Don't negotiate with him," I say, pulling on my husband's arm. "He's a liar. You can't trust him."

"Let me handle this," Jason says, stepping in front of me again. "I know what I'm doing."

"I would love to give you that gun, but it's kind of *my* insurance policy now," says Christian, coming over to me and touching my cheek with the gun. "As long as I have that murder weapon, you won't call the cops on me. Consider the ten mil my payment for helping your wife cover her bloody tracks all those years ago. I took a lot of risks to save her cute little ass."

"Do we have a deal?" says Jason. "Ten million and I get the gun."

I look at Christian. His hands go up to his face, and he scratches three times behind his right ear. That means he's nervous, which makes him vulnerable.

I take a chance and lunge for the gun.

# CHAPTER 55

What happens next is a big blur. I hurl myself at Christian. He swats me away like a mosquito and I go flying across the room. When I get up, Jason and Christian are rolling around on the floor knocking over lamps, tables and chairs. I reach for the heavy green jade Buddha statue sitting on our mantle. Despite all those fight scenes I've seen in movies, insinuating yourself into someone else's fistfight is not so easy.

As the two of them roll around on the floor, I try several times to hit Christian on the head, but only succeed in grazing his shoulder. He knocks Jason away, and throws me into a wall. When I look up dizzily, I see Jason and Christian are going at it again. That's when I remember, we have a gun in the house. I dash out of the room to our home office on the other side of the living room. The gun is in there inside a wall safe.

I'm shaking so hard that I screw up the combination with each attempt. Finally, after three tries, the lock clicks and it opens. I can hear the two of them still crashing around in the other room. Suddenly, there's a loud crash followed by the sound of glass shattering. I grab the gun from the safe and run back down the hallway.

As I get near the family room, I spot Christian's gun on the floor in the hall. He must have dropped it during their scuffle. I run past it and into the family room and nearly pass out when I see my husband on the floor. His face is covered in blood, and Christian's standing over him kicking him in the stomach and head with all his strength. Jason's not moving.

"Stop!" I scream, holding the loaded gun directly on him. Christian's back is to me, and he kicks Jason again.

"Stop it now or I'll shoot! I swear!" I scream again, as I fire the gun over his head.

The bullet goes into the ceiling. It gets Christian's attention. He spins around.

"Put that down," he says dismissively, and starts to walk towards me.

"Don't come any closer," I say. "I'll shoot."

"You're going to hurt yourself, Abbie," he says, with his hand outstretched. "Now, give me the gun."

I shake my head and point it directly at his chest.

"Stop where you are," I say, glancing down at my husband, still sprawled out on the floor. Tears roll down my face. This is all my fault.

"Let me have the gun," Christian says, taking another step towards me.

Jason moans and I let out a breath. He's alive.

"Put the gun down," Christian says, angrily. "You don't know how to use it."

All the rage and anxiety I've been carrying since I was fifteen comes to the surface and I stand up straight and tall.

"That's where you're wrong!" I yell. "I know exactly what I'm doing."

"You're not going to shoot me."

As I look at Christian, everything is so clear to me.

"You know what?" I bark, while taking a shooter's stance, legs apart and feet firmly planted on the ground. "You manipulated me when I was a kid. Now, you're trying to do it again. I've been running from you for twenty years. I'm not running anymore."

"Let's talk things out," he says, with his hand extended. "Now, hand me the gun."

"No," I say, waving the weapon at him. "I'm the one in control now. Not you. I'm calling the shots. How does that make you feel?"

He smirks. I fucking hate that smirk. He's losing control. He doesn't like being told what to do, especially by a woman.

"You're not going to shoot me," he says, getting red in the face.

"I've killed before," I say, taking a step towards him. "Once a killer, always a killer. You broke into my home and assaulted my husband. It was self-defense."

Christian laughs. "You don't have the guts. You may have been a badass when you were fifteen. But now you're soft. Too much of a privileged life. You couldn't kill a spider."

With all the adrenaline pumping through my body right now, I feel like I'm going to jump out of my own skin. Jason moans again, but still appears to be unconscious. I've got to get him to a hospital.

As I'm trying to decide my next move, Christian lunges at me, trying to get the gun. I sidestep out of the way, and he trips and falls. Both of my hands firmly on the gun, I turn towards him pointing it at his face.

"I'm giving you one last chance," I say. "Get the fuck out of my house right now."

Christian gets up off the floor and comes at me full force. I take a step backwards and cock the gun. "If I killed my own mother, I can certainly kill you. You want to take that chance?"

Unbelievably, Christian starts to cackle, which unnerves me even more. From the look on his face, it's obvious that he's highly agitated. He's someone who always needs to be in control. Right now, he's lost the upper hand, and he knows it. He's looking for an opening.

"You think you're some big-time assassin just because you killed that old bitch?" he shouts, the veins on his forehead and neck bulging.

Calmly, I take aim. "This is your last chance. Now, get out of my house, or I'll shoot you the same way I shot my mother."

"Are you fucking kidding me? You didn't kill that old hag," he says, taking another step towards me. "You didn't have the guts to do it. I had to do it."

"What?" My legs go suddenly wobbly.

"She was going to put me in jail. I was nineteen years old. I would have been in prison for twenty years. I would have been an old man when I got out."

"What are you saying?" I whisper, my hands holding the gun now shaking.

Jason lets out another groan, but Christian's and my eyes are locked on each other.

"It was supposed to be so easy. I was going to steal your mother's jewelry and cash and get the hell out of that town. Everything would have gone as planned, if she hadn't come home early. She walked in and saw me rifling through her safe and started screaming. I wasn't about to go to prison over her, or you. There was a loaded gun right there in her safe, so I grabbed it and fired. It was her or me."

My brain is about to explode. I can't process what I'm hearing. None of what he said fits into the narrative I've been carrying with me, weighing me down for the past twenty years.

"But the gun was in my hand," I say, not believing him. "I shot her. I was alone in the house with my mom."

"I gave you a few pills. You were popping so much shit back then, you had no idea what you were taking. I wanted to make sure you were out of the way while I helped myself to your mother's jewelry and cash."

"I don't understand."

"I didn't plan on killing her, but then she came at me like a caged animal, so I pulled the trigger three times. Problem solved."

Rage bubbles up inside me like a volcano about to erupt. I try to process what I've just been told.

"When I realized she was dead," says Christian, "I got the idea to make you believe you did it. I carried you into her bedroom and put the gun in your hand."

"You killed my mother?"

"Try to keep up. I figured if you thought you were responsible for her death, you'd keep your mouth shut."

"All these years, you let me believe I killed my own mother?" I scream. "Do you know how it's tortured me every minute of every day? *You ruined my life!*"

"Doesn't look that way to me," he says, his eyes sweeping around the room. "You live in a freakin' castle. Get over yourself."

Jason moans a third time.

"I need to get him to the hospital," I shout. "He needs a doctor."

"Now, here's what we're going to do. You're going to be a good girl and make a ten-million-dollar wire transfer from your account to the account number I gave you the other day. When that's all done, I'll be on my way and you can tell Jason whatever—"

From the corner of my eye, something moves. Suddenly, Jason rears up and tackles Christian from behind. They fall out into the hallway, both reaching for Christian's gun, which is still lying on the floor where it landed earlier. They both grab for it as they roll around the hallway out of my sight.

I'm still holding the gun I got from the safe, but am afraid to shoot for fear of hitting my husband. As I step into the hallway, there's a loud bang.

I see both men slump to the floor, and for a second everything's completely quiet. Neither of them moves. With the gun in one hand, I run over to them. Christian is lying on top of my husband.

"Jason?" I shout, as I kneel. "Can you hear me?"

Jason's head moves and he pushes Christian off him. I help my husband stand and we cling to each other while looking down at Christian's lifeless body on the floor.

There's a bullet wound in Christian's chest oozing blood, just like my mother. His dark eyes are wide open. I check for a pulse, but I know I won't find one. That's when I lose it completely and sink to the floor sobbing.

"I'm so sorry," I say, burying my face in my hands. "I put you and the girls in so much danger. I never meant to do that."

"What was he talking about?" says Jason.

Covered in his and Christian's blood, my husband sits on the floor and wraps his arms around me. "It's going to be all right. We'll get past this."

"Did you hear what he told me? I didn't do it, Jason," I say, crying uncontrollably now. "I didn't kill my mother. I loved her. I was just going through a bad time. He convinced me that I did it. Then he acted like a big hero, covering it up and pretending to protect me. But I didn't do it. I didn't kill my mother."

Jason holds me closer. "I heard. I couldn't move, but I heard everything. Everything's gonna be okay."

# CHAPTER 56

We sit on the couch. Jason puts his phone on speaker and punches in a number.

"Eastport Police Department," says a female operator.

"This is Jason Sterling at 151 Foxcroft Road. There's been a shooting at my home. A man broke into our house and threatened my wife and me with a gun. He physically attacked us. When I tried to get the gun from him, it went off. I think he's dead."

"Have you checked for a pulse, sir?" the woman says.

"Yes. There's no pulse. He's dead."

Five minutes later, four squad cars and an ambulance with sirens blaring pull into our driveway. Soon after, a police photographer and a pair of detectives arrive. Jason does most of the talking. He explains how Christian Wendt was a business associate from New York.

"He was pitching me and my group on making a substantial investment in his energy company," says my husband, as I gently dab a wet cloth on some of his cuts.

"Why do you think he broke into your house?" says the taller of the two detectives.

"Recently, my group had been signaling that the investment wasn't going to happen," says Jason. "I guess he went crazy."

"If you were conducting business in New York, how did he end up here in Eastport?" says the same detective.

"Christian told me he was looking at real estate in the area, so we invited him to our Memorial Day barbecue," says Jason. "After that, he knew where we lived and the layout of the property and house."

"I see," says the cop, taking notes.

"I got home from work early and surprised him. When I walked into the house, he was threatening my wife with a gun."

"Ms. Sterling, did you let Mr. Wendt into the house?" asked the shorter detective.

I shake my head. "No, absolutely not. I don't know how he got in. I was working at my desk when I heard a noise. When I looked up, he was right behind me. That's when he grabbed me."

"Our guys checked all the doors and windows," says a uniformed officer walking into the room. "There's no sign of a break-in. The victim must have come in through a door or window. Was your security system turned on?"

I nod. "We always keep it on. It requires a six-digit code."

"Any cameras?" says the cop.

I shake my head. "No, we didn't want our children growing up being photographed."

The detectives interrogate us for over an hour, while we lie numerous times and try to hold ourselves together. We recap our time spent with Christian, including when he showed up at the soccer jamboree and at our kids' camp. We also tell them about Sophie Boyd, or whatever her real name is. Jason and I reveal nothing about my mother's death or the history I had with the dead man on the floor.

At a little before 11:00 p.m., Christian's body is wheeled out of our house on a stretcher.

"I think you should let us bring you to the ER, Mr. Sterling, so they can take a look at you," says the older detective. "That's a nasty cut you've got. You may need a few stitches."

Jason assures them he'll seek medical attention. The police seem satisfied that the whole incident is a straightforward

271

self-defense scenario. They treat us like victims . . . because that's what we are. They instruct us to stay in town, and ask that we go to the police station in the morning to make an official statement.

It's late when they finally leave. After I put some antiseptic on the gash on my husband's forehead, Jason goes upstairs to take a shower.

I look around the first floor. The house is a total wreck. I straighten a few pieces of furniture and attempt to put the room back together. As I wipe up Christian's blood from the wood floor, it triggers something. My mind flashes back to the day my mother died. The memory is amazingly vivid and I start to shake. For the first time since it happened, the memory is different.

My feelings of guilt and remorse are now replaced by blinding rage. Dizzy and wobbly, I sit down at the kitchen table, not trusting my legs to hold me up.

*Travis killed my mother. Every day, I've hated myself. Twenty years of self-loathing, mixed with the fear of someone finding out. Now I know, I never hurt her.*

I pound my fist on the table, bury my face in my hands and cry harder than I've ever cried before. I cry for my mother, for myself and for my family. When Jason comes into the kitchen, I look up at him through my tears. The left side of his jaw is red and swollen and there's a little blood dripping from the cut above his right eye. I stand up and put my arms around him.

"Ouch," he says, pulling away from me. "I appreciate the love but maybe not right now. I'm sore all over."

I run to the freezer to find a bag of frozen peas and place it on his jaw.

"That should help with the swelling," I say, sitting him down in a kitchen chair and adjusting the iced bag on his face. "We'll go to the doctor in the morning and have him take a look at you."

Sitting at the table, we look into each other's eyes, neither of us speaking. Right now, being together is enough.

"The first time we met," my husband finally says, breaking our silence, "I sensed there was something you were holding back. There's always been a little piece of your heart that I never quite knew."

"I wanted to tell you, but I was so ashamed," I say, a tear trickling down my cheek. "I believed I killed her. He made me believe that."

"You should have told me. I could have helped. I would have protected you."

I shake my head. "I was afraid I'd lose you. I was also trying to protect you and the girls. I didn't want you to have to keep my secret. I didn't want to involve you in any of it."

"I could have been there for you."

"It was selfish on my part. I was so in love with you. I didn't want to give you up," I say. "If I had told you the truth as I knew it, you would have run away and I wouldn't have blamed you."

He reaches across the table for my hand and caresses it.

"Then you don't know me as well as you think you do," he says. "I'm in this for the long haul. For better or for worse, remember?"

I smile. A giant weight has been lifted from my body and soul. I literally feel lighter . . . giddy almost. *I didn't kill my mother. I loved her and I still do.*

I look at the clock on the wall. It's nearly 1:00 a.m.

"Let's go to bed," I say.

We get up from the table and walk to the stairs. I go first and Jason follows. Midway up, something hits me. I turn around and face him.

"We've still got a problem," I say grabbing his arm. "Christian said he had the original gun that killed my mother. He said, my prints were all over it. That gun was in my hand at one point. He put it there, but my prints were on it."

"How do we know what he said was true?"

"We don't . . . but I believed him."

"He lied about everything else."

I let out a breath. "When I knew Travis, he had this little 'tell' I always noticed. Whenever he was nervous or lying about something, which was often, he'd scratch three times behind his right ear. I never thought about it back then. Then, I saw him do it at the barbecue when he was lying about something, and it all came back to me. He did it again tonight."

"I'm not following. Why do you think he was telling the truth about having the gun with your prints?"

"Because he said that he put the gun in a safe place, somewhere that we'd never find it."

"So?"

"He didn't scratch. He was telling the truth. If he was lying about something that big, he would have scratched. He has that gun hidden somewhere. If someone finds it first and turns it in, I could still go down for my mother's murder."

"Then we'll have to find it," Jason says, looking down at me.

# CHAPTER 57

Jason and I lie in bed most of the night talking. I come fully clean to him on everything that ever happened to me. No more lies and no half-truths. Essentially, I spill a big pot of tea all over the table. When I finish the whole sordid tale, leaving out no details, he takes me in his arms and rocks me. I don't deserve him, but am so grateful to have him in my life.

The next morning, he and I drive down to the Eastport Police Department to make our official statements.

"Just tell the truth," says my husband, as he pulls into the police parking lot. "But leave out your backstory and history. The local cops won't connect the dots to Warwick."

"How can you be so sure?"

Jason turns off the engine. "Because my company did extensive background checks on Christian Wendt and Sophie Boyd when we were deciding whether or not to invest in their company. I don't know how Christian did it, but he had a long paper trail supporting all his claims about his education, company and identity. He was thorough; I'll give him that."

"But you were only looking at him from an investment perspective."

"True, but none of what we found led us back to Travis Ritter or Warwick, Connecticut. The cops won't find it either. I'm telling you, everything about him looked legit."

"Travis was a lot of things, but legit wasn't one of them," I say, in a half-hearted attempt at humor.

"When I first started having misgivings about Christian, I took another look at his background info. Trust me, we were potentially going to invest millions. If we didn't find anything, the cops won't either."

"You're sure?"

"There wasn't the slightest bit of impropriety on either Christian or Sophie Boyd. I even saw a picture of Christian when he was at Stanford, standing next to Bill Gates. Everything checked out."

We get out of the car and slowly cross the parking lot. Jason takes my hand before we walk into the police station. I've never been inside the building before. There's a tiny gray lobby with a wooden bench pushed up against one wall. A picture of city hall hangs on the opposite wall along with a few headshots of various police commanders over the years. A young male officer is seated at a desk, behind what I presume is bulletproof glass.

We identify ourselves, and are ushered into a small utilitarian room containing a metal table and six matching chairs. A few minutes later, the two detectives we met the previous night enter the room and take a seat.

For the next hour, we respond to the same questions we answered the night before. I suppose they're looking for any inconsistencies in our statements. That won't happen. Jason and I went over everything dozens of times last night and again, this morning. There will be no changes or deviations in our stories . . . ever.

By noon, the police tell us we're free to leave. It's lunchtime and a sunny summer day. We stop at the Eastport Deli, pick up a few sandwiches and walk over to the town park to talk. There's no one around so we're able to speak freely.

"What should we do about the gun?" I whisper, before taking a bite of my chicken sandwich. "If it's still floating around out there, anyone could find it. We'll always be looking over our shoulders, wondering if today is the day."

Jason takes a bite of his meatball hero before he responds.

"I've been thinking about that," he says, with a mouth full of food.

"And?"

"The way I see it is, we've got to let it go."

"That's your solution? Let it go? We can't do that."

Jason takes a sip of his lemonade and finishes chewing.

"Think about it. We don't know if Christian really had that gun. That was a pretty damning piece of evidence to hold onto all these years just for the hell of it. Since he was the person who really killed your mother, it was a huge risk. It doesn't add up."

"He said he kept the gun. I believed him."

"Did he ever show the gun to you?"

I think for a moment. "He sent me a grainy picture of *a* gun. But I don't know if it was *the* gun."

"Exactly," says my husband. "You know I always trust my gut. I think he was lying. Do you really believe he kept that gun for twenty years in case one day he might pull a scam on you? I don't buy it. Christian was a grifter. I've dealt with people like him before. They don't plan and execute twenty-year cons. They get in and get out with their money fast."

"What if he held onto it like a 'get of out jail free' card," I say. "My prints are all over it. Maybe he held onto it in case he had to exonerate himself one day."

"It's possible, but not probable. Look at how things unfolded. Once our investment wasn't looking good for him, then he showed us his bad side. He only brought up the gun when things started to go south. Before that, he was working his scam."

"You think he made the gun up?"

Jason finishes the last bite of his sandwich, crunches the wrapper into a ball and looks into my eyes. "I think he was a young kid who murdered a woman and wanted to get out of town fast. I don't think he would have kept the gun because he

277

*might* need it twenty years in the future. If it were me, I would have dumped it that same day and moved on with my life. I'm sure that's what he did, but he was counting on the fact that you couldn't know that."

"Right after I'd seen him sitting in a chair outside of St. Vincent's, he called me," I say. "He told me he was looking at the gun while we were on the phone. Maybe it's hidden there?"

"That doesn't make sense. How do you know he was still there when he called you? He could have driven somewhere else. Or he was lying."

"I guess."

Jason takes my hand. "We wouldn't even know where to start looking for that gun. Assuming Christian *did* keep it, the weapon could be anywhere — a bus station locker, a storage unit, buried in the ground under rock. Where would we even start to look?"

As his words pour out, they ring true. Over the past twenty years, Christian or Travis had lived all over. That picture he once sent me of a gun with a shamrock could have been taken a long time ago or just look like my father's old gun. If that gun still exists, it could be anywhere.

"So, we just let it go?" I say, my stomach twisting into knots.

"I don't know what else we can do," he says. "We don't want to draw any extra attention to ourselves. We'd also make ourselves crazy hunting for something that may or may not exist. If it is hidden somewhere, then it's someplace where it can't easily be found. The likelihood of us or of anyone else finding it now is remote."

I reluctantly nod. His rationale makes sense. It could be anywhere . . . or not.

"If he did have the gun," says Jason. "My guess is that he told no one else about it, not even Sophie. It would have been his prize, something he could hold over you. He would have hidden it well. The question is, can we live with the uncertainty of not knowing?"

I let out a breath. "I guess we'll have to."

# CHAPTER 58

After that awful night, the rest of the summer flew by. It's October now. The leaves are falling; the girls are back in school and life is back to normal. Jason and I are slowly putting the whole episode behind us. I'm not going to lie; it hasn't been easy. I'm still so angry. Travis made me believe I killed my own mother and was ready to set me up to take the fall. What kind of person does something like that?

I still have tremendous guilt about her death. I was the one who brought Travis into our lives. If I hadn't done that, my mom would still be alive. She'd be spending time with her grandchildren now. How could I have had feelings for him? He was a monster. Whenever I get into an emotional tailspin, I remind myself that I was fifteen and alone. I was a kid, and easily led. As Jason often says, give someone enough drugs and alcohol and you can get them to do almost anything. And . . . they won't remember most of it.

I'm not making excuses. I was the person who opened Pandora's box. Right now, I'm trying to understand my teenage self. Forgiving myself for bringing Travis into my mother's life is going to take time. But I'm going to face it head on.

In the meantime, I'm working hard at being the best person, wife and mother I can be. That's why, after a long break from volunteering, I'm on my way back to St. Vincent's today to work with the residents for the first time since everything happened.

When I stop to pick up Bianca, she only keeps me waiting in the driveway for three minutes, a world record for her.

"Right on time," I say, with a smile.

"I'm trying," she says, with a sigh. "I finally realized how exhausting it is being late all the time and rushing to get places. Not only that, people are usually annoyed. I don't want that dirty energy in my life. I've embraced the concept of punctuality."

"It is easier being on time," I say, as I drive down her street.

"How are you guys doing after that whole Christian thing?" she says. "I've hardly seen you since it happened. Are you still . . . ?"

"I'm okay. It's going to take a little more time for things to get back to normal, but we're good."

"I'm usually such a good judge of character. He seemed like such a nice person when I met him at your barbecue. He was my knight in shining armor that day."

"What are you talking about?"

"I picked up that enormous cake for you, remember? I was running late that day—"

"As usual."

"I'm working on it. Anyway, when I pulled into your yard, there were no places to park in the back by the party, so I had to go around front. I was carrying way too much stuff and as I was walking up to the house, I tripped and nearly dropped that massive cake. Christian ran over and caught it. Then, he helped me get it into the house. He seemed so nice."

Bianca's words give me pause.

"When Christian helped you with the cake," I say, "how did you go into my house?"

"Through the front door. I used the passcode you gave me. We took the cake into the kitchen. I dropped it off with the staff, and . . ."

I stare at my friend as her mouth opens.

"Oh, my God, Abbie," she says. "Do you think that's how he got the code to get into your house that night?"

"It has to be," I say, somewhat relieved as I turn my car into St. Vincent's parking lot. How Christian got into our house that last day was the one piece Jason and I couldn't figure out. We talked about it a hundred times.

"I let him in?" says Bianca, starting to get upset. "I'm such an idiot. Oh, my God. I'm so sorry. I didn't mean to. You have to believe me."

While Bianca de-combusts, I park the car near the front door of the senior residence and turn off the engine. I reach over and put my hand on my friend's shoulder.

"It's over now. You didn't know. You're not to blame. We brought Christian into our lives, not you," I say. "Shame on us for having him there to begin with."

"But I was the one—"

"Honestly, I'm glad to know there isn't a fault in our security system, or another way to get into the house. Jason had the security people go over every inch, and they had no idea."

"I feel terrible."

"Don't," I say, and I mean it. She didn't know. It was a hundred percent my fault Christian was there to begin with. But I can't tell her about that part.

We go into the building carrying fish bowls, gravel, containers of fish food and many plastic bags filled with live goldfish. After we greet the receptionist, we head off to our respective wings — Maple for her, Birch for me.

Pushing my cart down the corridor of the Birch Wing, I stop in to see Ms. Gill and Mr. Sala, who are both seated in a small living area near their rooms. They smile when I walk in and tell me they've missed my visits, which warms my heart. I guess coming here does make a difference.

After I set up their fish bowls, they each pick out a fish and select the color of gravel they want. Once we're done, Mr. Sala names his fish Nemo. Ms. Gill names hers Mary Anne, which makes me laugh. Who names a fish Mary Anne?

I continue down the hall greeting a few nurses and aides. One of them tells me there's a new resident on the floor. It's another retired priest, age ninety-nine, and he's in a wheelchair. I stop to introduce myself and set up his fish bowl. The old man doesn't say much. But when I let the little yellow goldfish slip out of the bag and into the glass container with green rocks, there's a smile on the priest's face.

"There you go, Father," I say, as an aide comes into the room to bring him his lunch. I look at my watch. It's only 10:30 a.m. They always feed them so early in this place. Who has lunch at 10:30?

I'm nearly done with my rounds and have saved Father Cleary, as always, for my last visit. After all these years, today I'm finally going to tell him the truth. I want him to know I didn't kill my mother.

I don't care if he's lucid today or not. I'm about to burst and I'm going to tell him. Also, if he knows I didn't do it, maybe he'll stop saying those scary things. I still can't risk having someone start to ask questions. I may not have killed my mother, but as far as the law is concerned, I technically am an accessory to murder. Also, there might be a gun somewhere with my prints on it. So, there's that.

I stop my cart in front of Father Cleary's room, pick up a glass bowl, a bag filled with water and a single yellow fish and some rocks. When I enter, Father Cleary's not there. I'm not surprised to see Nurse Peggy seated in a chair next to his bed, but she's bent over with her hands over her face. It's a weirder scene than usual, if that's possible. I clear my throat to get her attention.

Slowly, she removes her hands one at a time and looks at me. Her face is bright red. She's been crying. As much as I loathe this woman, the wet streaks on her skin tug at my heartstrings. I can't help myself, and ask her what's wrong.

She shakes her head. "He's gone. Father's passed."

*No. But I need to tell him the truth about what really happened. He has to know I didn't do it.*

I take a deep breath and place the heavy glass bowl and fish bag on a table.

"When?" I say.

"Last night. He died in his sleep, poor dear man. It was peaceful, the night staff said. They promised me that he wasn't in any pain. That's how Father deserved to go. He was a good man, a kind and righteous man."

While feeling an overwhelming sense of relief, I nod. Two things have haunted me since Christian died. The first, that gun hidden somewhere with my fingerprints on it. The second, and the one that keeps me awake at night, my decades-old confession to Father Cleary. The priest had said things to me alluding to the murder on numerous occasions. I always worried that he might tell others. After Christian died at my house, the last thing I need is for the police to start asking more questions.

Since the first time I encountered the confused priest at St. Vincent's, I've been scared about that. Every morning, I'd wake up wondering if that was the day he'd tell someone about my confession and they'd report it to the police. When Christian's death was all over the local news, the media called it a 'break-in gone wrong'. I constantly worried that hearing my name associated with any killing might trigger the priest's memory. He often had the local news on in his room. I wanted to tell him the truth, so he'd know I wasn't a bad person. Now, I won't ever get the chance.

"He was a wonderful, selfless man," says Nurse Peggy, breaking down into tears again. "Father and I were very close. I was his confidant."

After we both say a silent prayer together, I excuse myself and walk down the hallway to look for Bianca.

I review the facts. The old priest was cognitively out of it most of the time. The random things he said didn't make much sense to anyone, especially the parts in Latin. Most people who had contact with him probably shrugged off what he said as the confused rantings of a dementia patient.

Walking down the hall, I feel my entire body relax. All the loose ends that could tie me to my mother's murder are gone. My nightmare is finally over. I can breathe.

# CHAPTER 59

*Nurse Peggy*

Kneeling in the first pew of the chapel at St. Vincent's, I pray to the Virgin Mother to watch over Father Cleary's blessed soul. I never met a man with a purer heart. The gates of heaven surely swung open wide to welcome him home. It was truly my honor and privilege to take care of him these last few years.

My knees have gone numb. Kneeling for two hours will do that. It didn't bother me so much when I young, but my circulation isn't what it used to be. To keep my balance, I push myself up while holding onto the railing in front of me. Looking up at the large gold crucifix hanging above the altar, I make the sign of the cross and bow my head before turning to leave.

Slowly, I walk towards the back of the chapel, my mind deeply troubled. I'm not sure what to do with all the secrets Father Cleary shared with me. Because of his condition, I questioned how much of what he said was true. That beautiful man slipped in and out of reality so often. Sometimes, it was difficult to decipher a linear storyline from all the random things he said. I discounted much of it . . . except for one topic, a murder. Whenever he brought up the decades-old murder of a Warwick woman, he got extremely agitated. I figured he mixed up the locations and dates, or maybe he was remembering a movie and not real life. That happens sometimes with dementia patients. I just assumed it was his illness, but still, I always wondered.

Father also told me that not long after that poor woman had been killed, a teenage girl claiming to be the dead woman's daughter had come into his confessional saying that she did it. Again, his stories jumped around quite a bit, but that was the essence of it. I found the information rather incredible at first and once again chalked it up to Father's compromised mental condition. However, the whole sordid tale kept nagging at me.

Needing to put my curiosity to rest, I spent some time online doing my own research. You can imagine how surprised I was when I discovered Father's loose talk had some truth to it. According to an old newspaper article I found, there *was* a woman murdered in Warwick twenty years earlier. She'd been shot three times in the chest, right in her own house. The paper said it was a 'home invasion'. It was a dreadful story, and the crime was never solved. According to the newspaper, the murdered woman was named Midge Lester. There had been a lengthy investigation, but the police eventually declared her murder a cold case.

When I realized that some of what Father Cleary had told me was true, I didn't know what to do. Determined to leave no stone unturned, I went back online and dug a little deeper. That's when I stumbled upon some pictures of Midge Lester's funeral. Lo and behold, sitting in the front row of the church during the funeral service was a young girl with a very familiar face. I recognized her immediately. The eyes never change. According to the *Warwick Press*, the teenage girl in the photo was Midge Lester's daughter, Abbie.

The article corroborated all the stories Father Cleary had shared with me. Then I wondered . . . was it true? Was Abbie the teenager who confessed to Father? Did Abbie Sterling murder her mother twenty years ago?

Thinking that Abbie might be a killer made it hard for me to be normal or pleasant when she came to St. Vincent's. How do you look a murderer straight in the face and pretend nothing happened? I'm not wired that way. I make a practice of always telling the truth.

I often wondered why Abbie was at St. Vincent's all the time. I think she was worried that Father Cleary might reveal what she confessed. She spent an awful lot of time in his room. Once I had an inkling of the truth, I was afraid she might have intentions of harming him. If he was the only living soul who knew the truth about the murder, then I worried Father could be in danger. Of course, I had nothing tangible to go on, just my instinct.

I tried to scare her away by sending her some Russian dolls with an old newspaper article about her mother's murder tucked inside. I also once left a note on her windshield with a warning. But she was back at St. Vincent's the following week. Honestly, some people just don't take a hint.

I tried to ask Father about the murder and confession numerous times. But because of his deteriorating condition, it was hard to get a straight answer or one that made any sense. I never knew for sure what was true and what wasn't, until that day in the lunchroom.

We have a staff room on the first floor of the building. It's got a small kitchen with a fridge, a microwave, a white plastic table and four matching chairs. I usually eat my lunch in there and read for forty minutes until I go back on my shift.

That day, it was warm and sunny out. I was sitting alone at the table in the lunchroom next to a large open screened window. There was a nice comfortable breeze blowing gently into the room.

I was happily reading a murder mystery as I ate my tuna salad sandwich. I was just getting to the point where the killer was about to attack. All of a sudden, my reading was interrupted by some man outside blabbering loudly to a woman on his phone. He was right outside the window. He couldn't see me, but I could see and hear him. What made the whole thing even more annoying was that the man was talking on his speaker. People can be so rude.

I was about to lean forward against the screen and politely ask the inconsiderate man to move somewhere else, because he was disturbing me, when his conversation got extremely interesting. Instead, I sat back and listened.

When he called the woman by her first name, Abbie, bells went off for me. Since I had already done my own research on Abbie Lester Sterling, hearing the name Abbie made me all the more interested. You don't hear that name very often. It's a little old-fashioned, if you ask me.

After a few seconds, I recognized her voice. I was sure the Abbie the rude man was talking to was the same Abbie who visited Father every week. After a few minutes of eavesdropping, it became clear that she was the same person who confessed to murdering her own mother. At that point, I had a million questions. The first being, who was this man standing outside the window?

Until I heard that phone call, I never knew for sure if any of the random things Father had told me were true. That call confirmed it. Despite Father Cleary's cognitive challenges, it turns out he had many of the facts right concerning Midge Lester's death.

As I listened to the phone conversation, the pieces started coming together. From what I could surmise, the man outside on the phone had proof about the murderer in the form of a gun, and was threatening to expose Abbie. He told her he had the murder weapon in a very safe place and said he could 'see it right now'. He also said the gun had her 'fingerprints all over it'. Then, he threatened to turn her and the gun over to the police unless he helped him with some business deal.

I didn't quite understand the part about the business deal, but I could tell from the tone of Abbie's voice that she was scared. As I listened, I felt a little vindicated. I had always thought something was off with Abbie Sterling. Clearly, I had been right.

Now the question became, what do I do with all this red-hot information? Father Cleary broke his sacred vow by sharing Abbie's confession with me and possibly others. He would never have done that had it not been for his illness. I'm sure God will forgive him for that. But do I want to shine light on that and potentially damage Father's legacy? Should I contact the police or remain quiet and maintain Father's vow?

I'll admit it was wrong of me to listen in on someone else's private phone conversation. I should have made myself known from the beginning, or at the very least, closed the window. I suppose the temptation to overhear a little gossip temporarily overrode my otherwise infallible moral compass. But what's done is done. I can't un-hear what I heard. But maybe I can right a twenty-year-old miscarriage of justice. Father wasn't able to do that because of his vow, but that doesn't apply to me.

I remember that just as that overheard phone call ended, Robin, the admissions director, pulled up next to the man in her car. She was surprised to see him, and he told her he was there to 'take another look around the grounds for my mom'. Robin wanted to show him the new entertainment room and promised it would only take ten minutes. The next thing you know, the man's following the admissions director back into the building. That was my window of opportunity.

While he was on the phone, the man said he could see the hiding place of the gun from where he was. He might have been bluffing, but I went outside to look around anyway. Standing exactly where he'd been, I scanned the surrounding area. I didn't see anything out of the ordinary — no boxes or packages anywhere on the grounds. I walked over to a fountain with planters and a rock garden. I looked inside of things but saw nothing that resembled a gun.

As I started to go back into the building, I noticed there were only four cars in the visitors' lot. I wondered, could the gun he was talking about be in his car? He had mentioned New York City during the call. Only one car in the lot had New York plates. It had to be his.

I went over to that vehicle and circled it, keeping one eye on the main entrance of the building. Here in the country, people often don't lock their cars because there's very little crime. I tried one of the back doors. It was open.

Taking a chance, I looked in the back seat. It was filled with nothing but junk. I picked through it for a second, and then looked under the front seat and in the side pockets of the doors. There were dozens of old McDonald's and Burger King bags stuffed inside.

I glanced back at the building again and checked the time on my watch before I popped the trunk. I figured I had another couple of minutes before he came back. Working fast, I looked in the trunk. It was full of men's clothing, books, binders and a spare tire, but no gun.

Walking around to the passenger side, I opened the door and looked under the front seat. I also checked the well between the two front seats.

Nothing.

I was about to get out of the car when I realized I hadn't checked the glove compartment. I'm no master criminal, but if I had a gun that was damning evidence about a murder and I was using it for blackmail, I'd find a better place to keep it than my glove compartment. It seemed like a preposterous idea, and I almost didn't open it. But I'm so glad I did.

I flipped open the little door and found it filled with papers — receipts, bills with late notices, coupons. I quickly glanced up at the entrance again. All was quiet. I removed the contents of the glove compartment as fast as possible and discovered a small brown cloth sack. Inside was a thick plastic bag wrapped around a handgun.

I looked at the gun still inside the plastic and noticed there was a small green shamrock on the grip. I put it into my *Hamilton* tote bag right next to my book and water bottle.

Then I ran over to the rock garden, and picked out a few small stones. Carefully placing them inside the cloth sack to fill it out, I returned it to the glove compartment. Then, I stuffed all the papers over the bag, so it looked exactly the way it did before.

Minutes later and breathing hard, I was back inside the lunchroom. My heart was beating like a jackrabbit as I leaned against a wall to catch my breath. My shift started in five minutes, giving me just enough time to take the gun and put it inside my locker before I went back to work.

That night, I brought the gun home and was a nervous wreck having it in my house. I didn't know if it was loaded or not, and was too afraid to look. The truth is, I wouldn't even know how to open it. I was also afraid I might accidentally shoot myself. I don't know why, but I put it in my freezer overnight. I didn't want it anywhere near me.

First thing in the morning, I went down to our local savings bank and opened up a safety deposit box account. I left the gun in there. Judging from the mess inside of that man's car, he probably has no idea the gun is gone.

I've never taken the oath to keep the secrets of a confession. If Abbie Sterling killed her mother, maybe I should give the gun to the police. There's nothing stopping me. If she's a murderer, shouldn't she should pay for what she did? She broke the law. And what kind of person kills their own mother? That's a mortal sin.

I don't have the answers now but eventually, God will tell me what to do. He always comes through for me. In the meantime, I'm going to keep that gun in a safe place and my eyes on her.

# CHAPTER 60

*One year later*

*Abbie*

I can't believe it, but I'm actually getting ready for our annual Memorial Day barbecue again. After everything that happened over the past year, I wasn't in the mood to throw a party. Jason insisted. He wants things to be like they used to, but I'm not sure if that's possible.

"We can't let what happened define us," he said. "We've got to move on and reclaim our lives."

He's right; we have to make things normal again. If not for us, at least for the girls. So our life has resumed, with lacrosse practices and piano lessons. I've been working regularly with my community group on different volunteer projects, but no longer accompany Bianca to St. Vincent's. Too many bad memories, I guess. Thankfully, Luna and Grace don't know anything about what happened. On a positive note, my nightmares have disappeared, so I'm thankful for small blessings. Jason and I have tried to move on, put the past behind us and enjoy our life with our children.

Our barbecue is this coming weekend, and I'm in my usual pre-party frenzy. The liquor store just delivered several dozen cases of wine and the chairs and tables were dropped off this morning. We've even hired a magician with a live rabbit this year. It should be fun.

I'm in the middle of checking off everything on the caterer's list when the doorbell rings. It's UPS, with a rectangular package slightly bigger than a toaster wrapped in brown paper. I figure it's probably something I ordered for the barbecue, and stick it on the kitchen counter with the other party things. After I finish going over my food list, I reach for the package. It's covered by an inordinate amount of beige tape. Inside, there's a smaller box with a lid that I place on the kitchen counter.

I remove the lid and get a weird feeling. There's yellow tissue paper on top that covers the contents. Carefully, I peel it back. The minute I lay eyes on the contents, my heart begins to thump, and a rush of intense heat washes over me. It's a sixteen-inch doll. I run to the closet where I'd stashed the other dolls and pull them out. This new doll is a slightly different color, but it's the same type. I shake it. Something's inside the doll.

I remember when I opened the other dolls. Initially, I had a sense of delight as I went from one to another. This time, however, I'm terrified as I open up the first doll and find a smaller one inside. I'm five dolls in, and reach for the sixth and shake it. There's still something else inside.

I open the last doll. Like before, there's a small piece of paper spooled up inside. My legs get so wobbly that I sit in a nearby chair still holding the rolled-up paper in my hand. Slowly I unfold it, not really wanting to see what it is. When it's fully open, I look down and immediately jump back gasping. The paper falls from my hand and floats to the floor. Holding onto the edge of the kitchen table, I look down at the photo — it's an old handgun with a shamrock on the grip. Underneath the picture, there's a note written with a black sharpie.

*"You shall not murder, anyone who murders will be subject to judgment."*
Matthew 5:21–26

Dry air catches in my throat and lungs. It's not over.

## THE END

# ACKNOWLEDGMENTS

This has been quite a year for me and I want to thank all of my friends and family for their unwavering and amazing support. You know who you are. Onward and upward!

On the literary front, I want to thank my first readers, Peter Black, Diane McGarvey and Marlene Pedersen. Each of them always brings a different perspective and great advice. I don't make a move without their input. I'd like to thank Brooke Ciraldo for giving the manuscript a read. She caught a few problems and her comments were very helpful.

I'd also like to thank my amazing editor and friend, Kate Lyall Grant, at Joffe Books who cuts right to the heart of the good, the bad and ugly with kindness and smarts. I don't think there has ever been an insight or a correction she suggested that I disagree with. She makes each book better and better and I learn. Also, thanks to Jodi Compton who did the second round of edits and picked up a few more necessary changes. Jodi had the pleasure of experiencing my lack of comma and hyphen intelligence. But seriously, why do we even have hyphens?

Last but not least, thank you to the entire team at Joffe Books . . . marketing, publicity, administrative. You take such good care of my book on every front. Merci.

Finally the readers — thank you for taking time out of your day to read my story. I hope you enjoyed it. More to come!

# THE JOFFE BOOKS STORY

We began in 2014 when Jasper agreed to publish his mum's much-rejected romance novel and it became a bestseller.

Since then we've grown into the largest independent publisher in the UK. We're extremely proud to publish some of the very best writers in the world, including Joy Ellis, Faith Martin, Caro Ramsay, Helen Forrester, Simon Brett and Robert Goddard. Everyone at Joffe Books loves reading and we never forget that it all begins with the magic of an author telling a story.

We are proud to publish talented first-time authors, as well as established writers whose books we love introducing to a new generation of readers.

We won Trade Publisher of the Year at the Independent Publishing Awards in 2023. We have been shortlisted for Independent Publisher of the Year at the British Book Awards for the last four years, and were shortlisted for the Diversity and Inclusivity Award at the 2022 Independent Publishing Awards. In 2023 we were shortlisted for Publisher of the Year at the RNA Industry Awards.

We built this company with your help, and we love to hear from you, so please email us about absolutely anything bookish at feedback@joffebooks.com

If you want to receive free books every Friday and hear about all our new releases, join our mailing list: www.joffebooks.com/contact

And when you tell your friends about us, just remember: it's pronounced Joffe as in coffee or toffee!

9 781835 267660